Elegance and Evil

by

DK Coutant

A Cleo Cooper Mystery

Cover Art by *Teddi Black*

The Wild Rose Press, Inc.
PO Box 708
Adams Basin, NY 14410-0708
Visit us at www.thewildrosepress.com

Publishing History
First Edition, 2025
Trade Paperback ISBN 978-1-5092-6136-9
Digital ISBN 978-1-5092-6137-6

A Cleo Cooper Mystery
Published in the United States of America

Dedication

To my mother, Sylvia Ferriter, who flew from Florida to Seattle to support me as a debut author at Left Coast Crime. What a wonder you are. And to my kid brother, Jerry Coutant, the kindest person I know. Thank you for reinforcing my faith in humanity. And last but not least, to my beloved husband, Stephen Worchel. You and Beasley keep me happy, grounded, and excited about new adventures. What a wonderful life we have.

Acknowledgements

I have so many people to thank. All my friends and family that told me they couldn't wait for the next Cleo Cooper mystery: My fabulous editor, Ally Robertson, whose care and knowledge have guided me faultlessly along this path. Thanks to my amazing beta readers, Carolyn Meinel, Pamela Rees, and the wise and wonderful Retired Detective Casey Denhollander, who keep me on point, and as accurate as they can. Thanks to the Guppies from Sisters in Crime for their brilliant and ongoing encouragement and advice, especially Vicki Berger Erwin, my critique partner with an eagle eye. And I can't forget my long-running Tano Writer's Group. They hold me to a high standard and never praise good writing, only my best.

Chapter 1

New in Town

"Are you ready for this, Cleo?" Luc asked.

"Sure." Beginnings were intimidating. But, nothing ventured, nothing gained.

Luc pulled into the driveway of a traditional adobe house, typical of what I had seen here in Santa Fe, NM. A stocky man of medium-height, with hair pulled back in a small man-bun exited and locked the front door.

"Jon can be a bit insufferable sometimes, but his heart is usually in the right place," Luc said. Jon was one of Luc's closest friends, and a scientist who worked at a federal lab nearby. Luc was giving him a ride to the dinner party we were attending.

Jon swung open the back door of Luc's car. "This should be fun," he said sliding into the backseat.

I turned and smiled at him from the front passenger seat. "Hi, Jon, it's nice to meet you. Luc has told me a lot about you. I'm Cleo—"

"Cleo Cooper, I know. I've heard about you too. Anyway. Luc, did you get my email about the new grant I was awarded?" And Jon rattled on about the mega-grant he'd received for his latest research project.

Oka-a-a-a-y.

Luc pulled away from the curb.

"This grant will cement my spot at the top of the

1

food chain at the lab. The Defense Department is really interested in my ideas on further miniaturization of key components," Jon said.

"That sounds interesting. What kind of components? And how small do you think you can shrink them?" I asked.

Jon's gaze shifted to me. "You're just a psychologist, right?"

"Yes." But I suspected where this was going.

"Were your parents scientists?"

"No." My parents ran a diner.

"Then it is a waste of my time to try and explain atomic physics to you. Luc's parents at least taught him enough over the dinner table that he can understand the basics of my research. But a psych professor from a small university in the middle of nowhere—"

"Hey." Luc interrupted. "Cleo is a scientist, a social scientist. And she has conducted some solid studies. And I'm a psychologist too. So no looking down your nose at us because we don't get defense department grants. And, if you're going to bring up my parents…they claim that any good scientists should be able to explain their work to someone outside the field."

"And my university isn't in the middle of nowhere. It's in the middle of the Pacific Ocean, a gateway between East and West." I was on sabbatical from my university on the Big Island of Hawaii, and I wasn't going to let anybody talk smack about my island. Maybe coming to Santa Fe, NM, to work with Luc for six months wasn't such a great idea.

Jon sighed. "Whatever. I think I'd rather wait until we get to the party to explain my grant so I can see the look on Matias's face when he realizes I'll have the largest grant at the lab. He won't be able to get rid of me now. And he'll have to take me seriously."

We reached downtown Santa Fe and Luc pulled into a parking garage. Butterflies took flight in my stomach. I was usually comfortable in new situations. But Jon's obnoxious condescension had me feeling jittery. On our short ride from Jon's house to the garage, his bombastic wit had overwhelmed me.

I'd left a secure, comfortable career as a psychology professor, and a secure, mostly uncomfortable boyfriend, to create a new life. I arrived a week ago, and this dinner party would be my first opportunity to meet people. A lot of movers and shakers were expected, including Luc. I contemplated the man strolling beside me, his striking bone structure and tousled black hair. He was influential in town, and his Institute for the Study of International Relations lined up perfectly with my research.

Luc, Jon, and I traversed a crooked sidewalk that undulated over roots of old Siberian elms. My butterflies flittered again, and I hoped the walk from the parking garage to our hostess's home on the other side of the Plaza would rein in my nerves. I glanced at Luc. He'd invited me here to work on his project during my sabbatical. I wanted to keep the relationship professional, but his dark, smoldering eyes, broad shoulders, and kindness made my heart beat faster.

Luc must have noticed. "We're almost there, Cleo, not much farther."

Luc and Jon would know everyone at the party. Again with those damn butterflies. Luc smiled at me as we approached a crosswalk. Jon stepped off the curb ahead of us as a dark gray Lexus turned on to the street we were crossing and sped up.

"Watch out!" I grabbed Luc's arm to hold him back from the crosswalk. I winced, expecting the car to hit Jon who was already in the street but managed to maneuver out of the car's path.

"What the…that driver only missed you by inches." My hands shook from the adrenaline surge. The Lexus ran through a red light as it raced away. "Is someone out to get you, Jon?" I bit my lip as my heart thumped and my mind caught up with the fact I'd almost witnessed someone's death.

"Maybe." Jon grinned. The forty-ish nuclear physicist bounded forward to the other sidewalk. His legs bounced with a child-like spring. As he stepped out of the street he threw his head back and let loose a loud "Ha."

"I guess a brush with death has made him a little giddy," I said.

"Either that or Jon has been taste-testing his marijuana cookie recipe again." We took the last steps out of the road. "It was probably somebody texting while driving. You should have looked before you stepped into the crosswalk, Jon," Luc said. "But, if Cleo's right, and that driver was trying to run you down, the tough call is narrowing who does *not* want to knock you off."

I took a deep breath to steady myself. "How can you guys joke? It scared me to death, and I'm not the one who almost died."

"Who's joking?" Jon asked with a laugh. But his laugh wobbled. He blinked rapidly. "Luc's probably right. It was somebody texting, or drinking. But both Matias and Kyle hate my guts, could be either one of them. What do you think, Luc?"

"A tough call. You annoy so many people." Luc

smiled fondly.

We resumed ambling down the sidewalk. The shaking in my hands subsided. I glanced up the street, but the Lexus didn't reappear. Maybe it was my imagination and the car didn't aim for Jon.

"Is Kyle still living with Ginger?" Luc asked.

"Surprisingly, yes. I thought she would have tossed him out by now. He'll be there tonight, as well as Matias, to hear my big grant news." Jon's grin returned. "This should be fun."

Luc let out a low whistle, nudging me gently with his elbow. "Better keep your head down, Cleo. Sparks could fly."

Great. I had hoped to meet some nice people and make some connections, so I wouldn't depend on Luc to get acclimated. *Is everybody going to be at each other's throats?*

"Here we are." Luc touched my elbow gently with his right hand while extending his left to open a wooden gate elaborately carved with a detailed mural of a Mexican village.

I looked beyond to the creamy pumpkin-colored pueblo structure. Old wood broke the adobe into sizable chunks, so while the house was large, it didn't devour a guest. Well-trained roses and wisteria wound up far above my head around high frames of mesquite wood which offered sweet-smelling shade. The front door was constructed from some exotic wood, with dramatic zebra stripes punctuated by a natural sunburst pattern in the grain. Bespoke, oversized windows appeared to curve with the walls. I'd never been in a house of such obvious wealth. My confidence faltered.

I looked at my companions.

"You first, my dear." Jon bowed with a dramatic flourish. "I want someone to hide behind if people start throwing things."

Chapter 2

The Dinner Party

Despite the grandeur of the surroundings, our hostess, Ginger, conveyed the warmth of an adoring aunt. I liked her immediately. Tall and slender, her large green eyes twinkled at me from under chic bangs that almost hid the laugh lines I considered signs of a life well-lived. I hoped to be as happy and confident when I was her age. Jon whispered something in her ear and Ginger tipped her head back in a delighted giggle. Every silvery-blonde hair fell back into its place when she focused on me.

"Luc, this must be your Cleo." Ginger's smile was wide and genuine.

Luc's Cleo? *Luc's discussed me with Ginger?*

"Yes, this is Cleo, and Cleo, this is my dear friend, Ginger." Luc looked at me with a strangely shy expression on his face.

Ginger winked at Luc and grabbed my hand. She led me around the room, introducing me to everyone. A dozen names and faces I struggled to memorize, and we circled back to Luc. Ginger apologized for monopolizing me and kissed me on the cheek before moving on to circulate amongst her other guests.

"I got names of everybody, but not many details. Who are all of these people?" I asked Luc. "Anybody in particular I should try to get to know?"

"Ginger is a good connection for you, although she'll be busy tonight. She and Samia, that's the dark-haired woman with her now, they're co-directors of a center that helps Native American women who are victims of domestic violence. They're motivated, and have worked hard to get it up and running. But I think they're struggling to agree on the path forward. Neither one of them has a background in psychology or cross-cultural relations and I think they'd benefit from your expertise, if you're interested."

Ginger and Samia broke off their conversation. Ginger lifted a hand in dismissal and returned to chatting up her other guests. Samia's eyes followed Ginger's departing back, her mouth turned down.

Maybe some tension in that workplace?

A man threaded his way through the crowd to stand beside Samia.

"And that is Matias, Samia's husband and a friend of mine. He's a good guy," Luc said.

Matias wrapped his arm around his wife and whispered into her ear. Her face lightened and brightened as she kissed his cheek.

"Is that the Matias who's angry with Jon?"

"Yes. It's a crazy misunderstanding, but Jon won't let it go. And it could cost Matias his funding, and potentially his job." Luc's mouth tightened. "Matias is the head of an important federal lab, and one of his workers made a mistake. Instead of following regular channels to report it, Jon decided to accuse them of fraud as a whistleblower. He…"

"Dinner's ready, if you would like to come this way." Ginger waved us in the direction of an adjoining room.

Luc rolled his shoulders. "I'll explain the rest later. Let's find our seats and enjoy the evening."

Matias had approached and tapped Luc's elbow. Luc introduced us.

"It's delightful to meet you, Cleo, but do you mind if I borrow Luc for a quick conversation."

"Of course, go. I'll find my seat." I shooed them away and both men slowly moved off, deep in conversation.

Ginger caught my attention. She herded the guests with an elegant charm. "Come, come, Teresa says the food is ready. Let's eat it while it's hot." Ginger was behind Jon, the farthest person from the dining area, who was in an animated discussion with a young blond man, who had been introduced as Kyle. She rested her hand lightly on Jon's shoulder urging him toward the dining room. "You can finish telling him about your latest project over the first course. Don't let Teresa's signature dish get cold."

Jon laughed and threw his hands in the air. "I'm coming. No art is worth missing out on Teresa's cooking." He linked arms with the hostess, placing his free hand on her arm. "Ginger, darling, are you ready to make that trip with me into the mystical heart of the wild desert?" Jon turned his back on Kyle without a backward glance.

Kyle didn't follow. A muscle clenched and released in his jaw. His eyes narrowed as they followed Jon and Ginger.

At least I knew why Kyle hated Jon. He was jealous.

Kyle noticed my gaze and shrugged. "Typical. He runs away from an argument he's losing."

I didn't know how to respond to that. I flicked my thumb and middle fingers of one hand and followed the others into a room with a wide plank wood floor and creamy adobe walls.

There were no windows as it was an internal room, but each wall had a large oil painting of a landscape: Ghost Ranch, New Mexico; the cliffs of Dover; the French Riviera; and a South American jungle. A table made from a long slab of wood thicker than the width of my hand stood in the center of the room. Heavy linen placemats in bright Mexican patterns were set with sterling silver, stoneware, and crystal. The juxtaposition of casual and elegant was oddly peaceful, despite the tensions that ran through the guests.

Name tags had been placed on the twelve-foot-long table. Luc was already seated next to our hostess. Matias, who appeared to be in his forties with light brown hair going gray sat on the other side of Luc. I found my name tag near the far end of the table between empty seats reserved for Kyle at the end, and Samia.

Good, that would give me an opportunity to chat with her during the meal.

I couldn't resist glancing down the table at Luc. He leaned in and spoke intensely with Matias who glowered at Jon who sat on the other side of Ginger.

Kyle yanked out the chair next to me.

I offered a smile, hoping to pull him out of his mood.

It was lost on him. His eyes never left Ginger and Jon. Kyle sat down heavily.

Samia, a strong-featured woman, slid into the empty seat on the other side of me. Her luxurious dark hair tumbled over her shoulders. She said hello, before her gaze floated around the table. Her mouth tightened as she took in her husband, Kyle, and Jon.

"I hope Luc manages to discourage my husband from throwing his plate at Jon." Samia unfolded her napkin. "I do not know what Ginger expected, enticing those two to break bread together."

Her eyes flitted back to me, and she winked. "With the overload of testosterone in the room, it appears the women will have to be the grown-ups tonight." Her smile broadened. "You are Luc's new…" She appeared to search for a word. "…colleague. Yes?" Her eyes crinkled enough to make me wonder what other noun she had considered.

"Yes. I'm a cross-cultural psychology professor on sabbatical. It's a safe, secure job, but…I'm getting restless in my ivory tower. I'd really like to take a more hands-on applied approach where I'm actually solving problems rather than just writing academic papers that I'm not sure anyone reads."

"I can understand that," Samia said. "When I finished my PhD, I wanted to work in a lab, not a university." She cocked her head to one side. "But, I was married and we had two salaries. There is security in academics and a lot of professional risk in trying to solve world problems. Often power brokers and funders are motivated to keep the status quo."

"Exactly."

"I'm not sure I would have had the courage to accept such an unstable financial situation if I was on my own."

Like me.

A colorful, crispy salad arrived in front of me, preventing another round of butterflies. I dug in.

Sometime between when the salad plates had been removed and the main course was brought to the table,

Kyle stopped attempting to burn holes into Jon and Ginger with his glares. With less intensity he contemplated me.

"Sorry, I was a little distracted when introductions were going around. I'm Kyle." He lifted his wine glass for a sip. "Who are you again? And how are you connected to this motley group?" His tone was light as he replaced his glass to the table.

"Cleo. Cleo Cooper. I'm a professor on sabbatical from my university in Hawaii. I'm here in Santa Fe working with Luc Bastien's International Relations group."

"What are you working on with Luc?"

"I'm on the refugee and immigrant team."

Kyle lifted one eyebrow in question. "Refugee and immigrant team? You don't look like a refugee to me."

"I'm an academic. My research explores effective ways to integrate refugees into their new culture. I'm here in Santa Fe for a semester and still learning how I can contribute."

Samia leaned in. "This is the Hawaiian *wahine* that Luc recruited. Remember him telling us about her at Ginger's last party?"

I'm sure I blushed and took a sip of my water to cover. "Actually, I'm not Native Hawaiian. I grew up in Virginia. I've been working in Hawaii for five years but that still makes me a *malahini*, a newcomer." I smiled to soften the correction.

"Well, as I said, I'm Kyle. I'm an artist and web designer. In that order." He gestured toward Samia. "Matias, the head of the lab is married to the lovely Samia. And, I have to say, Samia is definitely the more interesting, as well as beautiful half of that couple." Kyle raised his wine glass in Samia's direction.

Samia graciously tipped her head at Kyle. "How astute you are. But do I remember correctly that you grew up somewhere near Cleo? Are you not also from the south?"

Kyle grimaced. "Arkansas. About a thousand miles away. I couldn't get out of there fast enough."

"I haven't spent time in Arkansas, but I loved growing up in our small town in Virginia." My heart panged as I remembered doing my homework in the family diner. The smell of pot roast and oyster fritters drifted out from the kitchen as Mom smiled at me from behind the counter every time I glanced in her direction. Dad was usually cooking in back, but often slipped me a slice of pecan pie during slow times.

As the main course was brought to the table it gave me a chance to blink away tears and breathe through the wave of homesickness that had caught me by surprise. Samia startled me when she patted my hand.

"I, too, am far from my homeland. It reaches out and seizes us at unexpected moments, does it not?" Her eyes tightened as they followed the plates being delivered to the table. A second later she continued, "You are in for a treat. I do not know if you have heard, but Teresa, Ginger's cook is incredible. Ginger serves amazing food." Once again her eyes sparkled.

Samia did not exaggerate. The appetizer, roasted broccoli on ricotta-topped garlic bread bites drizzled with a spicy-sweet sauce, was followed by a lovely, spiced lamb tagine with apricots, over couscous. As I savored the flavors, voices at the other end of the table grew louder.

Ginger's brow creased and she pointed her fork at

Jon. "It is a real problem. Native American women are subject to incredibly high rates of sexual violence. The Indian Law Resource Center reports 50% of native women experience it, and in the vast majority of those cases, the perpetrator is never punished."

"So you're going to bring the MeToo movement to the Pueblo?" Jon's lips curled.

Ginger speared a piece of broccoli. "Don't be a jerk. Native American women are at a massive disadvantage. There's a complex web of national, state, and reservation laws that work to protect perpetrators. It's maddening, and my Foundation started the Center to end the maltreatment." Ginger's gaze flew to the woman next to me. "Right, Samia?"

Samia stiffened. "Yes, we need to fix the system to help these women. As well as immigrant women from other countries who also need our protection."

"I know you want that, Samia." Ginger's voice sharpened. "But as I have explained to you, Native American women are in situations even more disadvantaged. Like the case of a white guy who entered the reservation and raped a native woman. The Rez can't touch him because of the stupid restrictions, and the feds have declined to pursue it. That needs to change. And we need the Center to stay focused."

An uncomfortable silence descended on the table at Ginger's tone. The atmosphere heavy, Jon broke the mood.

"Hey, Kyle, you used to date a native woman, didn't you? What was her name? I hope you aren't one of the men Ginger and Samia are aiming to take down. Are you?" Jon's eyes twinkled with mischievousness.

Kyle's face reddened.

Jon laughed again. "I'm kidding. You hadn't had a date in years before Ginger took pity on you."

Ginger's face softened and with a cat-like expression, she playfully elbowed Jon. "Leave him alone."

"As you wish. Now that I've secured a promise from you to join me on this adventure, I am at peace with the world." Jon shot a sideways look at Kyle.

Jon clearly delighted in tormenting poor Kyle; no wonder Kyle hated him.

Kyle sat up straight and leaned toward Jon's end of the table. He flexed his fingers as if he wanted them around Jon's neck. "What? Where are you going with him?"

Ginger waved a hand in Kyle's direction. "Don't worry. Jon has been trying to convince me that if I'm going to be an effective leader for my Center, then I need to visit Native American women who live in remote areas. It's not a bad idea, really. And nothing to concern you, dear." But she tilted her head and fluttered her lashes at Jon.

I understood why Kyle was jealous.

As I was thinking Kyle was going to climb across my plate to throttle Jon, Teresa carried a tray into the room.

"I made your favorite dessert, Senor Kyle, Flan de Naranja." Teresa set a plate in front of the young man with a flourish.

Ginger clapped her hands. "See, Kyle, I wanted Teresa to make you something special to celebrate the new painting you finished."

Kyle leaned back, pulled his hands down by his sides, and smiled stiffly. "Thank you, Teresa, Ginger. It smells amazing."

But his hands tightened into fists.

Teresa set a creamy buttercup yellow flan, nestled in a honey-colored sauce with a twist of orange slice resting on top before each of us. The tension at the table receded as guests delighted in the dessert. The storm had passed.

Apparently, this was not to Jon's liking.

"I tell you, Ginger, there are beautiful pueblos for hiking. Acoma, Tesuque…and the Navajos have Rez Golf." Jon's grin was infectious. "I know you love to golf."

"Yes, I do." Ginger's mouth curved up.

"The Navajos have started their own version. In the desert, with livestock as hazards and old carpet torn out of an office building packed down for greens. I swear the next Tiger Woods will be Navajo."

Several heads swiveled toward Jon.

"Indians. Playing golf. Give me a break." Kyle scowled.

Jon held up one hand and put the other on his heart. "I swear it's true. The Navajos are athletic, and I guess the old guys, after playing basketball for years, wanted something a little easier on the joints. They started designing rez golf courses. I think most are free, and one of them, Wagon Trail to Lone Pine is open at night. With glow in the dark golf balls." Jon grinned and lifted an eyebrow. "Isn't that amazing? You have to try it, Ginger. Let's go this weekend."

Ginger's eyes lit up. "It sounds interesting. And it would be a good opportunity to talk with some of the Navajo Nation women's support groups." She glanced at Kyle.

I followed her gaze and flinched at his clamped jaw and the veins popping out of his forehead. I leaned away from him in case he jumped up to reach across the table to strangle Jon.

"Kyle, I'll only be gone three days, and you have your new show opening. That's been taking all of your time lately. You won't mind, will you, darling?"

Jon smirked, obviously pleased with the havoc he had created.

Chapter 3

The Drive Home

"Well that was interesting," I said as Luc and I backed out of Jon's driveway. After dinner we'd strolled uneventfully back to the parking garage and driven Jon home.

"Jon was in rare form tonight." Luc focused on the road but shot a quick glance in my direction. "He likes to get under people's skin, but I've known him forever and he's a good guy deep down. He has no tolerance for anything he sees as injustice or hypocrisy. Like being a whistleblower at the Lab. He's driving Matias crazy, because as head of the lab he has to defend his team, but Jon is convinced that one of the team members was sloppy with federal dollars. I mean, some people think Jon likes to stir up trouble, but honestly, I think he only does it when he thinks that person deserves the trouble."

"What's the deal with him and Kyle? What has Kyle done to deserve Jon's derision?"

"Jon thinks…and the emphasis here is that Jon *thinks* that Kyle is using Ginger."

"Using her how?" Ginger, with her golden hair cut into a chic bob, and flawless skin I'd love to have, even though I'm twenty years her junior. She appeared to be a beautiful, confident, wealthy woman, very much in control of her life.

"I think I mentioned that Jon creates art as a way to relax when he isn't doing his nuclear-physicist thing at the lab." He glanced at me again.

"Yeah. And you said he's won a few prizes at recent art shows for one of them."

"Right. Kyle, on the other hand, is a website designer who paints in his spare time. He is really good at website design, one of the best in town. I want to hire him for our institute's website. But his paintings—well, they don't win awards. Kyle desperately wants to be an artist, and I'm not an expert, but according to Jon, Kyle just isn't that good."

A quarter moon rose on the horizon as we left the lights of downtown.

"Where does Ginger come in?"

"What I've heard is that Kyle spent a year trying to find a gallery to sell his art, but no one was interested. Ginger hired him to do the website for the Center her foundation funds, and suddenly she and this younger guy are a thing." Luc shrugged. "I'm not saying Kyle doesn't care for Ginger. People of different ages fall in love. But as Jon points out, suddenly Ginger is financing one-man shows for Kyle's art. And these are lavish shows. If you think her dinner party was amazing, these Kyle-shows as Jon calls them are high-class extravagant affairs, even by Santa Fe standards. People are going for the party, not the art, according to Jon."

"How does Jon know Ginger?"

"Santa Fe isn't that big. People who like parties will bump into each other sooner or later. And Jon and Ginger like parties. Jon admires Ginger's great big embrace of life. She has been fortunate and wants to share her good fortune with people who have not been so privileged. Jon appreciates that. Ginger likes and trusts him because she recognizes that's why he respects her."

The streetlights became fewer and fewer as the highway curved despite being only a mile from town.

"How did you get hooked into this crowd? Are you a person who likes parties? Or were you looking for funding from Ginger?"

"I've known Jon since before high school. I hadn't seen him for years, but we reconnected when we realized we were both here in Santa Fe. I met Ginger through Jon. I agree with his assessment; she has a big heart," Luc said. "I probably should've hit her up for my Institute, but I'm not comfortable with that. I'd rather apply formally for grants and not lean on friendships. We've been lucky so far. The grants have been hitting. So I haven't needed to resort to that."

We were on Tano Road now, winding through the dark lit only by our headlights. I caught sight of the back legs of a coyote slipping behind a pinon tree on the edge of the pavement. I glanced at Luc's profile in the reflected light of an oncoming car. He and I discovered a physical attraction at a conference last year. We didn't act on it, but there was definitely a spark. And a friendship had grown during our email exchanges afterward. My beloved dog died last year, and Luc was the only person who seemed to understand the depth of my grief.

But, I didn't come here for him. This was a great professional opportunity. When I made the decision to accept a temporary consulting position at his new institute, I gently mentioned that I didn't want a relationship to interfere with my career. Our relationship would need to stay professional. That line had grown fuzzy over the last couple of weeks, and even fuzzier this evening. Luc had respected my wishes. I was the one having a hard time sticking to my decision. An irresistible urge to reach over and run a finger along his jawline or grab a fistful of hair above the back of his neck gripped me. I wove my fingers together in my lap to stop myself. Luc smiled, as if he could read my thoughts.

As we turned onto our road Luc licked his lips and said, "I would invite you to my place, but…"

I watched him in the darkened car. He slowed in front of the driveway to the casita I currently called home and stopped. At the top of Luc's short dead-end street was his neighbor's casita that I'd rented for the six months I'd be in Santa Fe. The rental market was tight, and I only scored this one because Luc was friends with the owner and offered it when Luc mentioned I couldn't find any temporary housing. It was convenient for work, but not so convenient for me to resist those dark eyes and that sexy mouth.

I laid a hand on his arm that rested on the steering wheel. I couldn't stop myself. "You better leave me here."

Luc's face grew serious, and he looked like he wanted to say something. But his jaw tightened, and he nodded.

I reluctantly slid out of the seat. I didn't want to walk away, but I should walk away. I started to close the door, then pulled it back open, and leaned down to look at him.

"I know I'm sending mixed messages. I'm sorry. I also realize I can't go on like this with one foot here and the other…" I didn't need to complete the sentence. "But I want you to know that I appreciate your patience and understanding."

"I'm not sure you can call it understanding. Because I don't." Luc's somber expression relaxed. "But, if you aren't ready, you aren't ready. And I don't want to push it. I find it encouraging though that you aren't oblivious to what is happening between the two of us." Luc smiled. "And I'm right up the street when you come to your senses. Now, go to bed, dream of me, and why don't we go for breakfast tomorrow morning?"

I laughed and suggested a time to meet. Lingering on the driveway, I watched Luc's taillights as they flickered past pinon trees on the way to the end of the street and into his own long driveway where I lost sight of them. Houses on this street were situated on four or five acres, but the walk to Luc's house couldn't have been more than 500 yards. I resisted the urge to walk up the road and catch him before he entered his house. Stop him. Grab a fist full of his hair. Kiss him. Then he'd take my hand...

I closed my eyes, shook my head, and with heavy steps entered my casita.

****

Luc picked me up, bright and early the next morning and we drove to a café downtown. The smell of chili peppers and sausage greeted us as we entered. A young woman seated us and brought the coffee in a flash. It was good coffee, which made me happy.

Luc excused himself to go to the counter and buy a newspaper. I grew up in a family that read a print newspaper every morning. My friends and colleagues found it weird that I always bought a local paper when I traveled. I considered it a window into the communities that I visited. A warm, cuddly feeling curled up in me knowing that Luc enjoyed a morning paper, too. We passed sections back and forth while we waited for our food. Drinking my morning coffee and reading the newspaper was a favorite ritual of mine, and the intimacy of sharing it with Luc soothed me. I snuck a glance at his face to see if he sensed it, too.

Apparently not. His forehead creased and his mouth formed a tight line as he read the front page.

"Bad news in the paper?" I asked.

Luc groaned and set the paper on the table. "There's a big article on the lab. Poor Matias. I know one of his researchers was sloppy, but the reporter is writing as if this guy is guilty of criminal embezzlement. It puts Matias in a tough position."

"Is this the situation that Jon exposed with his whistleblowing?"

"Right. This researcher who goofed up is one of the top scientists at the lab. He's making ground-breaking discoveries in robotics. But he often forgot to submit receipts for his equipment. And some of the equipment has gone missing. He has a lot of temporary postdocs who have come and gone, and he thinks the missing equipment might have gotten mixed up with their personal equipment. Also, he hosted a big conference last year, and some of the equipment was used in demonstrations, but not signed out. Like I said, sloppy, but not criminal. Matias is sure of that. But our local paper has good investigative journalists who are salivating over a possible scandal at a world-famous lab. With the white-hot spotlight of the press on the lab, Matias is being pressured to fire this guy."

Luc stopped talking as the waitress approached with our food. We thanked her, and when she stepped away Luc leaned toward me as he reached for his fork. His voice low, he said, "I like Matias *and* Jon. Both of these guys are smart and honest. But I'm afraid they'll end up destroying each other." Luc sighed and dug into his western omelet.

My mouth watered as I considered my Santa Fe hash browns, golden brown slivers of potato, oozing with Hatch green chili and melted cheddar cheese. I scooped a bite on my fork and watched steam swirl off of it. While I waited for my food to cool I asked a question that had been bothering me.

"I thought whistleblowers were supposed to remain anonymous, to protect them from powerful players that didn't want their misdeeds revealed. Kind of this situation exactly. How did that break down? How did Matias find out Jon was the whistleblower?" I took my first bite of hash browns. Heavenly. I closed my eyes and savored it.

Luc had a mouthful of omelet. He shook his head and rolled his eyes while he swallowed then took a drink of water before answering. "You've been around Jon enough to know he craves being in the spotlight. He filed it secretly, but when it blew up in the press, he couldn't stand that people didn't know he was the whistleblower. And Jon is powerful in his own way. He's an expert in his field and has multi-million-dollar grants in his name that the lab can't take away. Matias doesn't have much power over him, so Jon doesn't have much to lose."

"Did he go to the press?"

"No, he doesn't care if the general public knows. He wanted the people he reported on to know who brought them down. At one of Ginger's parties with mostly lab people, he let it *slip* that he was the whistleblower."

"Wow. Were you there? Was blood drawn?" I took

another bite of my cheesy-chili hash browns and thought back to the tension of last night. I could imagine how furious Matias must have been when he found out.

"No, I was out of the country. Thank goodness. I was visiting family in Switzerland when all this broke."

"That's right, you were born there. Lucky you, to have a reason to go to Europe every year." I took another mouthful of hash browns.

"I moved here with my parents in high school, but stayed after they returned. I like the States, but Europe will always feel like home. Except for breakfast." Luc contemplated his plate. "I could never get a hot breakfast like this at home unless I went to a hotel." Luc forked another bite of his omelet. "I love American breakfasts."

"You would have liked my parents' diner." I sipped my coffee.

"Tell me about it," Luc said. "I'd love to get the inside scoop on an American diner, and your childhood."

Chapter 4

Lunch with Samia

An azure blue, cloudless sky lured me away from my laptop. Luc's institute didn't have a lot of office space so I worked from the casita most of the time in front of a large window with a view over a pinon forest and distant mountains. I sighed and reread the email from Ben.

"Everything is fine here. Hope with you too."

Short and uninformative, like talking to Ben in person. We had been living together in Hawaii. Like me, he was a professor at the University. He was a super nice guy and my parents loved him, but his unwillingness to travel became a sore spot between us. And that sore spot revealed our major problems with communication. We were using this sabbatical to take a break. I owned the house in Hilo where we had lived together, and Ben occupied alone while I was gone. I would be going back to Hawaii when this sabbatical was over; maybe I would move back in with him. Or maybe he would move out. I tried to keep in touch. I'd sent him an email last week telling him I'd settled in and a bit on life in Santa Fe. I'd also asked how he was faring.

I closed my computer, poured another cup of coffee, and relocated to the small patio off my casita. The brevity of Ben's message rankled me. I stretched my neck and took a sip of my coffee. Was it really irritation? Or guilt? I hadn't acted on my desires for Luc, but wow, I had desires. I sent Ben the chatty email last week right after Luc and I had one of our close encounters. It was a guilt email. Maybe Ben could read the guilt in the message. Maybe that's why his email was so…impersonal. Or, maybe that was just Ben's way. Spending time with Luc was different. We found a million things to discuss. He asked me about my thoughts, dreams, and ideas. Not something Ben ever did. Maybe Luc was my new normal, and that's why Ben's email irked me.

My phone rang, and I jumped. I ran my fingers through my hair to chase my thoughts away, glad for the escape from where they had led me. I went back inside to find my phone. I didn't recognize the number, but it was local, from Santa Fe.

"Hello?"

"Cleo? This is Samia. We met last night at Ginger's dinner. I sat next to you? Do you remember me?"

"Samia. Of course." An image of the elegant dark-haired woman flashed in my mind. She was a molecular physicist, and the wife of the director of the lab. The calm in contrast to the raging temper of Kyle who had been on the other side of me.

"Luc gave me your number. I hope you don't mind. But since you are new in town, do you want to go to lunch? I work with a bunch of men at the lab, so I don't pass up a chance for some girl chat." A gentle laugh came through the phone.

"That sounds great." Really, great. I missed Rikki and Gina, my gal-pals in Hawaii.

"Are you free for dinner? Matias has a late meeting

and I thought perhaps we could grab something in town."

"Sounds good. Where shall I meet you? I don't know many places yet."

We settled on a time and place and said our goodbyes. With a lighter heart, I reopened my computer to finish up what I needed to do before I drove into town to meet my new friend.

****

I walked into Maria's New Mexican Kitchen, and saw Samia, already seated. I wound my way through the tables as she stood to greet me.

"I'm so glad you were up for this." Samia embraced me warmly and kissed me on both cheeks. "I truly love my life here in the States, the freedom to work and run my own life without anyone else's permission." Her lips twisted ruefully as she returned to her seat. "But I miss the female gatherings in Saudi. We could uncover and let our hair down. We felt decadent wearing makeup and flipping our hair around." Samia chuckled.

"That sounds nice." I smiled and picked up a menu. "How did you wind up in Santa Fe?"

"I was fortunate that my parents allowed me to attend university here in the U.S. My father worked at the embassy in D.C. so they lived here when I started, and allowed me to stay for my degree after they moved back. I wanted to save the world by developing a new, powerful, green energy. That aligned with the King's proposed goals. I was accepted into a prestigious program that brought honor to my family and the King." Samia stirred her iced tea.

"I met Matias during college and married him against my parents' wishes." A shadow came over Samia's face. "I miss them, but I cannot imagine going back to a life where I can't leave the house without my husband's permission." She waved her hand around the room. "Like this. I can call a new friend and meet you here, where they serve alcohol, without having to ask anyone. If I want a margarita, I can have one without being thrown into prison." Samia shrugged. "I like being able to make my own choices."

Samia's focus shifted from my face to something behind me. She frowned. "Raul? Is something wrong?"

A fiftyish Latino man stopped at our table. His skin was brown, his hair black with gray strands in his beard and temples. His dark eyes were troubled.

"Samia, I'm sorry to bother you when you are here with your friend." The man waved a hand in my direction. "But I must speak with you about my nephew. Manuel is a good boy. That girl who said those things, she must be lying." The man clutched a baseball cap in his hands.

Samia's mouth hardened into a firm line, but her eyes remained soft. Her tone was kind when she spoke. "I know you are fond of your nephew, but you have to trust that Ginger and I will get to the bottom of this. And I do not think this is the time or place to discuss this situation." Samia lifted one eyebrow. "Do you?"

Raul stood there, gripping the hat in his hands as if his life depended on it. His countenance begged Samia for something, but no words escaped. He sighed heavily. "I guess I will see you at the Center Wednesday as usual."

"I'll be there. We can talk more then if you would like. But, I hope you aren't going to ask me to go against Ginger. We can't ignore the accusation. We have to investigate. If you are so sure Manuel is innocent, then his innocence will come to light."

Raul stepped away without answering, his mouth grim and his brows furrowed as he joined a young Latino man, probably in his early twenties, standing near the exit. The younger man glared at Samia. He vibrated with anger. Raul laid his palm on the young man's chest. I couldn't hear what was said, but Raul frowned and moved his hand to the shoulder of the younger man, urging him to turn around. Raul was successful and they disappeared through the door.

"Who was that?" I asked.

"Raul," Samia said. Her eyes fixed on her empty placemat, as if she envisioned something unpleasant. "He works at the Foundation's Center." She barked a laugh and looked up at me. "Who am I kidding? He keeps the Center running. Ginger's foundation decided to fund a Center here in town to help native women who have been attacked or beaten. She asked me to co-run it, when she found out I'd volunteered to help immigrant women resettle here.

"At the Center, we get the women help, whatever they need. Legal help for restraining orders, we pay hospital bills after an attack, and Ginger puts a lot of pressure behind the scenes to get the legal authorities to follow through on prosecutions. But we are housed in an old building. It is beautiful, Old Santa Fe style, lots of adobe and tile, but it always has something breaking or wearing out. Raul can repair anything. I don't know what we would do without him."

Samia smiled sadly. "But it is not only his ingenuity or handyman skills. He is a kind soul. And our clients, who are often afraid of men after what they have been through, they seem to feel safe with Raul. They see him as a protector. He has barred the entrance from more than one young man who threatened one of our girls." Samia shook her head. "That is why this is so tragic. He dearly loves his nephew and wants to protect him, but Ginger is not convinced that Manuel is innocent. I considered letting this one case go, out of respect for Raul, helping the girl, but not issuing reward money for information, or hiring investigators to search for more evidence. But Ginger will not allow it. As much as she appreciates Raul, she vehemently objected when I broached the idea of not digging into the case against Raul's nephew, Manuel. She called it a slight slap on the wrist."

"A slap on the wrist? What was Manuel accused of doing?"

Samia sighed. "I've said too much. Sorry, Cleo. All of this is confidential. I'm not supposed to be talking about any of it."

"Of course," I said. We grew silent as the waitress approached with our food. When she left, I took a bite of my chili rellenos. The hot cheese burned my tongue, but it was worth it. "Wow, this is amazing."

"Yes. Maria's is known for their margaritas, but I come for their food." She took a chip and dipped it into the red chili sauce that covered her blue corn enchiladas. But before placing it in her mouth she pointed it toward me. "I would not put it past Jon to have stirred that whole situation up." Samia popped the chip into her mouth and reached for her fork, as I struggled to turn my mind away from my green chili rellenos to our previous discussion. The one she had ended.

"Jon stirred up the situation with Raul's nephew? I don't understand. And you realize you told me you couldn't talk about that with me. Right?"

Samia waved me off. "I cannot give you details of the allegations, but I can tell you I think Jon could be behind it."

"How exactly?" I asked.

"He has a lot of influence over Ginger," Samia said. "Ginger is the only person who thinks Jon is as brilliant as Jon thinks he is." She stabbed her enchilada. "Please understand, Ginger is no fool, but she puts great store in Jon's opinion. I could not comprehend why she would not take Raul's word that Manuel had learned from his mistake. But if Jon set her against Manuel, that would explain it." Samia dug into her food again, but with her fierce expression I don't think she enjoyed it.

I hesitated. "You know these people and the situation better than me, but don't you think you might be giving Jon too much credit? In the short time I've known him, I can see he's irritating, but would he truly stir up false charges?" As soon as the words were out of my mouth I remembered. That was exactly what Samia and Matias thought Jon was doing at the Institute.

Samia's eyes blazed, but her voice was ice cold. "You are right. You do not know these people as well as I do, and you do not know the stupidity of the furor that Jon has brought to the Institute. This feud between Jon and Matias has to stop. It is beginning to affect Matias's health. Jon has attacked my husband enough. I will not have it."

Samia's hand came down hard on the table.

Water sloshed out of my glass.

So much for my hopes for some light-hearted girl time.

Chapter 5

Ginger

Ginger cranked the air conditioner higher, but it was maxed out. With one hand on the steering wheel, she pulled her silk blouse away from her chest with the other. Her sunglasses were useless against the unrelenting glare of the Arizona sun. Her head began to throb.

Ginger sighed. She needed to call her niece back but dreaded it. She'd want to discuss the will again. Ginger liked Mimi but her entitlement issues were becoming wearisome. As she contemplated how she would break the news, the road in front of her shimmered and appeared to stretch forever.

No one crossed her path on this pot-holed, lonely road through the middle of the desert. She drove slowly. The bumpy road rattled her teeth. Ginger picked up her phone to see if any texts had popped up. No signal.

That was probably a good thing. Ginger's lips curled in a bitter smile. Right now she rivaled Jon for pissing off people.

Jon was furious with her, like Samia, Kyle, and her niece. Teresa hadn't said anything but trouble was brewing with her. She'd even managed to upset gentle, hardworking Teresa,

Ginger's mind slid to people at the center…like Raul. And Manuel. Her mouth tightened.

All those men who thought they could use and abuse and kick around her clients. She had received enough threats to know how much they hated her.

She vowed not to rest until those guys paid for the pain they'd caused. So what if she collected a few haters? This blonde Wonder Woman would do what she had to do. She laughed at the memory of her last Halloween party, and the Wonder Woman costume she'd worn.

A thumping noise sounded from the front of the car. Ginger gripped the wheel tightly and glanced at the dashboard.

"Damn," she said. A red light flashed. How long had that been going on? Kyle nagged her to pay attention to those things. Maybe she should've listened.

The scent of hot metal filled the car. Crinkling her nose and furrowing her brow, Ginger tried to remember how long it had been since she'd passed a gas station? An hour? Two? Should she push on and hope to see a gas station or some sign of civilization, or pull over and let the car cool down? The car made the decision for her and slowed. Ginger slammed her ankle-booted foot on the accelerator, but nothing happened.

She did the only thing she could and steered the dying car onto the thin shoulder. The right two wheels sank into deep sand that bordered the pavement as the car came to a stop.

"What to do?" Ginger whispered in the silent car and tapped her index finger on the steering wheel. The air conditioner had quit running when the car died. Remaining in the car with windows rolled up wasn't an option. Ginger opened her car door and stepped out. The 112-degree heat hit her like a blast from a rocket ship. She checked her phone. No signal. Ginger shaded her eyes and surveyed the empty road behind her.

Nothing. No sign of life. She made a 180-degree turn and scanned the road ahead of her. Again, nothing. She inspected the Porsche Cayenne she'd bought last year. Steam seeped out from under the hood.

Her fists tightened and she kicked the front tire, hard.

"Ow." Now her toe hurt. Feeling silly she leaned back into the car and grabbed the Gucci silk scarf she had tied around the handle of her bag. She used it to wipe the sweat that dripped down her brow and neck.

She should check the engine. On TV when a car overheated they opened the hood.

Ginger crawled back into the car, already at sauna temperature, and examined the area under the dash. She pulled every lever she could find. Finally, one pull caused the Cayenne's hood to pop open.

Ginger climbed out and strode to the front of the car. She gripped the hood to pull it up.

"Ouch." Ginger yanked her hand back and shook her scorched fingers. Screw it. She didn't know what she'd do with the hood open anyway.

Waggling her painful fingers slowly, Ginger considered the direction she'd been traveling. The road quivered in the heat. She narrowed her eyes at the steaming Cayenne. She shrugged and entered the car to get her bag.

Ginger opened her little cooler to see if another bottled water had escaped her notice. Empty, except for a little melted ice. Jon had warned her to bring plenty of water. Who knew she would need more than two bottles? There were a few swallows left in the one she had thrown on the passenger side floor. It was warm but she unscrewed the cap and carefully poured the melted ice from the cooler into the plastic bottle. A few drops spilled, but she captured most of it. Ginger put the cap on and shoved it into her bag.

She clambered out of the car again and dug into her bag. She unearthed a notepad and pen and scribbled a note telling anyone who found the car that she needed help and which direction she would walk. She left the note on the front seat.

Ginger hitched her bag up more securely on her shoulder and started walking. Her Italian suede boots were overkill, but they'd offer her feet some protection. With any luck there would be a gas station or a town just out of sight.

****

Hours later, Ginger couldn't be bothered to dig her phone out to check for a signal. A hot wind buffeted her. But it cooled her a tad as the sweat evaporated. The howling sound reminded her of being on the sailboat with Roger in the middle of that terrifying storm. The empty, desperate sound brought a stab of fear to her heart. Ginger shivered, despite the heat. On that expedition, all she could see was water and no land.

Now, all she could see was land and no water.

That was when Roger had his heart attack. They'd made it to the dock and rushed him to the hospital.

He'd survived to see the shore, but not home.

For all the good that did him.

Ginger yelled at the wind, "You won't get me." Then whispered, "No, you won't get me."

The wind paused, then roared again with a gust almost knocking her over, blowing sand on her exposed arms and in her face. She reached a hand up to protect her eyes, but it was too late. They burned and stung. She scrunched her lids tight. Sand scratched her eyeballs. She tasted grit in her mouth. And for a second, she thought she heard the wind laughing.

Chapter 6

It's Over

It had to be done. I flicked my fingers as I stared at my phone. The guilt was giving me a stomachache. I'd been dithering for days and had one nightmare after another last night. This wasn't one of Ben's teaching days and I should have called this morning, but I convinced myself mornings were a bad time to break up with someone. And with the time change between Hawaii and Santa Fe that excuse worked until late afternoon. I slogged through a report to a funding agency I needed to finish, describing our findings.

That was done.

Slumped at the desk at my casita I checked the time, 4:00. A little early, but I poured myself a glass of wine and stared at my phone. Maybe I didn't have to call. Maybe with us being on a break, it was understood that we could see other people.

But this thing with Luc felt important. He wasn't a meaningless fling. At least not for me. I believed on his part too.

Ultimately, the critical issue was where my feelings had pulled me.

I had loved Ben, and part of my heart still belonged to him. The big sea change was that I no longer saw my future with him. The future he and I had discussed never quite coalesced. He was drawn to stability and isolation. Part of me liked that, but another, bigger part of me longed for adventure and travel. I loved nature, but also cities, architecture, and navigating a new culture. And I no longer wanted to fight an uphill battle to share that with Ben. That was why I needed to call him. That was what I needed to tell him.

I took a swig of wine and picked up my phone. I dialed, but a flash of pain knifed my heart on the second ring and my finger hovered over the hangup button.

Too late.

"Cleo?"

"Uh, yeah. Hi, Ben. It's me." I swallowed hard. "How are things there in Hilo?"

"Fine." His voice was sharp. "Did you want something?"

Well, bless his heart, he was going to make this easier for me. "We need to talk. If now isn't a good time I can call back later."

Ben sighed. "No, now is fine. What do you want to talk about?"

I pictured him pushing his chair back from his computer, and the resigned expression he wore whenever I brought up relationship issues. I took a deep breath to calm my shaking hands. "I know we decided to take a break, but until recently I expected we would pick back up again and try to fix our problems when I got home to Hawaii."

Ben's chair squeaked. He must have changed positions quickly. "Until recently? What does that mean?"

"It means I don't think our problems can be fixed."

"Cleo. Wait. I mean, what's going on? I know you

get restless, but I've been patient with you. We had a good thing. Are you prepared to walk away from that?"

"You have been patient with me. But patiently expecting me to change, to settle down. And I've been expecting you to change. I don't see a happy future together for us if we're both expecting each other to become something we're not."

Silence on the line stretched to what felt like an hour. A tear rolled down my cheek. This is what I wanted. Right?

"It sounds like you've made up your mind." Ben's voice was tired, defeated. "But for the record, I would never have thrown our relationship away like this." His voice hardened. "I've never betrayed you and I've never held you back. There's nothing I can do to stop you, but I hope you don't regret this. If you walk away, don't expect me to be here waiting for you when you come back at the end of your sabbatical."

I ran my fingers through my hair. He had a right to be angry, I guess. "Yeah, I know. You've been great." My voice sounded flat to my own ears as I remembered all our discussions that were like talking to a wall.

Another pause. This wasn't how I wanted to end this conversation, but I couldn't think of anything to say.

Ben broke the silence. "The house is yours. I'll start hunting for a new place to live tomorrow."

"There's no rush. I'm not going to be back for another five months. Stay." Ben's chair squeaked again. I waited for him to respond. When he didn't, I blathered on before I could stop myself. "Rents in Hilo are expensive. Staying in the house will give you a chance to save some money before your expenses go up. You know that half the mortgage and utilities is less than you'll spend on rent."

Ben must have been thinking the same thing. "Okay, and it will also help you while you're paying rent on your sabbatical. I guess that's better for both of us." He paused and his chair squeaked again. "I'll stay here until you get back...unless I find a bargain that I need to act on quickly."

"Of course. Whatever works best for you."

There didn't seem to be a lot to say after that, so we hung up without any goodbye endearments. But then, Ben had never been much for endearments, goodbye or otherwise.

I set my phone down and sighed. I stared at my barely touched glass of wine before picking it up and carrying it to the couch. I opened a cotton throw blanket resting on the back and curled up underneath barely getting it to my chin before the flood of tears commenced.

Chapter 7

Meanwhile…

Meanwhile, somewhere in the Sonoran Desert a Gucci scarf snagged on a barrel cactus. With each jerk of the wind, the delicate silk shredded a centimeter. A desert spiny lizard perched on a nearby rock watched the dancing scarf, as two vultures wheeled and spun overhead. Waiting.

Chapter 8

Missing

I awoke with a pounding heart to an unfamiliar ringtone. I blinked at the sun streaming through the high windows in Luc's bedroom. It took me a minute to orient myself. Somehow, last night, I'd found myself crying on his shoulder. Luc was a good listener and encouraged me to talk and get the Ben break-up out of my system. Sometime after that, the consoling had crept into a yearning. A craving for Luc. This was the first time I'd spent the night at his house.

Luc picked up his phone, "Matias? Is something wrong?" He sounded much more alert than I felt.

I peeked at my watch, 6:15. I quietly got out of bed and collected my underclothes, sweater, and jeans that were strewn across the floor between the door and the bed. As I slipped into my clothes I glanced at Luc, sitting up, bare-chested. My stomach flip-flopped and I ached to crawl back under the covers with him. But the wave of desire was washed away by a wave of guilt. I hadn't made it twelve hours after my breakup with Ben before I jumped into bed with Luc. My mother would be appalled.

"Why are you so worried? She wasn't at the board meeting?" He was quiet again as he watched me dress, but he appeared distracted by whatever Matias was saying.

"Okay, okay, I'll make some calls and see what I can find out. But I think you're worrying for nothing. She's a grown woman and allowed to skip out on a meeting, or not answer calls from someone she thinks might be annoyed with her. I understand you and Samia are worried, though, so I'll do some checking around."

Luc put his phone down. "Where are you going in such a rush? Let me make you breakfast." A slow sexy smile slid onto his face as he lifted one eyebrow. "Or you could come back to bed, and I'll make you breakfast later."

A cocktail of desire and guilt coursed through my veins. I clamped a lid on my thoughts. "Who is Matias worried about? I didn't mean to eavesdrop, but I couldn't help but overhear."

The playful smile on Luc's face disappeared. "Ginger. She was expected at her foundation's center for a meeting with Samia yesterday afternoon, then at a board meeting last night, for the Friends of the Lab group that supports Matias's organization. It isn't like Ginger to skip meetings without letting someone know. They called her last night and again this morning, but no answer on her cell or home phone. Kyle isn't picking up either." Luc shrugged. "My guess is she's having problems with Kyle and ducked out of town for a couple of days. It seemed to me at dinner the other night those two weren't getting along. What did you think?"

"Yeah, Kyle seemed aggravated with Jon, but a lot of that appeared to be because Ginger was spending so much time with Jon. I mean, I don't know either of them well but that's how I interpreted it. Your theory makes sense."

Luc climbed out of bed.

I sucked in a lungful of air to stop myself from moaning. Damn, he was gorgeous.

"I'll call Jon as soon as it's a decent hour. Since he was the one stirring up trouble, he probably knows where she is." Luc stepped into jeans that fit per-fect-ly.

"Right. Yeah. Right." I stepped away from temptation. "Wasn't Jon going to the Navajo reservation with Ginger? Maybe she decided to stay a little longer? From what Samia explained to me, Ginger focused on helping Native American women who have been victims of sexual violence. Maybe she found an organization to partner with there."

I walked to the mirror to brush my hair. Luc, still shirtless, came to stand behind me. He wrapped his arms around my waist and tickled the back of my neck with his lips. "Yeah, I'll call Jon. Later." Luc's teeth nibbled my left ear. The brush slipped out of my fingers as Luc's hands slipped me out of the clothes I'd barely put on.

Two hours later, Luc had made us a breakfast of avocado toast, fruit and cheese, and I had made coffee. I was particular about my coffee. I didn't want us to begin a new relationship on the wrong foot if he made bad coffee.

After breakfast Luc picked up his phone to call Jon. "They were supposed to get back from their Rez Golf trip two days ago. I'll see if he knows what her plans were after she got back," Luc said.

"Good idea. Maybe she caught a cold on the trip and is home in bed. He'd know if she was feeling bad when he dropped her off."

I went to the kitchen and poured another cup of coffee while Luc called his friend. I didn't want to eavesdrop, but I was curious why Ginger wasn't answering her phone. Could she be hiding? But from who? Did she and Jon have a fight on the trip? Lord knows that wouldn't be hard to do. Or were she and Kyle arguing because she went to the desert with Jon? I didn't know Ginger well, but she seemed like the kind of woman who wouldn't shirk her responsibilities or hide from the world because of an argument. This situation worried me.

I drank my coffee. The warm velvety taste soothed me as I swallowed. I was letting my imagination run away with me. She probably had a cold and turned her phone off so she could sleep. How funny that my mind jumped to interpersonal problems. *Projecting, maybe, Cleo?* I thought of my irritation with Ben and grimaced. Yes, I'd probably projected my relationship angst onto Ginger.

I sipped my coffee again, but almost choked on it when Luc stalked back into the room with angry eyes and a tight jaw. I managed to safely swallow.

"What did Jon say?"

"He didn't go with Ginger to the desert." Luc's voice was terse. "After humiliating Kyle in public, Jon backed out at the last minute."

"Why?"

"He says the dust-up in the newspaper stressed him out and to relieve his anxiety he needed to stay home and work on his art. Evidently…" Luc's voice turned sarcastic. "Evidently he is at his most creative when he's stressed." Luc's lips squeezed together as if struggling to hold in a withering comment about his friend.

"Did Ginger cancel? Or did Kyle go with her? Wait…if she canceled does that mean she's been missing for four days?" My foreboding returned.

"No, she didn't cancel. She went by herself according to Jon. I called Kyle to confirm but it went to voicemail. His message said he would be unavailable until his art was ready for the show." Luc scowled. "What is it with these guys? Putting their art above a woman, whether a lover or a close friend. Ginger is amazing. She deserves better."

My heart stirred and before I could think, I set my coffee down, took three steps to reach Luc, and kissed him on the cheek. "You are a good guy. Do you know that?"

The frustration on Luc's face lifted and he smiled. He wrapped one arm around me and kissed me on the top of my head. "I like having you around the house. Do you know that?"

A warmth flooded my cheeks. Before I could answer, Luc removed his arm and took a step away, one eyebrow raised and a crooked smile on his face. "I better call Matias back before I do something I won't regret."

I blinked at a rush of disappointed arousal. I missed the brief bodily contact we'd shared. I picked up my coffee before I could reach out and pull him back.

Luc winked at me and reached for his phone.

****

"Samia? This is Luc. I promised to call Matias back after I'd talked to Jon." Luc listened before giving a low chuckle. "Agreed. They're both behaving like four-year-olds. I hate acting as the go-between, but Jon loves to antagonize Matias. I think they'll mend their differences quicker if they have as little direct contact as possible until this situation is settled."

Luc listened again.

I refilled my coffee cup. I'd never sleep tonight if I kept this up. But I needed to do something. As I poured the last few drops of the pot into my cup, Luc spoke again. "Maybe you're right. I guess the worst thing that can happen is we'll be embarrassed if she only decided to stay an extra few days or her phone broke or something." They said their goodbyes and hung up. Luc's focus shifted to me. "Samia is going to call the police and report Ginger missing."

"The police? She's that worried?"

"Yeah. Samia tracked down Kyle at his workshop this morning and he doesn't know where Ginger is. He's been sleeping at his studio working on his painting, and I guess he was still mad that she left on the trip in the first place. He was waiting for Ginger to come looking for him."

I bit my lower lip. "If Kyle is still mad, maybe Ginger is too. I'm not sure why Samia is so eager to get the police involved in what may be a lover's tiff."

"What Samia pointed out to me is that the Center, she, and Ginger receive threats regularly."

"The one Ginger described at dinner the other night? It helps victims of violence, mostly native women, right?" My mind flashed to my dinner with Samia when Raul approached to plead his nephew's case. And the young man who smoldered at the door, waiting for Raul.

"That's the one. Ginger's been making waves with some angry men who don't have much respect for women. When Samia put it that way, it makes sense to be safe rather than sorry."

"Is Samia calling them?"

"Yeah, probably as we speak." Luc enveloped me in his arms. "Now we wait to hear from Ginger or the police."

I wrapped my arms around his waist, my face smushed into his shirt. "And hope for the best."

Luc kissed the top of my head. "And hope for the best."

Chapter 9

Worried

I analyzed data all afternoon. We'd received survey and demographic information on refugees crossing the U.S.-Mexico border from one of Luc's team members in Nogales, Arizona. We'd worked on it last night, before…heat rose to my face. I stretched and soaked in the view of the late afternoon sky through Luc's giant floor-to-ceiling windows. After finally pulling ourselves out of bed for the second, or was it third, time Luc suggested I work from his house while he went to town for meetings. My delicious, satisfied mood from this morning had faded and a heaviness settled on my heart. My relationship with Luc was off to a delectable beginning, but I also grieved for the death of mine and Ben's.

I heard cawing and walked outside to soak up some late sun. Yards here in the high desert didn't have grass. Pinon, juniper, and occasional cacti or large boulders decorated Luc's property. There was a chill in the air, but the adobe walls radiated the heat they'd absorbed all afternoon. A movement in one of the pinon trees beyond the courtyard caught my attention. An enormous black crow landed on a top branch. Six or seven more crows followed until the spreading branches on the crown of the pinon tree drooped under their weight. The largest bird observed me with an intelligence I found unnerving. I shivered and breathed in the scent of pine mixed with a hint of smoke. Someone had their fireplace going. Fall came early to the high desert. My phone rang. I spun around to go back inside where I'd left it, relieved to escape the intense stare of the crow.

"Hey, Rikki. I'm so glad you called." The sky was darkening with the end of day, and the murder of crows had given me the heebie-jeebies.

"Howzit, chica. I've been thinking about you. What's been going on? You ready to come back to Hilo yet?"

Rikki's sunshine broke through my somber mood.

"You are tonic to my spirit, girl. What's happening in Hilo?"

"Hang on there; I'll tell you Hilo news in a minute. Why does your spirit need tonic?"

"Well, a woman I met, and liked, is missing." I took a deep breath. "And Ben and I broke up."

"What? You and Ben? Broke up broke up? Like for keeps? I thought you guys were giving each other some space? Whoa, wait a minute. You started dating that guy in Santa Fe, didn't you?"

"Yes, broke up for keeps." A tear leaked from one eye. "And yeah. I really like Luc and felt like I needed to let Ben go before I could follow the Luc-thing, wherever it's going to go."

"I'm sorry. I guess. I mean Ben is a nice guy, but if you weren't feeling it then it's good you cut the cord. And *did* you follow Luc's thingy?" Rikki laughed.

"Rikki." I laughed with her. I couldn't help it. "Shame on you, girl. You're so focused on sex you missed the fact that a woman is missing." But I didn't want to scold Rikki, and I didn't want to fixate on Ginger. To lighten the mood, I told her about the crows and made fun of myself for getting spooked by them.

I expected Rikki to laugh at me, but her voice grew serious. "I'd get chicken skin if I saw a murder of crows. There are a lot of cultures that view crows as mystical."

"Really? What magical powers are they supposed to have?" I tried to drag this conversation back to normal Rikki-cheerfulness.

"Early European cultures believed crows were harbingers of death. I've read some people say if you see one crow fly across your path it's bad luck. If you see two crows fly across your path it means good luck. But if you see six or more crows…someone will die. But I think crows are common in many parts of the world and I don't think death rates are any higher there."

"Having a group of crows greater than six, perched outside watching me, I am relieved to hear you say that."

"Native American beliefs often involved a crow as more of a trickster or someone in disguise. Someone trying to pretend they're someone they're not."

I shivered. Rikki's parents were anthropologists, and she had been raised on these legends. Who could be in disguise? "You're freaking me out. Let's change the subject. I spilled on what's happening here. It's your turn to catch me up on Hilo gossip."

"Pele's on the move again."

Pele was a Hawaiian deity, the goddess of volcanoes and by extension creator of the Hawaiian island. If Pele was on the move, a new fissure of a volcano had opened.

"Pu'u O'o, again?" I asked, referring to a volcanic cone on the eastern rift of the Kilauea volcano. That cone had been flowing off and on for the last couple of years.

"No, the floor of Pu'u O'o collapsed, and the lava shifted farther south. There were a lot of small earthquakes in Leilana estates, more than usual, and then a fissure opened. You know Gina has family down there."

Gina was married to a police officer in Hilo and related to half the island between her family and his. She and Rikki were my best friends. They inducted me into outrigger canoe paddling and open-ocean distance swimming when I first landed on the Big Island. We regularly met for drinks, or a morning walk and talk. I missed them. And last year when a former student had been killed, and one of my favorite students was accused of the murder, I had called in Rikki and Gina to help me find evidence to save him. We called ourselves the Scooby-Doo crew. They were my peeps. I was concerned for Gina and her family if the lava flow was headed their way.

"I hope this doesn't turn into another Kalapana type of event," I said. Kalapana was a quaint little town with one of the island's most beautiful beaches. Until Pele decided to visit back in the eighties. Now the town was covered in lava.

"Yeah. Me, too. But the geologists are already considering evacuations if the lava keeps opening fissures. They warn it might cover the road this time."

We were quiet for a minute. My thoughts on all the people who lived on that part of the island.

Rikki broke the silence. "I gotta go teach a yoga class. I just wanted you to hear about the lava before you saw it on national news."

"Thanks, and please keep me up to date, and if I can help."

We said our goodbyes and hung up. I looked out the window and found the murder of crows still perched. The crow king, as I thought of him, continued to watch me with his piercing eyes.

Chapter 10

Law on the Rez

Special Agent Joe Rivera pulled off the road, more out of habit than because of any need to get out of the way of oncoming cars. He pulled in behind a Tohono O'odham nation police car that was already parked. An officer stood several feet away observing a medical examiner kneeling over the body of a woman. Joe wanted to smile when he realized the ME was Annie, but he maintained his professional demeanor.

He took a swig from his water bottle, screwed the cap on tight, and slowly opened his door to the heat. The Tohono O'odham police officer lifted his eyes to Joe as he approached.

"*Sha Pui Mas Ma?*" Joe said, using one of the few O'odam phrases he knew.

The officer nodded, and responded, "*Mana sape, api hik?*"

"I'm good. What do we have today?" Joe asked.

"I've got phone calls and paperwork after I deal with some hooligan kids. *You* got a dead body. Not Indian. Looks like a white woman with money. Not our jurisdiction."

"Has the medical examiner given a cause of death?"

"I have *not.*" Annie spoke loudly from five feet away, as she shifted her attention from the body to Joe.

"But my early guess is that she died of heatstroke." Annie shook her head. Her long, black, straight hair tied back in a ponytail flipped over her shoulder with the movement. "You would think these people would have the sense God gave them to bring water with them into the desert."

Joe grinned. He'd met Annie on his last case in this part of the state. She was good: professional, compassionate, and hard-working. She also had a killer smile when she deigned to bestow it on a person.

But back to work. Joe spoke to the Tohono O'odham officer. "Do you have any idea how she got out here?" Joe's eyes scanned the horizon. There was nothing but desert in all directions as far as the eye could see.

"Not yet. Either the ME will be able to tell if she was thrown or dumped from a vehicle, or we will find her car abandoned somewhere. That's where I'm off to next. I thought I'd go one direction." He lifted his long arm and pointed east, then dropped it waved a hand westerly. "And you go that way".

"I just came from that direction," Joe said.

"Yeah, but this road splits about ten miles out. I'm guessing you only came on one of those roads."

Joe smiled sheepishly. "Yep. And I guess the first person who finds an abandoned car radios the other."

"Right."

As the two men walked to their cars, Joe called to Annie, "Do you need a ride? How'd you get out here?"

"I rode with him." She stood up, stretched her back, and lifted her chin in the direction of the patrol car that was pulling out onto the road. "He happened to be in town when the call came through and offered to drive me out. My team is on the way, and they'll give me and the body a ride back to the morgue after they collect all their evidence." She glanced at her watch. "They should be here any minute." She rolled her shoulders and pulled an evidence bag out of her pocket before she waved him off and kneeled back down to work on the body.

Joe sighed and climbed into his car.

Chapter 11

Mama

"Hey, Mama," I said when I answered my phone.

"Hey, sweet baby girl. Your daddy and I have been talking about you. Were your ears burning?" My mom grew up and lived her entire life in a small town in Virginia.

"I hope it was all good."

"Oh yeah, we were just saying how glad we are that you aren't in Hilo right now. We were watching the news last night on that volcano there. Hoowee, I thank my lucky stars you aren't there now, sweetie. Of course, we are worried about poor Ben. Is he in any danger?"

I took a deep breath. I guess now was as good a time as any to tell them. "Actually, Mama." I winced, then plowed on. "Ben and I broke up. He's fine though. Our house and the university are not in the path of the volcano."

"Oh, Cleo, no. Honey, what was wrong this time? We thought Ben was a good man for you. I mean we love having you back in the USA—"

"Mom, Hawaii is in the United States, the 50th state, remember?"

"Yes, I know. But it feels like another country and it's so far away from home. Your daddy and I understood when you wanted to go there for a while, but we worry.

The only thing that reassured us was thinking you had finally settled down with a good man. Someone who would bring you back to our ocean after you had a little adventure there in Hawaii." Her voice softened and I heard a sadness in it. "Why did you run this time, honey?"

I swallowed. "Mama, you have to trust me. It wasn't working. It wasn't what you and Daddy have."

"Your daddy and I didn't have it trouble-free when we got started. You didn't see that. You were too young to understand. But your daddy and I, we struggled and stuck together and *now* we have what we have, the relationship that we have. We didn't have it then, back in the early days."

I swallowed hard again and cleared my throat. "I have to go, Mama. Lots of work to do today. I'll call you soon." A tear rolled down my cheek.

"Sweetheart, I'm sorry. I let my mouth run on. I'm sure you have your reasons, it's just that…well, sweetie. You always seem to run away at the first hint of trouble. I was glad of that when you went through your bad-boy phase. But when you find a good man, you need to change your tactics, baby girl."

Wow, could my mother be right? Was breaking up with Ben a mistake? My stomach twisted into a knot. We said our goodbyes and hung up, both of us sadder than when I had answered the phone.

Chapter 12

Sad News

Kyle, Luc, and I met at Luc's house for the afternoon. Kyle had worked up some ideas on the website for Luc's Institute and wanted to make a formal presentation. It was Luc's decision, but he wanted my input on it. Kyle wore a dress shirt and tie, his sleeves rolled up. He was usually a jeans and T-shirt kind of guy. This outfit made him appear older and more intense. I was surprised he didn't dress this way more often.

"Sorry it took so long for this initial presentation," Kyle said. "As you know, I have the art show coming up, and I was committed to finishing my work for that before I did anything else. Thanks for your patience. Today, I've brought examples of three approaches we could take for your website. Each has advantages and disadvantages. I have a recommendation, but I'd like to get your initial feedback before I tell you which one is my favorite." Kyle flashed us a smile.

Luc's phone buzzed with a text. "Sorry." He reached for the phone to mute it when another text came through. He glanced up quickly at Kyle. "Just a minute," he said, and quickly texted back. He laid his phone down and glanced at Kyle, then me before standing up. "That was Samia. She has something important she needs to tell us. She's on her way over. Maybe I should make some coffee or something." He shoved his phone in his pocket and dashed to the kitchen.

Kyle and I exchanged a look. "That was weird," he said.

I agreed.

Kyle chewed his lower lip and scowled.

Then it hit me. Samia must have news on Ginger. The police must have called her since she filed the missing person's report.

"Have you always wanted to be an artist?" A weak distraction, but he appeared worried.

Kyle stopped chewing his lip and shifted his gaze to me. "Yeah, I have. I bussed tables at the hotel where my dad worked. But I hated that and found a job cleaning an art gallery."

"I think you told me you grew up in Arkansas?"

"Yes, Hot Spring, Arkansas." Kyle's brows furrowed and he chewed his lip again.

"From cleaning an art gallery to web designer to having your own art in a gallery, that's quite an impressive path you've taken," I said.

Kyle shrugged. "There was also a stint as a mechanic. One of my dad's buddies thought I needed a better paying job than cleaning at the gallery, so he hired me to work in his garage. I hated it. All that grease and grime, and I was always banging up my fingers or knocking my head on something. But that motivated me to study computers and web design. And that's how I met Ginger." A fond smile came over his face. "She hired me to design the web page for her Institute, and we fell in love."

Luc carried a tray with sugar, milk, and four cups into the room. He wouldn't meet Kyle's gaze. "The coffee must be almost done," he said and returned to the kitchen.

Noticing the four cups, instead of three, I called out to Luc, "When are you expecting Samia to get here? Where did she call from?"

"She left her office ten minutes ago, but couldn't get a signal. You know the spotty coverage we have around here. She said she was a few minutes away."

A knock came at the door as Luc carried a pot of coffee out to us. I opened the door to an unsmiling Samia.

Her mouth set in determination, Samia stood, elegant and poised, in black pants and a goldenrod silk top.

"Hi, Samia," I said.

"Hello." But her eyes searched behind me as she responded to my greeting. I stepped back and waved her into the room. Her eyes locked on Kyle, who seemed startled by the attention. He glanced at Luc and then me. I gave a slight shrug to indicate I didn't know what was going on either.

"Kyle," Samia paused. She swallowed, cleared her throat and started again. "I've had word of Ginger."

Kyle's eyes opened wide and the corners of his mouth curved up. "Great. Where's she been? Is she coming home soon?"

Samia's large, beautiful eyes filled with tears. "I am sorry, but Ginger is dead."

Kyle took a step back as if he'd been punched. He dropped into a chair and folded over, head buried in his hands, elbows braced on his knees.

Luc placed a hand on his shoulder. "What did the police say?"

Kyle looked up sharply. "Police? What police?"

"I was worried when Ginger disappeared that one of the abusers she has been pursuing might have harmed her. But that doesn't appear to be the case."

"It was Jon." Kyle jumped up, grief transmuting to fury. "I tell you, it was Jon. He knew he couldn't have her and killed her to stop her from being with me."

Luc and Samia both stepped in front of Kyle before he could charge out the door. I think they feared he would drive off and do something he would later regret.

Samia extended a graceful, but firm hand and placed it on Kyle's chest. "No, it appears it was a tragic accident. Ginger ended up in the southern part of Arizona, on the wrong highway and her car overheated. She tried to walk for help but was overcome by the heat and died of heatstroke. I'm sorry." Samia pulled her hand back.

The fire drained from Kyle. Luc stepped close enough to put a hand on Kyle's shoulder. "Would you like to stay here tonight?" Luc glanced in my direction, and I nodded. "I don't think you should be alone. Give yourself some time to recover."

Kyle's shoulders drooped. "No. I want to go home. I need to go home. I should have gone with her. I'll never forgive myself."

"What do you say, I go with you then. I can help you get settled in. Make sure you have food in the fridge," Luc said. "I can drive."

"I'll pack up your stuff." I moved to stack the folders and notes that Kyle had laid out for his presentation. I closed his laptop and slipped it into its sleeve.

"Thanks, Luc, but I don't want to leave my car here."

"I'd like to help too, Kyle." Samia stood on the other side of him and mirrored Luc by also placing a hand on his shoulder. "Ginger was my dear friend, and she would want me to help you. I could call her relatives and let them know, if you'd like. I can follow you and Luc and drive your car home. Then, when we have you settled, Luc can give me a ride back here to my car. How does that sound?"

Kyle sighed. "That's probably a good idea. I'm pretty shaky. Ginger didn't have any blood relatives, just one by marriage, Roger's niece, Mimi. But that would be good if you could break the news. I...I'm..." He swallowed hard, and his eyes glistened with tears. "Thanks, guys."

The three of them organized keys, and I carried Kyle's laptop and folders out to Luc's car.

"I'm so sorry, Kyle," I said, as I opened the passenger side door for him.

After he was inside, Luc, who stood on the driver's side with his door open, blew me a kiss. "I'll text you once we get him settled."

I raised a hand to wave, then shade my eyes from the bright sun as I watched the two cars pull out of the driveway. I followed their path up the winding dirt road before returning to the house.

Poor Ginger. Poor Kyle. My heart ached for them both. How could this be? What was she doing in Southern Arizona, so far away from the Rez Golf she was going to on Navajo land? Just days ago Ginger was vibrant, and full of plans. Just minutes ago, Kyle was confident and excited to present his ideas, not realizing the woman he shared his life with was dead. A tidal wave of vulnerability engulfed me. Anyone could be taken away from me in a blink of an eye. I thought of my parents. They were getting older. Close to Ginger's age. Not old yet, but older. How long before I lost one of them? My eyes filled with tears. I didn't leave things good with my mom on that last phone call.

My phone rang and I jumped. Was it Mom with bad news?

I grabbed it so quickly it almost slipped through my fingers. Not Mom, Rikki. I breathed a sigh of relief and hit the green button. "Hey, Rikki. Wow, how did you know I needed cheering up? I had psyched myself into a super-dark moment."

"My spidey-senses told me you needed a call, girlfriend. I got the vibe." Rikki's voice bubbled from my phone.

"Really? A vibe?"

Rikki snorted. "I do yoga, not psychic readings." She laughed. "I want to hear what drove you to the dark side, but first, I have news that may cheer you up."

"Yeah? What's up?"

"Gina is preggers."

Gina, the third of our three musketeers had been trying to get pregnant with her cop-husband for several years. A grin split my face. "That's fantastic. I bet she and Kawika are over the moon happy."

"More like over the toilet. Poor Gina's got bad morning sickness. But she smiles through the vomit. And still paddles."

Gina's uncle was head of the halau that I paddled with in Hawaii. Gina and I were in the same six-person outrigger canoe. I wasn't surprised that a rough pregnancy couldn't keep her off the water.

Rikki also updated me on the volcano. "New

fissures are starting to open. And in neighborhoods. We haven't lost a house yet but the vog is pretty toxic. They are asking people to evacuate a few areas and if they stay they are supposed to wear gas masks."

"Really? It's that bad?" I had experienced vog, the official name for smog produced by a volcano. When Madame Pele belched the days could get hazy. But I hadn't faced vog so bad that gas masks were recommended. But no new fissures had opened up when I was on-island.

"It's that bad." Rikki's normally sunny voice was somber. "That's all the news from the Big Island. What's happening with you? Why did you need cheering up?"

"Do you remember from our last phone call that a woman I met here was missing?"

"Yeah. That was the day you saw the murder of crows."

"Right. She's dead."

"Dead? What the heck, Cleo? Did you find another dead body? People are going to think you're a jinx or something." I could hear worry in Rikki's voice, even as she tried to make a joke of it. "Do we need to reunite the Scooby-Doo crew again?"

What I wouldn't give to have Rikki and Gina here. "No. I mean, come for a visit if you want. I'd love to see you. But I don't think it's a murder this time. They think she took a wrong turn in the desert and her car broke down. She died from heatstroke. She was a kind, intelligent woman trying to help others and make a difference in the world. It's sad."

"Well, let me know if you need us. Remember, Ali's death last year looked like an accident at first. Gina and I can hop on a plane if you need your crew there. Gina might be puking the entire trip, but you know she would come if you needed her."

"I know. You guys are the best. Tell Gina I hope she feels better, and I'll be back in Hilo before she gives birth. My sabbatical is only for six months. Never mind; I'll call her and tell her myself."

We said our goodbyes and after hanging up I tried to call Gina, but she didn't pick up. I laid my phone down on the table and ambled out onto Luc's patio and gazed at the mountains. We had mountains on the Big Island, but they were the youngest in the island chain. Green and graceful Mauna Loa and Mauna Kea were usually shrouded in clouds. It was a rare day to have their slopes fully exposed. Here in Santa Fe, there was rarely a cloud in the sky. I could drink in the shadows created by the angular, red, brown and green peaks of the Sangre de Cristo Mountains, the southernmost subrange of the Rocky Mountains.

My mind drifted back to Gina. *Hapai*. Pregnant. I smiled. My tough, sometimes cynical friend was finally going to have her baby. She would be a great mother. The baby would soften her. I couldn't wait to hear her use baby talk. She who made fun of adults who cooed at babies. I looked forward to teasing her when I caught her doing it. I happily anticipated Gina's baby. I'd get to hold her or him. And babysit. It would be fun to be an auntie. But I was also a little sad.

This time last year I was considering the possibility of Ben and me having a baby. I destroyed that option. Would I ever have my own child, or would I always be the auntie? My mind slipped to Luc. Too soon to ruminate about a baby with him. Time to focus on something else.

I walked into the kitchen to see if Luc had ingredients for a casserole. Wasn't that what grieving people needed? Food they could stick in the freezer and pull out when they wanted it. That was a way I could help.

Chapter 13

"To Ginger"

Samia carried a platter of grilled lamb from the kitchen and placed it on the dining room table. Matias followed closely behind with a platter of grilled vegetables.

They had invited us to this dinner before Ginger went missing. It had only been two days since we received the news of Ginger's death. Luc had called Matias to see if we should cancel or postpone. Samia had insisted we come over. She had also invited Kyle, but he had declined.

"Dinner is served," Samia said. "Would you mind pouring the wine, Luc?" I'd filled the water glasses while Samia and Matias finished the food, and Luc had opened an Italian Primitivo he'd brought. He poured it into four roly-poly Waterford crystal glasses already set on the table.

Once everyone was seated, Matias raised his glass of wine. "To Ginger, an amazing woman whose life ended much too soon."

We raised our glasses. "To Ginger."

We dug into the food. Samia had used middle eastern spices I wasn't familiar with, but I loved. Dinner was delicious, but the mood somber. A fire crackled in the living room. At 8,000 feet elevation, the hills around

Santa Fe were cool at this time of year, while the Sonoran Desert could have temperatures well over 100 degrees. Ginger probably wasn't prepared for that heat. After complimenting Samia on the meal, the conversation faded until Luc asked the question we had all been thinking.

"How could this have happened? Have we heard any more from the police about how Ginger died?"

Samia shook her head. "The officer called me when they found her, since I had reported her missing. But when he found out that Kyle had been living with Ginger, I think he has been giving Kyle the details." She took another bite and her brow furrowed. After swallowing she continued. "Although Ginger had a niece. I wonder if the police know? The niece, Mimi is her name, is probably the next of kin. Kyle and Ginger were not married, but they have lived together for…almost a year, I think. Mimi is coming to town next week. Her trip was arranged before Ginger died. The three of us were supposed to go to lunch." Samia sipped her wine. "I wonder if she will still want to go? When I broke the news of Ginger's death, she said she would come to help Kyle deal with everything, but I do not even know if Ginger told her about the lunch. Or if she will want to go, even if she is aware of it."

"Check with Kyle," I said. "Or the niece if you still have her number."

"Right, I have her number on my phone. And I wanted to reach out to Kyle anyway. See if he had any plans for a funeral or celebration of life, or anything."

"Did Mimi tell you if Ginger had any other family?" I asked. "I know Kyle said she was the only one, but maybe there was someone Ginger forgot to mention to him."

"Ginger did not have any blood relations," Samia said. "No siblings and she never had children. Mimi was Ginger's husband's sister's girl. But the sister-in-law died shortly after Ginger's husband. I believe it was only Ginger and Mimi after that. I have met her before when she was visiting. If Mimi and Kyle do not have any ideas on a ceremony, I can contact her cook, Teresa, or one of the staff at the foundation. Ginger treated her employees like family." Samia's eyes filled with tears. "She was such a kind person. We lost a treasure when Ginger died."

Riiiinnnng.

The landline rang loudly. Samia and Matias both cocked an ear. Luc and I continued eating. An answering machine picked up after the first ring.

"Samia? Sorry to bother you, but there has been a break-in here at the Center…"

Samia pushed her chair back and rose from the table to pick up the call as the woman's voice continued on the answering machine speaker.

"Thank goodness Raul was here to stop them and prevent them from entering, but the alarm had already been triggered. Raul waited for the police…"

Samia picked up the phone and silenced the speaker. "I am here, Sandra. Did you say the police came?" Samia's face tensed as she listened to the voice that no one else could hear.

Matias leaned into the table and spoke with a quiet voice. "Am I a terrible husband if I'm relieved it was her Center calling with a problem and not the Lab?"

"The power couple." Luc chuckled softly.

"I don't know how much power either of us has. We

seem to put out fires and jump up to answer phone calls in the middle of dinner. Not much power-wielding going on around here." Matias poured more wine around the table.

Samia hung up the phone.

Matias cleared his throat and looked at his wife. "Do you have to go, or did Raul and Sandra handle it?"

Samia waved one hand in his direction as she sat down and spread her cloth napkin back across her lap. "They have it under control. The burglars didn't get in, and since I wasn't there, I can't add anything to the police report."

"Does your Center get broken into often?" I asked

Samia speared a piece of meat with her fork. "No. In fact, I have always thought the alarm was a waste of money, but Ginger was a stickler for security. She worried some of the clients' confidential information could be stolen. That is why there are several layers of locks. Not only on the filing cabinets, but the rooms with records, too. And all the doors and windows have alarms."

My mind wandered to the encounter with Raul I had witnessed when Samia and I had met for lunch. Raul was polite and respectful, but he wanted help for his nephew. What was the nephew's name?

As I struggled to remember the incident, the conversation had moved on. I looked up from my plate to see that everyone was staring at me. What had I missed? I gulped the bite I had been chewing and smiled. "Sorry, did you ask me something? I lost myself in your cooking for a minute, Samia. It's amazing."

Samia laughed. "What better compliment could a chef receive?" Her smile faded, and her voice lost its effervescence. "We were discussing the volcanic eruption in Hawaii. Is that happening anywhere near where you lived? Have you heard anything?"

"Yes. The volcano that opened new fissures is on the Big Island, my island. My house and the University are probably safe, but a lot of homes farther south are in danger." I explained what I had learned from Rikki in our phone call earlier in the week.

Matias brought in dessert as I described the volcano. When the baklava was set in front of us and coffee poured, Luc spoke.

"Samia, Matias, do you remember when Ginger took that trip to Hawaii? She came back with koa bowls for everyone, including Teresa, her cook."

Everyone around the table smiled. And more than one eye glistened as they each shared their favorite Ginger story.

I wished I had more time to get to know her. I think I would have really liked her.

Chapter 14

Agent Rivera

Joe picked up his phone on the second ring. "Special Agent Rivera here."

"I've got your lab report on the abandoned car, Joe. Your victim's fingerprints are all over it. And license and insurance match the ID in the wallet you found. It's her car." The call was from one of the techs who had collected evidence on the scene.

Joe had thought as much when he found it and the note she had apparently left on the front seat. He didn't want to mess with any evidence before the crime scene people arrived, but he saw the cooler and empty water bottles in the car along with a briefcase that looked like it might have belonged to the elegantly dressed dead woman. "That makes sense. The M.E. found nothing inconsistent with death by natural causes. And with her car, and the victim's note, that shows she wasn't dumped. Unless you found sabotage to the car, we can mark this as death by misadventure."

"That's the thing," the tinny voice came out of the phone. "There was sabotage. A small hole was drilled into the radiator. It was clearly made by a drill and not debris, from the edges of the puncture and the placement. Someone wanted her car to run smoothly for some time before breaking down."

Joe sat up straight in his chair. "Well, well, well. That's a horse of a different color. Maybe I should take a drive to Santa Fe. I'll give the police there a head's up that I'm coming. But, I need to do my homework here first. When can I get your report on evidence from the car?"

"I should have that ready for you later today, if I don't catch another case."

"I appreciate that. See you this afternoon." Joe terminated the call and pulled a legal pad out of his right-hand drawer. He scribbled his thoughts down feverishly. He had believed this was nothing more than a silly woman unprepared for the desert. He had only taken sparse notes.

Joe's eyebrows drew together. He needed to make up for his sloppiness by recording every detail of what had transpired since the initial call. Then he'd go through her briefcase and everything from her car. He tapped his pencil against the desk, frustrated. He would make up for his initial slackness. Her killer would not get away.

Chapter 15

The Will

"My talent is hiring the right person," Mimi said, an impish smile on her face, honey-colored hair falling gracefully over one shoulder and down her back in deceptively natural, but perfect, waves.

Samia's brows drew together lightly. "You hire people? For what company? For what jobs?"

Mimi's laugh rang delicately, like an entry bell to a candle shop. "Why, whoever will pay me. I organize events of all kinds. I organized a motorcycle event in downtown Manhattan, a fundraising ball for the Metropolitan Museum, and an inauguration event for a popular New England senator." Her smile grew larger. "An event organizer is what I put on my resume, but 90% of what I do is finding the right person for the right job. Caterers and janitors are only the first step. I had to find motorcycle mechanics, tire repairers, leather repairers, and masseuses for the motorcycle event and a hundred different odd jobs that will assure every motorcycle rider and their guests have a great time. That is the key to successful event planning."

Luc laughed. "That sounds challenging. I had an electrical problem last year, and it took a dozen calls to find a good electrician that could fit me in. The recommended ones were booked months in advance."

"And that's just the legal jobs." Mimi put her hands together in a silent clap and leaned in. Her voice dropped to a dramatic whisper. "One of my first events was for a movie director, who shall remain nameless. He wanted a marijuana buffet with at least twenty different strains, in a state where pot was still illegal." Mimi straightened up with a big smile on her face. "And I made it happen."

Jon snickered. "Now that's an event I want an invitation to next time."

Kyle scowled.

"That's amazing." Samia glanced sideways at me. I don't think she was referring to Mimi's hiring skills as much as she was stunned that someone could make a living, and a good living to hear Mimi tell it, by hiring people with other people's money.

The door to the conference room opened and Ginger's attorney strode in. Everyone fell silent as all eyes watched the distinguished-looking Hispanic man with a boyishly handsome face and a touch of gray at the temples enter the room. He set a thick file on the desk, then sat down himself. He poured a glass of water from one of the pitchers near him on the table, cleared his throat and then, and only then, did he lift his eyes to contemplate the rest of us in the room.

"Let me explain why I have asked you all here."

Mimi giggled, then slapped her hand over her mouth. "Sorry. Nerves, I guess. It sounded like a line from a movie." Another giggle had to be stifled, then blushing, she said, "Go on. I'm fine now."

The lawyer cleared his throat again and smiled at Mimi. "It is not uncommon for people to laugh during times of stress. I promise, you're not the first person I've heard laugh at a solemn occasion. And not because they were happy." He surveyed each of us sitting around the table. He paused as his gaze settled on me. Probably trying to decide who I was and why I was there. Then his eyes dropped to Luc's hand, resting on mine. He nodded. I presumed he recognized Luc had brought me for support.

He cleared his throat and opened the folder in front of him.

"I want to be clear that this will has not been through probate and is not part of a public record. We have filed with the court and it will take approximately six months to a year for it to be finalized. But Ms. Ginger Hanlon left a sealed copy with my office to be read soon after her death, so her beneficiaries would know what to expect and could plan accordingly. I'm not sure if you are aware, but Ms. Hanlon updated her will every year. This gathering is not something we ordinarily do—bring all the beneficiaries together at one time like this, but Ms. Hanlon was a long-time client and a good friend. It was a special request on her part. I promised her I would carry out her wishes."

He pulled an envelope out of the folder, slit it open, and pulled out a document.

"I will start with the small bequests. To Ms. Teresa Martinez and Mr. Raul Garcia, she leaves $200,000 to each of you and her heartfelt thanks for your kind and faithful service."

Teresa and Raul, who were sitting next to each other along the back wall, and at the words, Teresa clutched Raul's hand, before she brought a tissue up to dab at her tear-filled eyes. Raul remained motionless, but his eyes also swam with tears.

"Mr. Jon Suvorov and Mr. Kyle Paige will each

receive a painting from Hanlon's collection." The lawyer's eyes shifted to Kyle. "Mr. Paige, Ms. Hanlon wanted you to have the painting by Elizabeth Russell from her Heatseeker collection. She bought it at the Bay Area Art show because she knew how much you loved it. She hoped it would bring you fond memories of that weekend. She finished by writing, 'It will make me happy that you will continue to enjoy it after I'm gone.' " The lawyer turned his gaze to Jon. "To Mr. Jon Suvorov goes the David Hockney painting."

Jon beamed. "Good ole Ginger. She knew how much I loved that painting."

Kyle shot Jon a withering glare.

The lawyer cleared his throat again. "She has also left $200,000 to the Santa Fe Artist Aid Association with a note that it should be divided evenly between the two of you to support future shows of your work. It can only be spent to support your shows, and if it is not used within three years, it reverts to the general fund for artists."

The lawyer lifted his head from the document. "The three-year time clock would, of course, not begin until the will is probated, and the money distributed to the charity."

"I won't have a problem with that timeline." Jon smirked at Kyle.

Kyle stuck out his chin. "Me neither."

"Moving on, Mr. Luc Bastien, Ms. Hanlon leaves $500,000 for your new Institute. She does this in appreciation of the wonderful work you do." The lawyer looked at Luc, a fond smile on his face. "She insisted I read that part to you. She told me it was important that you understood your work was valuable."

I glanced at Luc. He squeezed my hand and blinked away tears. With a bittersweet smile, he dipped his head to acknowledge the attorney.

The lawyer flipped a page and continued. "Ms. Hanlon leaves her house and all the objects within to her niece, and only living relative, Ms. Miriam Margaret Adair." The lawyer regarded Mimi kindly, "But you will need to remember that you cannot take possession until the will is probated. Mr. Paige will be accorded some period of time to vacate but perhaps if we put our heads together we can find some mutually beneficial arrangement with the court to assist with the coordination and handover of the property."

"Some of the things in the house are mine, so Mimi doesn't get everything in there. But it's a big house. I think we can work something out so she doesn't have to stay in a hotel until probate."

"Thanks." Mimi smiled at Kyle.

The lawyer glanced at the page in his hand before flipping to the next page. "Those are all the small bequests."

I was stunned. *Luc's $500,000 bequest was a small one?*

"Now I'll move on to the bulk of her estate." He looked up at everyone around the room with raised eyebrows. "It is large. We are instructed to sell off all of her other properties and when added to her holdings, which, when the will was updated a couple of months ago, were estimated to be…" He flipped to the next page. "Roughly…a little over two hundred million dollars."

Samia gasped, and even Jon's jaw dropped.

"After everything is sold and tabulated, the estate is to be divided evenly between two beneficiaries, her niece, Ms. Miriam Margaret Adair; and Ms Hanlon's Foundation. She further directs control of the Hanlon Foundation be transferred in its entirety to you, Ms. Samia Keller."

Chapter 16

Watching Lava

I closed my laptop and rubbed my eyes. I was
working at the casita for the day. I needed to write up a
summary of the immigration data I'd analyzed last week.
Luc had back-to-back teleconferences scheduled at his
house for projects that didn't include me. I wanted to
give him his space and I would get more work done here
without Luc as a distraction. My stomach fluttered. What
a distraction he could be.

My mind wandered. A break was in order. A break
that didn't involve walking to the end of the street and
Luc's house. I reopened my laptop and clicked on the
Big Island news bookmark. Most of what I found were
videos and updates on the volcano. My house in Hilo was
in lava zone Three, relatively safe compared to parts
south, like Pahoa which was lava zone Two. I switched
to Facebook and found former students and friends of
friends who lived in areas near the newest fissures. They
posted videos of the latest flow.

I couldn't pull myself away from the screen. The
slow, inexorable movement of the lava as it folded in on
itself when it hit a rise in elevation. The black cake batter
crust overrun by fluid, scarlet-orange, was hypnotic. And
the sounds…the quiet, popping and crackling as it
consumed branches, a whine as it pushed a door open on

a shed, followed by the unhealthy gurgling as it consumed an old wheelbarrow propped against a chicken wire fence connected to the shed.

My survivor's guilt tasted like bile in the back of my throat. Here I was, ensconced safely in Santa Fe, while Gina's family lived in a risky lava zone One. I hoped it wasn't one of her uncle's sheds on the video. My thoughts progressed to all the people who lived in Puna. Even if the lava didn't hit a home, if it crossed the road, it would cut off lower Puna from friends, family, and livelihoods. A forty-minute drive into Hilo became a four-hour drive into Hilo. Rikki led yoga classes down there. How many of her clients would be cut off? And my poor students…a lot of them lived in Puna. It was hard enough for many of them to get their education. With electricity and internet cut off, they wouldn't even be able to take online classes until it was restored. And when the utilities were re-established, and the internet was back up, depended on Pele.

My thoughts drifted to Ben. He would want to help. I considered calling him, but I didn't know what to say. Images of last night in bed with Luc flashed in my head. My face grew hot at the memory. I lifted a hand to my cheek. How could I talk to Ben with the memory of Luc's hands on my body fresh in my mind?

Ben and I were really over. My stomach clutched up—I hadn't thought about Ben all week. Had I been in his thoughts? Did I want to be? Was I ready to move on…not just experience something different? How would I feel if Ben slept with someone in Hilo while I was here? It was only fair. He had every right, but my mouth puckered. *I'm sure he hasn't. Has he*? No…Rikki or Gina would have told me. *Wouldn't they*?

Sheesh. The Big Island had a volcano erupting, disrupting the lives of people already living close to the edge, and I was obsessing about my love life.

"Priorities, Cleo," I said aloud.

I should call someone, anyone. To offer support, see if I could help. I wouldn't be able to refocus on work until I'd done something. I pulled out my phone and called Gina. She picked up on the second ring.

"Howzit, chica."

"Hey, Gina."

"We miss you at paddling, girl. The new steersperson's not too good."

It was nice to be missed. "Miss you too, girl. How's the pregnancy going? Feeling any better?"

"Oh, little Thumper is a force to be reckoned with. He or she wants Mom to know who is boss before they get here." I heard a smile in Gina's voice.

"I hope you feel better soon. But hey, I watched some videos of the volcano posted on Facebook. Wow, Pele is on the move."

The joy drained from Gina's voice. "Yeah. I think she means it this time. This could be another Kalapana situation. We are up to eighteen new fissures opening. And they've closed Highway 11." Gina's voice grew quiet. "My cousin probably lost her house. They had just finished building it and moved in with their new baby eight months ago. Last week, civil defense gave their neighborhood a mandatory evacuation notice. She hasn't been able to get back down there to check, but that flow took out a lot of houses."

"I'm sorry. Can I do anything to help?"

Gina sighed. "The island is pulling together. Somebody's got a wish list or something set up with an online store. I'll text it to you. In addition to diapers, towels, and clothes, the big need is gas masks and filters for the masks."

"Air quality is that bad?"

"Bad? It's toxic in Puna. It's only really, really bad here in Hilo. To be honest, we have canceled paddling the last two weeks because the vog level was dangerous. But, sorry, girl, I just realized what time it is, I'm due at my ob-gyn appointment in fifteen minutes. I gotta run. Miss you."

"Bye, Gina," I said, but I'm not sure she heard it before she hung up.

The situation on the Big Island was dire. At least now I had a plan. I pulled up the website Gina had texted to me while we talked and ordered a couple of gas masks and a dozen filters.

That was not an order I ever thought I'd make.

Chapter 17

An Email

Joe ran his fingers through his hair. None of this made sense. Why was Ms. Hanlon on that road leading to the most barren section of the Sonoran Desert? He was most of the way through reading all the documents in her briefcase and they all pointed to her having business farther north in Shiprock. That was hours away in the wrong direction. How could she have gotten that lost? It didn't square with the sabotage to her car, or the receipt from a swanky hotel in Phoenix. He was missing something.

Joe's eyes were bleary from reading. He pushed his chair back and strolled into the break room to get a cup of bad coffee. He gazed out the window. A tumbleweed with a plastic bag clinging to it blew across the parking lot. He stretched his neck and went back into his office to review the stack of documents he had already read. His victim was one of those do-gooders who wanted to save the world. She had depositions from Native American women who had been raped. Unfortunately, the names had been blacked out. Probably to protect their confidentiality, but it was going to make his work more difficult. There were clues from some locations and landmarks mentioned in the depositions about where these women had been attacked. He would have to work backward to see if he could find out which jurisdiction they were in, and if the local tribal police knew who these women were. Men who raped or assaulted one woman and got away with it weren't likely to stop there. One of these women that Ginger Hanlon was trying to help could know the identity of Ginger's killer. But would she discuss it with a man?

Joe sighed and sat down at his desk to read the stack of documents he hadn't completed yet. It was going to be a long afternoon reading these accounts of abuse.

Twenty minutes later, Joe sat up straight, his chair screeching a complaint at the sudden movement. This was interesting. He reread the printout of an email one of the techs had found in the victim's car and piled onto the rest of her documents. This piece of paper was crumpled on the lower right side, probably from her holding it tightly with one hand while driving with the other. Someone had emailed her directions that put her on that notoriously deserted road. The instructions promised her she would reach an Indian village that was unreachable on that road. *Could it be a mistake? I don't think so. Not when I put that together with the sabotage of the car. Finally, a possible lead.* Best of all, the victim had printed out the entire email so the sender's email address was visible.

"BrillianceInAllThings, boy, this sender has an ego. They only signed it J, but that should help narrow it down. Carlotta," Joe called out to his assistant in the next room. "I found something you need to dig into."

Chapter 18

Cleo's Offering

After ordering the gas masks, I went back to work. I switched from my data write-up to finishing the slides I had promised Luc I'd prepare for his presentation next week. It was to a private funding agency. If he received the money he was asking for, there would be funds for a position for me. Or someone with my qualifications.

I was committed to going back to UH Hilo after my sabbatical. Faculty on sabbatical were obligated to return for the length of time they had been gone. I'd have to go back for at least one semester. Luc had been encouraging me to return to Santa Fe after that to work with him. That's why he worked long hours on grants and fundraising appeals for his fledging Institute.

I appreciated his enthusiasm, and the idea was appealing. But it was a major decision. I was settled in Hilo with friends and more stability than I'd usually had in my adult life. I had job security at the university. And I owned my home, well, with a little help from the bank.

Thoughts of my house triggered a realization that I hadn't spoken with Ben since the volcano flared up. I had told him there was no rush for him to find a new place. With the highway to Puna covered in lava, hundreds of families must be displaced. He would never find anything now. Broken up or not, I wasn't going to kick him out of the house. And the house had a guest room if it came to that. I should call and let him know. I would hate for him to stress over finding a new place.

I picked up my phone and called him before I chickened out. I suddenly had a dry mouth and tried to swallow a sip of water before he picked up.

"Cleo?" Ben answered, his voice brisk.

I hadn't expected him to pick up on the first ring.

"Cleo is that you? Did you mean to call me?"

I swallowed. "It's me. On purpose." I set my glass down. "I've been hearing news of the volcano. The lava over the road and the heavy vog. I just wanted to make sure you're okay."

"I'm fine. Yes, there is heavy particulate matter in the air, but I don't need to drive into Puna. As you know, most of my work is either here in Hilo or on Kona-side."

Ben was a marine scientist who worked out of Hilo Bay or on the west side where there was another nice bay with easy access for the research vessel, unlike the south island, where the lava was flowing.

"But a lot of my students are struggling." Ben's voice finally softened and I heard the squeak of his chair. He still hadn't oiled it.

"Yeah, Gina's cousin is waiting to hear if lava took her house. It sounds like there are a lot of people that may be homeless."

"That's why you called? You're afraid I won't be out of here when you get back?" Ben's voice hardened again.

"No, no, not at all." I tried to break in, but Ben continued as if he didn't hear me.

"You don't have to worry. I'll figure something out. And this lava won't last forever. It could stop any day."

"Wait. *No.*" I almost yelled into the phone.

Ben stopped talking. An icy silence reached across the ocean and desert that separated us.

I took a deep breath and continued in a quieter voice. "I called to tell you not to worry about moving out. Things must be chaotic there and housing shortages are going to be a real issue. Right now, I'm sure people who evacuated are camping on couches and spare rooms of relatives and friends, but eventually, if they can't go home, they'll have to find a new place to live. What I called to say is…" I took a deep breath. What exactly did I want to say? What was I willing to commit to? "What I wanted to say is that let's play it by ear. We are both grown-ups and even if we aren't together, the house has three bedrooms and there's room for both of us to live there if we need to. If there is a housing shortage. We could manage for a while." I took a deep breath and slowly let it out. That situation would be awkward, but what else could I say?

"Right. Okay." I heard surprise at my words. "That's decent of you, Cleo. Thanks."

"Well, I hope I'm a decent kind of girl." I meant it as a joke, but Ben's silence made me wonder if he took it that way.

After a couple of beats, he finally spoke. "Okay. Great. Thanks again, Cleo. Gotta get back to work now." Ben hung up before I could respond.

We once had a loving, affectionate relationship. What happened to us?

Chapter 19

Joe's Therapist

Special Agent Joe Rivera knocked on the therapist's door.

"Come on in." The woman who rose to greet him was in her mid-sixties. Her hair, more gray than black, was pulled back in a bun and the smile on her face widened at the sight of Joe. Her blue-green suit was rumpled and she exuded energy.

Joe smiled at the woman he had at first resisted, but then come to admire. "Dolores, you ate lunch at your desk again. What are you always telling me about that?"

Dolores laughed and re-wrapped a half-eaten sandwich. "Do as I say, not as I do. And besides—I work with the good guys. That's easier."

Joe's smile faded. They moved away from her desk toward two armchairs on the opposite side of her office. These mandated meetings with Dolores, the federal psychologist hired to keep federal agents from losing it, began after a case last year. Joe had hunted a kidnapper who had stolen two teenage sisters from their beds. For three days and sleepless nights, he tracked them, only to find one tortured, catatonic fifteen-year-old, chained next to her sixteen-year-old sister who had bled to death the day before from unspeakable injuries. That case had messed with Joe. He shook his head to rid his brain of the image.

Joe glanced up and found her studying him. He forced a smile onto his face and moved to take his normal seat. "The saxophone lessons are helping."

He concentrated on relaxing his shoulders. Pulling them down from their creep up to his ears, as she had taught him. Dolores had recommended that Joe find something—anything, to do in his time off that would keep him from thinking about the job twenty-four-seven. She had suggested painting, woodworking, or music. Joe had discovered a used saxophone at a garage sale the following weekend, and a musician was born. That same weekend he'd called someone about giving him lessons and never looked back.

"In fact, my teacher asked if I wanted to join his band for rehearsals."

"That's great." Dolores' smile widened, then sobered.

Joe knew the drill. This was when she would push him to test his resilience.

"Any new cases troubling you? Anything we should talk about?"

Joe leaned his elbows on the top of his thighs and stared at his tightly clasped hands. "Yeah, there is."

The therapist didn't speak, and a heavy silence settled on the office.

Joe took a deep breath. "A woman was found dead on the rez. Heat exhaustion, her car died, and she didn't have any water." Joe shook his head. "I thought it was death by misadventure. A tourist, who wasn't prepared." Joe's gaze jerked up to the therapist. "But it wasn't."

"No?"

"No." Joe sat up and leaned back in his chair. "The

car had been tampered with and was found at the other end of Arizona than where she was supposed to be." He raised his index finger. "But, we found an email from someone who sent her bad directions. Directions into the middle of the Sonoran Desert. And, we found a receipt for a swanky hotel in Phoenix, which was not on her planned route."

"You have a suspect? That was quick."

"No. I lost a day assuming it was misadventure." Joe lips puckered. "The victim was a lady. A woman, close to sixty, with a lot of money, living in Santa Fe. And there is a younger boyfriend. But…" He relaxed and leaned toward his therapist.

Dolores smiled. "What?"

"The email of bad directions didn't come from the boyfriend. It came from a friend who is also male. It could be a romantic triangle." Joe shook his head. "It could also be something completely different." He hunched over and clasped his hands again. "But this woman, see. She wasn't just some old rich lady. She was a good woman. She ran a foundation that tried to help native girls that have been raped."

Joe's face hardened. "She was trying to help these girls. She was trying to get justice for them. Bring their rapists to trial. And I think she may have had enough money and enough political pull she might have been able to do it." He scowled. "And I'm thinking one of those perpetrators may have wanted to stop her."

Joe looked up and read concern on his therapist's face. He forced himself to straighten up and take a deep breath. He managed a smile. "No worries, Doc. I'm fine. I'm just going to take me a little trip to Santa Fe and sort out what's what.

Chapter 20

Lunch Interrupted

I ordered my tuna-pesto panini and searched for a place to sit. The patio tempted me, but I needed to work. I chose the long table inside with my back against the wall. While I waited for my food, I opened my laptop to revise and flesh out the project proposal Luc and I had brainstormed earlier this morning. I had only made it through the first point when I heard the scraping of a chair being pulled out next to me. I glanced up and saw Kyle. He seemed better than a couple of days ago at the reading of Ginger's will.

"Hard at work, I see." Kyle winked.

Yes, he was definitely in a better mood.

Before I could answer, a smiling young man delivered my food. "Is that everything you wanted?" he asked.

"Yes, it looks great." I closed my laptop.

"I didn't mean to disturb you," Kyle said. "If you want to keep working, I can move down the table."

"No, no, a girl's got to eat." I nodded toward the chair he had pulled out. How are the preparations for your art show going? Do you need any help getting set up?" I took a bite of my panini.

Kyle shook his head and grimaced. "No, the gallery owner canceled it after Ginger died. I asked him to postpone instead, but he said no. In honor of Ginger he didn't want to go through with it. Sounds stupid to me, but I don't get a say." His gaze drifted to my food. "You've found my favorite spot for a quick lunch." He sat down next to me.

"My first time here," I mumbled, four fingers in front of my mouth so I could talk with my mouth full of panini and not gross him out.

"As soon as you finish eating, I'll let you get back to work, but there is something I wanted to talk to you about. Seems like kismet to see you here."

I swallowed my first bite and looked from my panini to Kyle's face. "Do you want to discuss the website?

"No, not the website. An FBI agent called me this morning. Ginger's death wasn't an accident. He thinks she was murdered."

I dropped my panini on the plate. "That's unbelievable. I thought she died of heat exhaustion in the desert." I watched Kyle for clues as to how he was taking this. To find out your lover was murdered must be worse than an accidental death. My mind raced. Maybe not. Kyle's expression was excited-angry, rather than heartbroken. Maybe if he had someone to blame, the anger would help him deal with Ginger's death.

"Do they have someone in custody?" I asked.

"Not yet, but the agent is coming to Santa Fe to investigate." Kyle raised his eyebrows. "And I told him it was probably Jon who killed her."

"What?"

"The FBI agent said Ginger's car was sabotaged, and an email signed with a J, from Jon's email address, giving her instructions to the remote place in the middle of the Sonoran Desert where they found her. The FBI agent asked me who I thought J was and if I knew the email address." Kyle sounded smug. "I told the agent it was Jon. Obviously, he lied about going with her, damaged her car, and then left her there to die." Kyle stuck his chin out confidently. "It's only a matter of time before Jon is arrested."

Hmm, I wasn't so sure. "If Jon was with Ginger, why would he email her directions? And Samia told me Ginger had left a note in her car telling which direction she was walking. If Jon left Ginger there to die, wouldn't she have put that in the note too?" I shook my head. "I don't know, but maybe we should let the FBI agent do his job."

Kyle's smile faded. "I get it. You have to defend him. Luc and Jon are friends, but there's something you should know. He has a dark side under all those jokes he makes."

Ugh. First Samia and now Kyle. I didn't want to get dragged into another feud someone had with Jon.

"Luc has known him for a long time, so I'm sure he's seen all of Jon's sides, dark and otherwise. And I don't know him." I lifted my panini to my mouth for another bite, hoping he would move on to something else.

"Does he know that Jon's father was a Russian spy?"

I closed my mouth without biting and set the panini back down. I glanced sideways at Kyle, skeptical.

Kyle mimicked a Boy Scout salute. "It's true. I swear. Ginger told me. I can't believe they even allow him to work at the lab. I've heard they have a lot of grants and contracts with the Defense Department."

"Even if his father was a spy...what does that have

to do with Jon?"

"He's deceitful, I tell you. His father was deceitful as a spy, and he taught those skills to his son." Kyle stuck his chin out. "Jon told lots of lies to Ginger. Mostly about me, but probably about you and Luc, too."

I took a deep breath. "I don't know why he would tell lies about me. He doesn't know me. What makes you think he has told lies about you?"

"He was trying to turn Ginger against me. He was jealous of our relationship. I think he wanted her to sponsor his art, but she liked mine better." Kyle's upper lip curled. "She loved me and my art. He was trying to take her support away, but he couldn't."

How tragic. Ginger was a trophy to Kyle. Smugness, not sadness, emanated from his face. I'd lost my appetite. Maybe my waiter would wrap my panini up to go.

My phone rang. It was Samia. Normally I'd turn it off and call her back when I was alone. But Kyle's vendetta against Jon, and lack of respect for Ginger, was tiring. I appreciated the interruption.

"Sorry, but this is Samia, and she has something she needs to tell me that she says is important. I need to take this." A little white lie. I had no idea why Samia wanted to talk to me, but I didn't want him to think I was blowing him off. Which, of course, I was.

"Sure, I'll go order." Kyle stood and moved to the counter.

"Hi, Samia. What's up?" I asked.

"I'm here at the foundation. An FBI agent called. He said Ginger was murdered and he is investigating. He had some questions about Ginger's laptop and the files he found in her car. It made me think. Maybe I should try to…Oh, I do not know. Somebody should figure out everything she was working on and follow up. We can not leave our clients in limbo. But I feel like I am invading her privacy prying in all her drawers and files." Samia's voice faltered.

"The federal agent has the laptop?"

"No, but he is driving here tomorrow to get it. He told me not to touch it. But Ginger reliably backed up her files on the cloud each day. I think I know how to access that. If not, Sandra can help."

"Do you want more help? There might be information in those files that point to a suspect. But you're right, this is possibly confidential. I have a lot of experience working with data at the University. I can help you set up a blind coding system if you want. And while we're at it, we can keep an eye out for any offenders that might have had a grudge against Ginger. I can't help thinking there could be something in her case files related to some of the angry ex-boyfriends that reveals a motive for her murder."

"Do you mind?" Samia asked. "It is a little scary to hunt for that information by myself. I have some ideas of where to start, but you are a psychologist. You might recognize something I would not. Are you free tomorrow? Oh, I just realized I was on the phone with the detective longer than I thought and I need to get back to the lab for a meeting."

"Sure. Text me the time and I can meet you tomorrow."

We said our goodbyes and as I hung up, Kyle returned to the table with a coffee and a paper bag labeled pear-almond tart.

"Everything okay? he asked.

"Yeah. The FBI agent called her too. I'm going to

help her set up a confidential system tomorrow so we can study the case files at the Center and see if anything points to someone with a grudge against Ginger."

Kyle's eyebrows raised. "But she hasn't found anything yet?"

"No, but she has some ideas of where we might start."

Kyle pounded the table. "I tell you, that's a waste of time. Jon is the killer."

I didn't want to talk about Jon, or Ginger, or death. I didn't want to get sucked into the shadowy underbelly of Santa Fe like I did last year in Hilo. Investigating a murder was dark business. At this point in my life, I'd like to focus on getting the most out of my sabbatical in Santa Fe. Developing a coding system for Samia was one thing, but listening to accusations depressed me.

I took a deep breath and let it out slowly. "Kyle, it's great to run into you, but I really need to get back to this proposal if I'm going to finish a first draft today."

"Sure," he said. "I got this to go anyway. I have errands to run. Talk to you soon, Cleo." He raised his hand holding the paper-bagged pastry in a wave.

I waved back before taking another bite of my panini. It was cold, and I had lost my appetite. I set it down and resumed my work.

****

An hour later, I packed up my laptop and sauntered downtown to stretch my legs and explore Old Santa Fe. My mom's birthday was in a few weeks. I could look for a gift. I walked past the large territorial-style Roundhouse, the only round State Capital building in the country and circled toward Loretto Chapel with its miraculous staircase. I continued on to the Plaza, ducking into shops if something in a window caught my eye.

I found a pair of silver earrings with a little chunk of gorgeous turquoise. Posts, not dangly, so Mom could wear them to work at the café she and my father ran. I held them up to my ear. Yes, she would love these. I flipped the tag. The price was more than I planned to spend, but my mom never indulged on frivolities for herself. For me and my dad, yes, but not herself. If she was going to get nice earrings, they would have to come from me. I smiled imagining her telling me "you shouldn't have," and handed over my credit card. I would economize somewhere else. Like now. Since I'd wrapped up my panini and it was stowed in my bag, I had planned to get a coffee at one of the enticing coffee shops I'd passed on the way. But not today. The money for today's coffee would go to Mom's earring fund. I tucked the earrings into my bag and stepped out of the shop.

The day was blustery with gusts that swirled leaves around me. I tucked my chin into my coat. Winter was coming. I waited for the traffic light before I crossed to the Plaza on the other corner. I noticed Jon exit one of the excellent coffee shops I'd skipped. I raised my hand to call out to him when he turned back to hold the door open for someone behind him. Mimi. She walked through, carrying a Lucchese's bag and smiled up at Jon, playfully nudging her shoulder into his chest. And from here it looked like she laid her head on his shoulder for a moment.

It struck me as an intimate gesture.

One of Jon's hands came down to Mimi's lower back and gently pulled her away from blocking the doorway to the coffee shop. She gazed up at him as if expecting a kiss, but Jon's hand dropped, and he said something I couldn't hear. Mimi laughed and the intimacy ended. She stepped away and they strolled off in the opposite direction of me. I let them go.

What had I witnessed? They didn't kiss or hold hands, but the closeness of their bodies and Mimi's focus on Jon's face left me with the impression of a romance.

Was Mimi picking up where her aunt left off? Living, at least temporarily, with Kyle and flirting with Jon. But was Mimi going to take it further with Jon than I think Ginger would have? But what do I know? I only met Ginger once. And if Mimi had an affair with Jon, what business was it of mine? I chuckled. I was becoming too immersed in this Santa Fe intrigue.

Chapter 21

Chinese for Dinner

Luc and I sat across from each other in a hole-in-the-wall Chinese restaurant.

"I ran into Kyle today," I said.

"He had a rough morning. Did he seem upset?" Luc asked.

"Not as upset as I'd expect him to be after hearing Ginger was murdered. He made some wild accusations about Jon to the FBI agent. He really hates Jon."

"What?" Luc's eyes opened wide. "Ginger was murdered? The FBI called? That must have happened after I talked with him."

"I guess. I was having a late lunch when I saw him."

"Wait a minute, why is the FBI involved? Everything I know about the FBI I picked from television or the movies."

"The FBI has jurisdiction for major crimes in Indian Country like murder, sexual abuse, and kidnapping. From what I understood from Ginger at her party, her Center was in large part set up to help native women who were victims of major crimes. The FBI has jurisdiction, but doesn't always investigate," I said.

"That's right, I remember Ginger explaining that."

"But you're saying Kyle was having a bad morning even before he got that news?" I asked.

"Right, he came by to work on the website problems. We had barely started when Mimi called him. Those two have not been getting along."

"Oh? That surprises me," I said.

"Kyle says Mimi has been cataloging Ginger's art and valuables. And Kyle's stuff is getting mixed in her list." Luc opened his menu. "She called to ask which painting Ginger had bequeathed to him. I didn't see why Kyle was getting so upset. But he needed to vent. We didn't get much work done after that."

"Maybe he's grieving, and every time Mimi asks him about one of Ginger's possessions it reminds him Ginger's never coming home. Maybe all Kyle's anger toward Mimi and Jon is just his way of dealing with his grief," I said.

Luc's mouth curved into a smile. "You are good at sizing people up. Anybody ever tell you that you would make a good psychologist?"

A goofy-happy feeling came over me. I felt sorry for Kyle, but it felt peaceful sitting here with Luc.

"I'm glad you like this place. It isn't fancy, but the food is good and…" he hesitated. "I'm glad you like it."

I sensed I'd passed a test. I didn't know what the test was, but I had passed.

The owner came out with a loaded tray and my stomach growled. As she handed us our chopsticks Luc's phone rang. He groaned and pulled it out of his jacket pocket.

"It's Samia," he said and silenced his ringer. "I'll call her back after we've eaten."

I'd scooped my first bite into my mouth, and my phone immediately rang. Luc's eyebrows raised as I pulled my phone out of my bag and swallowed. Was I not going to get through a meal without phone interruptions today? "Samia calling me now."

He laid his chopsticks down. "This might be important. Maybe you should pick up."

I answered my phone.

"Samia? Hi, Luc and I are at dinner. What's up?"

"Matias is out of town on a trip, and well…" Samia's voice twisted before she paused.

"Has something happened?" I asked.

Luc looked up from his food.

"I received a call. A threatening call. This person, a man…he knew where I lived and that I was alone." Samia's voice wavered.

"What did he say?" I asked. Luc studied my face, but I focused on Samia. I'd explain it to him after the call.

Samia's voice was barely audible. "He said I should go back to Saudi if I don't want anyone else around me to die. He said I should drop whatever I was doing and go home to my parents."

My eyes met Luc's. "How about Luc and I come over, Samia? Do you feel like Chinese?"

Luc nodded and waved at our waitress.

"Would you mind?" Samia said. "This has never happened when Matias was gone. Or been this direct."

"There have been other calls?"

"Yes," her voice sounded tired, but a little stronger. "Would you mind bringing an order of Mu Shu chicken with you?"

"One order of Mu Shu chicken," I said.

Luc gave me a thumbs up.

"Done. We'll be there in about thirty minutes."

****

We passed stately Ponderosa pines as we drove into the foothills of the Jemez mountains. It took a little longer than the thirty minutes we had promised because we had to wait for the Mu Shu chicken. But we were warmly ushered in by Samia when we arrived.

Samia pulled out black stoneware plates as Luc and I unpacked the food. We had wrapped ours for takeout so we could eat together. There was a chill in the air, and Samia suggested we take our plates into the living room and sit in front of the fireplace. A large stone mantel surrounded the fire and we seated ourselves on cushions at a low table in the middle of the room. Samia went to the kitchen to open a bottle of wine and I followed to help with the glasses.

"I told Luc what you said about the call. He had a lot of questions. I do too. I don't want to invade your privacy, but if you want our help…" I raised an eyebrow at Samia before I carried the glasses back to our low table and sat next to Luc on the floor.

Samia took longer than I expected to open a bottle of wine and Luc and I exchanged a concerned glance. Luc pushed himself up off his cushion as Samia entered the sitting area with the bottle and a tight expression on her face.

Samia focused her attention on filling our glasses. She avoided eye contact with either Luc or me. That action completed, she licked her lips and flashed a grimace at an unoffending wine glass before clearing her throat and raising her eyes to meet ours.

"I do not like to speak of this. For many reasons. Which I will explain. But I have interrupted your dinner and dragged you out here. I feel I owe you an explanation."

"You don't owe us anything," Luc said quietly.

"And you didn't drag us here. We offered," I said.

Samia set the wine bottle on the table and sat down across from us.

"You are kind people. Normally I turn to Matias when these things happen. But he is on an overnight flight from Europe, and I could not reach him. I should explain after worrying you." Samia swallowed and inhaled deeply.

"I was born and raised in Saudi Arabia by a wealthy, well-connected family. Because of that I was allowed more freedom, in the home at least, to be educated and speak my mind. My father doted on me and was secretly proud of my intelligence." Samia stared at her food and pushed it around the plate with her chopsticks as she spoke.

"I was allowed to study here in the U.S. for my bachelor's degree. I came with a girlfriend from Saudi. We had grown up together. Her parents let her come because my father was allowing me to come. We were supposed to watch out for each other and keep each other in line following sharia law and customs."

Fascinated by Samia's history, I took a bite of my food without tasting it.

"Adara was more daring than I. She became involved with a woman's group that encouraged her to seek equal rights in Saudi. She posted things on Facebook that challenged the king to give women more rights." Samia's mouth twisted bitterly. She raised her eyes to meet ours. "That did not go over well, as you might expect."

"The royal family worries about what a young woman writes on Facebook?" Luc asked.

"Of course. Dissent of any kind is illegal. Protests of any kind are illegal." Samia toyed with her food. "Poor Adara, her family demanded she return home immediately. They married her off within weeks of her return. She did not receive her degree because we were in the middle of the semester. Fall of our senior year. My parents were disappointed that I had let Adara get herself into trouble. I am not sure how I could have stopped her, but that was beside the point. I had embarrassed our family by being connected to someone who had expressed criticism of the royal family."

Samia sipped her drink. "At that time, I met Matias. He was wonderful—intelligent, supportive of the difficulties Adara was having, and respectful. He was not at all like the stories I had heard about American boys." Samia smiled. "I convinced my parents to let me finish my senior year and get my degree. Of course, I said nothing about Matias. My mother was not happy, but my father allowed it with the understanding that after I earned my degree, I would return to Saudi and marry." Samia looked at us with a plea in her eyes. "I would have promised anything at that point to stay in the U.S. a little longer. I was months away from earning my degree and I was falling in love with Matias. I knew the relationship could never amount to anything, but I wanted to enjoy it as long as I could." Samia shook her head.

"I was naïve. I went home during the winter break and ran into Adara at a woman's gathering. She had a black eye she had tried to cover with makeup. When I could get her alone I asked about it, but she refused to answer and walked away. I told my mother about her bruised eye when I got home. She scolded me for prying. 'What do you think a husband would do to such a willful girl?' my mother asked. I could not believe it. But I was young and foolish, and I pushed on. It seemed impossible that just six weeks after getting pulled out of school my friend was married to someone who hit her. But my mother told me I was stupid. Of course, that is what happens when a young woman acts out. She is shunted off to a husband who will take a firm hand with her, before she can embarrass the family further.

" 'You would do that to me?' I asked. I will never forget her face. 'You had better not ever embarrass this family,' she told me. Our family was more important than Adara's. If I caused trouble, my father could not protect me. His father would demand a harsher punishment. She would not tell me what that would be, but I was terrified. I was scared to death they would find out I was dating Matias. I have never been so relieved in my life as when my airplane took off from Riyadh."

Samia stared at her plate, one hand holding chopsticks, the other resting gracefully on the table.

Luc reached across and laid his hand on hers. "You are incredibly brave," he said.

Samia's eyes filled with tears. She squeezed his hand before removing hers to push back an inky lock of hair that had fallen over one eye.

"No. Matias was brave. I borrowed his strength. We married in secret the day before graduation. My parents had come to see me graduate and take me home. Instead of attending our graduation ceremony, Matias and I drove across the country to Berkeley where Matias had been accepted for a post-doc position. My parents did not realize I had fled until my name was called at the ceremony and I did not walk to the stage. I left them a letter at their hotel explaining I was sorry for disappointing them, but I had married an American and was staying in the U.S."

"Wow," I said. "That must've been the most difficult decision of your life. At what age, 22?"

"I was twenty-one. It did not seem like a difficult decision at the time. I was having nightmares about Adara and what would happen to me if my parents ever found out about Matias. And…" Her face softened. "I was in love."

"But why would they wait until now to threaten you?" I asked. "You've been married for years, right?"

"Eighteen years last June. But they did not wait. I have been receiving calls, letters, texts, and emails from family and friends since then. They started almost immediately. At first, they coaxed and made me feel guilty because I had hurt them. Would I come home for a visit to reassure them I was happy and healthy? I almost went. I had booked a flight to go back for Ramadan about two years after our marriage.

"The night before the flight a cousin in Saudi texted me and told me not to come. She had overheard her father and our grandfather talking. Her father had been tasked with punishing me when I arrived. They would never have let me leave the Kingdom."

No one spoke for some minutes. The silence, like a heavy blanket, suffocated me. The Chinese food had grown cold, and our wine glasses were barely touched. It was inconceivable that this intelligent, sophisticated, beautiful woman had family members prepared to physically punish her for falling in love. Those ideas should have died out in Shakespeare's time.

Luc recovered his voice first. "You have been getting these calls for eighteen years?"

"No. When I backed out of my trip, that is when the threats started. Every time I would post a happy picture of me and Matias on Facebook, trying to show my family he was a good man, and I was happy, I would get threats. First, mean, awful, nasty comments from my male cousins, but then the phone calls began. Demanding I return home to Saudi." Samia sighed. "Then I read about Saudi women who violated family traditions and ended up dead after returning home. And the Saudi journalist, Jamal Khashoggi, who was murdered by the Prince in the Saudi embassy in Turkey…that terrified me. I don't feel like I can visit a country within his grasp and be safe."

Samia stared at her plate. "After that, I quit social media. I considered venturing back online, but in 2019 Twitter found that two Saudi employees were spying for the royal family on expats like me." Samia exhaled heavily. "That panicked me. I broke off all posting on social media and the calls became less frequent. I do not think I have had one in ten years. I cannot believe it is happening again." A tear rolled down her cheek.

I took a deep breath too. This was wrong. Samia didn't deserve this, no one did. "Can you remember anything about the voice? Did you recognize it? Was it male or female? Did they speak Arabic or English?" I asked.

Samia lifted her eyes to mine with interest. "Yes. Now that I think…tonight the caller spoke English. Eighteen years ago the calls were in Arabic."

"So maybe it wasn't your relatives this time," I said. "Is there anyone here in the U.S. who would want to terrorize you?"

Samia shook her head, then abruptly sat up straight.

"No, but I had a thought. Could Ginger have been killed because of me? Could the Saudi government have gone after her because she gave voice to my concern for women's rights?

"Ginger wanted me to work on the social media platform for our organization. But I could not. I just could not. She and I did not always agree, but once I explained…" Samia paused. "Ginger understood. She let me work in the background. She did not want to expand our mission, as I did, to immigrant women who suffered harassment and abuse, but she did not push me to expose myself. Could they have killed Ginger?"

"I don't know. But we may find a connection in the files," I said. "I also think it's something we should tell that FBI agent when he gets here."

Chapter 22

Thoughts on the Road

The flat sandy desert with nothing more than a few gray chamisa bushes and misshapen juniper trees had rolled on for what seemed like ages. Joe's mouth was dry, and the wind buffeted his car as he drove. When he passed the exit for Acoma pueblo resort, the earth lifted and gave topological vivacity to the desert. It reminded Joe of Annie, the ME. She had hiked there one weekend and told him it was amazing. At the time, he had almost invited her to go back there with him. But they were in the morgue, one of her techs walked up, and the moment passed.

Maybe I'll text her tonight and mention I drove by her hiking trail. I could invite her to come back with me some time for a hike, and dinner...and maybe an evening at the resort/casino...Shoot. Who am I kidding? He hadn't found time to ask her out for a first date, and she wasn't the type of woman you texted to ask out. Besides, he had a murder to investigate. Best to keep his mind on the case.

He'd scheduled an interview with the live-in boyfriend. Joe had the feeling the boyfriend was a mooch, but he knew better than to settle on a person too early and resisted his early bias.

Speaking of trying not to judge, my techs traced the

email with the wrong directions back to an arrogant, piss-ant scientist. I'd love it if that cocky SOB was the killer.

But Joe sighed, the guilty party was almost never who he wanted them to be. It wasn't a good idea to judge or hope someone was guilty or innocent before he had all the facts. That was Joe's approach. Check out all the motives, all the alibis, all the means. Even from his brief telephone conversations with the boyfriend and the snotty scientist he could tell those two hated each other.

Is a love triangle at the root of this case?

That was listed in Joe's notebook as a possibility. But he didn't want to settle on that yet. While he was in Santa Fe he also wanted to check out the Women's Center the victim ran, as well as her co-director.

That co-director seemed a little stiff on the phone. Feeling guilty? Or just nervous talking to the FBI?

Joe also planned to examine the clients at the center.

When you help abused women, there are likely to be some angry, violent men that'll have a motive for killing you.

Joe thought he might need some help with that. Confidentiality for clients sometimes caused a hassle. And the murder itself was complicated. He'd have to check who had the knowledge and means to sabotage her car while she was on a trip away from home. That would eliminate some suspects.

It was a challenge investigating the murder of someone so wealthy. Some people would be motivated to keep her alive, like a mooching boyfriend, and some would be motivated to bring about her early death, like whoever inherits that wealth.

Joe's stomach growled. He glanced at the clock on

the dashboard, lunch time. If his memory served, he could grab a laguna burger at the next pueblo. As he saw the exit coming up he flipped his blinker on and hoped there wouldn't be a long wait. He was starving.

Chapter 23

Jon Worries

We sat on the patio of a café on Canyon Road. Our table nestled next to a pinon tree embedded with jays. The pinon appeared to struggle to reach its branches through the taller, stronger juniper that was rooted next to it.

Jon twisted the napkin that had come with his coffee. He had called us last night and asked Luc and me to meet him for coffee. His normal irreverent expression, replaced with a worried brow and a grim line of thin lips. "The police have their eye on me. I know it. An FBI agent is driving here today from Gallup. He called me last night and said he wants to meet with me. I need your help." His eyes moved from Luc to me and back to Luc. "You probably think I'm paranoid. But, I'm not. Personal experience has taught me. If someone wants to frame you, it's not hard to do."

I sat up straighter in my chair. "You've been accused of a crime before? What was the crime?"

Jon glared at me. "No, I wasn't accused. But I've seen a frame-up at close quarters. I won't discuss that."

"You asked me…us, here. You asked us to help." I shrugged. "How can I help if you hold back information?"

Jon stared at me before he relented. "Cleo, you don't

know my past, but my family came from Russia. My father worked for Gorbachev first, then Putin's government until he realized the corruptness of Putin's administration. He watched as the GRU framed anyone who questioned Putin's policies." Jon glanced toward Luc then back to me. "Ask Luc; he knows my history. His family knows my family." Jon dropped the napkin he had been torturing to raise both hands to mold the air into a shape only he could see.

"My father..." Jon clenched his fists then dropped his hands and restarted his napkin-twisting. "My father was a Russian spy who became embittered of the Rodina, his homeland, and resolved to supply intelligence to the U. S." Jon's eyes begged me to believe him.

I nodded to indicate that I did.

Relief flooded Jon's face. "Russians are like elephants. They never forget. Ever since the FBI agent called and told me Ginger had been murdered I've been thinking. I believe it is possible that Ginger was killed to frame me. I am the only son of my father and the GRU still burns with hatred for him. Look at what they did to Skripal."

I remembered that case. Back in the nineties, Sergei Skripal was a double agent working in the GRU. Skripal had spied on Russia for the west. He was caught in the mid-2000s and convicted of high treason before being sent to a Russian penal colony. He was released to the west in a spy swap around 2010. The only reason I knew any of this was because of what happened eight years later. Skripal's daughter was visiting him at his home in England when they both fell seriously ill from nerve-agent poisoning. A nerve-agent developed in Russia. It was all over the news. Skripal and his daughter both recovered after months in a hospital. A couple of Russian GRU agents were charged with the attempted murders.

Luc leaned forward. "I don't know if it was the Russians who framed you, or if you were framed at all, and it's just bad luck. But I *do* know that you didn't kill Ginger. You would never kill anyone." Luc laid a hand on the back of Jon's shoulder. "You may skewer them with acerbic comments and make their life miserable…but kill someone?" He removed his hand and shook his head. "Never."

Jon smiled. A vulnerable smile instead of his normal smirk. "Thanks, Luc." Jon's eyes found mine. "I know you don't know me, but Luc's right. I may have a PhD in being a smart ass, but I'm no killer. I don't hunt or fish." He performed a dramatic fake shudder. "I can't stand the blood."

"From what I understand, Ginger didn't bleed. She died of heat stroke."

Both men, who had started to relax, stiffened.

Luc recovered first. "I get it. You don't know Jon. Fair enough, you don't have to take my word for him."

Jon glared at Luc. "Why the hell not?"

Luc grinned. "Because she can make up her own mind." Luc's gaze shifted to me as he spoke. "Cleo is not just another pretty face. She solved a murder last year in Hawaii, didn't you?"

My cheeks grew warm. "Ah, well, I don't know if solved is the right word. More like stumbled onto an important clue." I waved the comment off. "Dumb luck."

Luc tilted his head in my direction. "But you were trying to prove your student who was accused of a murder, was innocent. You were investigating when you"—and he raised hands using two fingers to make air quotes—"stumbled on," Luc dropped his hands, "that important clue."

Jon's gaze flicked to Luc, then back to me. "Really?" he asked. "You helped this student prove his innocence? I guess as a psychologist you understand motives and have probably seen your share of wack-jobs." Jon frowned. "I can't believe I'm asking this but Cleo will you help me? Help make sure I don't get framed for this?"

I let out a deep breath. "I don't know. I appreciate your confidence in me. But I had known Kai and Ali, the victim, for over a year. And I knew Hilo better than Santa Fe. I'll help if I can, but you guys shouldn't get your hopes up. I'm new here and only met Ginger once, and Jon…"

I met Jon's scrutiny. "I don't know you very well either."

"Cleo, believe me, I wouldn't be asking you if I didn't think I was being framed." Jon gripped the edge of the table tightly with both hands. "Please, could you investigate Ginger's death for me?" He shook his head. "No, not for me. I know I can be a jerk. Do it for Ginger. Whoever killed her deserves to go down. She was one grand dame." An infant of a smile appeared on his lips. "I know you didn't know her well, but you saw enough to know she was amazing, didn't you?"

"Yeah, I did. I didn't know her well, but I liked Ginger. And the more I hear about her, the more impressed I am."

Luc and Jon broke into wide smiles. Jon clapped his hands once and Luc leaned over and took one of my hands. "So you'll look into this? I'll help of course. If you want?"

I bit my lip. "I don't know that I'll be much help."

"But you'll try?" Luc's butter-soft eyes encouraged me, and he encircled my hand with both of his. "Because I have faith in you, Cleo. You have a fresh perspective. I know you'll figure out what is going on here." He released my hand. "Jon and I will help if you want, too. And he won't be his normal jerk self."

"At least I'll try not to." Jon winked and shot me one of his wicked grins.

I laughed. "Okay, okay. I'll try. Just don't expect miracles.

"Competence is important, but so is luck, and Luc thinks you are lucky." Jon threw his mangled napkin at Luc.

Luc patted my hand. "You have all the competence we need. And don't worry. Jon will hire a lawyer who will probably also hire an investigator, but we need some Cleo Cooper outside-the-box thinking here. Thanks."

I smiled at Luc but had an uncomfortable feeling inside. I would try to uncover who had killed Ginger. But I wasn't at all sure that Luc would like what I found. I had serious doubts about Jon's innocence.

Chapter 24

Girl Talk

"Hey, Cleo, this is Samia."

"Hi." I had not spoken with Samia since last night when Luc and I moved our Chinese dinner to her house—the night she had been threatened. *I should have followed up with her this morning.* A twinge of guilt twisted inside me.

"I have been working here at the Center all morning and was thinking about taking a hike to shake the cobwebs out of my head and the tightness out of my shoulders. Do you want to join me? There are some great trails halfway between the Center and your casita."

"Are you sure that's a good idea after your phone call? Is it safe for you to be hiking alone?"

"I refuse to be a victim, and besides, I will not be alone. You will be there."

"If you're sure." I rolled my head to shake out my shoulders. "I could use some untightening and de-cobwebbing too."

Samia laughed. "Great. Do you know the La Tierra Trails?"

"Yes, I drive by them all the time."

"Let's meet at the La Cuchara trailhead, okay? The phone reception is terrible in that area so we will not be able to call and find each other. But if you know where it is…will that work for you?"

"Sure, I've seen the sign for it."

"I will finish a few things here and meet you in thirty minutes."

I wrapped up my emailing and left to meet the woman I had high hopes would become a new friend.

Samia was tying the laces on her hiking shoes when I arrived. She stood to greet me.

"I am glad you could make it."

"Me too." I missed my regular walks with Rikki and Gina, my best friends back in Hawaii.

The weather was perfect for hiking, cool and brisk but a bright blue cloudless sky kept it from feeling too chilly. The juniper and pinon trees were spaced far enough apart to make it easy to negotiate the trail. The straggly trees were not tall enough to offer shade. Though, in this cool weather we didn't need it. The terrain was challenging, with almost constant elevation changes. We climbed up and down, into and out of arroyos. They were dry and not so steep as to prevent us from talking.

"I don't want to pry," I said. "But have you had another threatening call?"

"No. And Matias got home this morning. I feel safe with him here. He is a scientist now, but he was a soldier before he went back to graduate school. He is trained to protect." Samia smiled as she stared at the trail ahead. "Yes, when he is home, I am safe." She glanced over at me. "But I appreciate you and Luc coming over last night. The call terrified me. And with Matias away it was nice to have company."

"We were happy to do it," I said. I looked at her and immediately stumbled on a branch. I almost face-planted but caught myself at the last second.

"Careful," Samia laughed. "It is rough terrain out here. That is one of the reasons I love hiking these trails. I have to concentrate on the terrain. They are not too steep, but they are challenging and only five minutes from town."

I grinned. "I can see why you like the difficulty of the trails, but it is safer to do it pairs, don't you think? Especially with the spotty cell reception?"

"Why do you think I called you?" Samia chuckled and leapt across a three-foot arroyo.

I hesitated, then made the jump too.

"Soooo…" Samia said. "What is the scoop with you and Luc?"

The terrain had flattened, but I fixed my eyes on the trail ahead of me. "I don't know yet. It's early days for us."

Samia observed me. "But I am sure someone like you has, or had, a guy back in Hawaii. Right? Is that over? Is Luc just a fun fling while you are here, or did you end a relationship to be with him?"

"It's complicated," I said.

"Of course." Samia smirked. "It is always complicated."

We hiked another hundred feet, but Samia's presence was powerful. Her curiosity was palpable.

I sucked in a deep breath. Samia had revealed her history to me last night. Turnabout was fair play, I guess.

"Yeah." I walked on. Samia remained silent. "I had a guy in Hawaii. Ben. We lived together for almost three years. But we weren't in a good place when I left." I brushed some hair that had fallen in front of my eyes behind an ear. "We left it unclear whether we would stay together when I got back.

"And then with Luc...I had to end it with Ben. Which I did. Last week." My shoulders tightened so I rolled my head to stretch my neck. Our hiking pace didn't slow. "To make things more complicated. He's living in my house in Hilo and can't move out because a volcano is flowing and lava has covered a bunch of homes and roads. So, there's a housing shortage in Hilo now. Which will probably not be resolved by the time I go back at the end of sabbatical. And I will most likely have to live in the same house with him again." *Geez, how did I screw things up so badly?* "Like I said. It's complicated."

Samia stopped, threw her head back, and laughed. "I am sorry. I do not mean to laugh at your situation. I assumed my crazy Saudi background made me the queen of complicated relationships. But lava? Spewing volcanoes? You have me beat."

I stopped when she did. She put one hand on each shoulder. "I like you, Cleo. And you can always talk to me about ex-boyfriends or volcanoes."

"Thanks," I said. We walked on. "I admire what you and Matias have built together. It reminds me of my parents. Both of you are 100% in love and 100% committed. I hope one day to have that kind of a relationship." I shook my head. "I swear when I meet a nice guy, I try to make it work. Like Ben. He was a great guy, and I tried to make it work. But..." We came to another arroyo we needed to jump over. On the other side I continued. "As I reflect back, I think I always had one foot out the door. And then when a difference popped up, I ran."

"Maybe you ran for a reason," Samia said. "There

are a lot of divorces out there between people who were in love, then later found irreconcilable differences. Maybe your psychology training is sending warning signals to your brain that you do not recognize."

"What about you and Matias?" I asked.

"Oh, I was crazy in love with him, and him with me. In some ways, it was insane what I did…leaving my family and country for a guy from a completely different culture. But…" Samia's mouth curved up. "It worked. I do not mean that we do not have problems. It is just that none of them feel important enough to make me want to leave Matias."

"I hope I recognize that when I see it."

We hiked on in silence for a while. I took pleasure in having a woman friend to talk to. It usually took me a while to grow into a new friendship, but I had a good feeling about Samia.

We hiked for an hour. The sky was clear and sunny, but the chill in the air invigorated me. As we approached our cars I was sorry to say goodbye.

"Hey, Samia, if you don't have anywhere you need to be, do you want to come by my casita? I think I could scrounge up some cheese and crackers."

"I would love to. Poor Matias has to catch up on work at the lab."

Samia knew where Luc lived and since my casita was on the same street, I only had to give her the house number. We pulled up at the same time. Luckily, I'd tidied up this morning. That wasn't always the case.

I poured us two large glasses of water and set cheese and crackers on a tray. It was a main staple of my diet when I ate alone in the casita, so I had several kinds of cheeses in my fridge. I also found some grapes and added them.

Samia lifted her phone and flashed it in my direction to show me the time. "Now that it is after five, and I have been a good girl and rehydrated with the water, do you think we could open a bottle of wine?" Samia glanced at my countertop wine rack that held four bottles of inexpensive wine. She winked. "Cheese and crackers taste better with wine."

"Of course." Wine had also become a staple part of my diet.

I poured us glasses of a chardonnay and spread a healthy smear of goat cheese on a whole grain cracker. I bit off half the cracker and popped it into my mouth when I remembered something. I swallowed. "I've come up with a plan on how to blind code and review Ginger's files without violating confidentiality. Have you pulled them up yet?"

Samia swallowed a sip of wine and stared at her glass as she set it on the table. I put the rest of my cracker with cheese into my mouth, chewed, and waited.

"No." Samia reached out to swipe a rice cracker with the goat cheese before continuing. "That was the night I got the threatening call, so it slipped my mind. Then Mimi called this morning. She asked that she be allowed to go through all of Ginger's stuff before me to separate any personal documents." Samia popped her cracker into her mouth.

"That's a little strange, isn't it?" I asked. "In psychology, privacy is a major issue. I teach an ethics section in my research class. If there are confidential files, a relative or spouse doesn't inherit those. They would belong to the client or the practice, Ginger wasn't a psychologist, but I would assume the ethical rules would be the same."

"Right. That is what I told Mimi. She is a sweet girl, but ditzy. She said she would check with the lawyer. She did not want to violate anybody's privacy. But she also asked that I not go through it without her until she had talked to the lawyer." Samia sipped her wine. "That was this morning, and I have not heard back from her. I am going to wait a day to follow up. I do not know everything Ginger was working on and I do not want anything urgent to be waylaid too long."

"That seems fair," I said. "I'm surprised the police haven't confiscated the files. There might be information relative to a motive in there."

"An FBI agent called and asked us to seal the room. He is driving to Santa Fe today and will search it. I did as he asked, but I warned him that people had been going in and out of her office."

"She didn't keep it locked?" I asked.

"Not when she was at the institute. If she was in her office she had an open-door policy. She usually locked it at night, so I had not bothered to check it until a couple of days after her death. When I did, I realized she had forgotten to lock it before she left."

"You mean it was unlocked and anyone could have had access to her computer or files?"

Samia lifted her chin defensively. "Everybody makes mistakes. Ginger was usually good about locking up."

"Yes, but this puts a different light on things," I said. "Evidence could have been removed or planted. Like the evidence against Jon. That email that supposedly came from him."

"Jon? I am sure evidence against Jon was not

planted. He is an evil-being." Samia's upper lip curled in a sneer. "You are not trying to get him off, are you? He has been horrible to Matias and the lab." Samia's eyes narrowed as she leaned toward me. "That man deserves no help from anyone."

I knew there was resentment between Jon and the lab because of his whistleblowing, but I didn't realize Samia felt the same way. "Luc and Jon are old friends," I said. "Luc asked me to help Jon. I don't know if he did it or not, but nobody deserves to go to jail for something they didn't do."

Samia scowled. "Jon deserves any bad consequences he gets. The way he went after Matias and the lab, over a simple mistake. Jon was not worried about Matias getting punished for something Matias did not do. Besides, I am not convinced Jon is not Ginger's killer."

The depth of Samia's anger stunned me and I struggled with how to respond. Before I could say anything she stood abruptly.

"I should go," she said, her mouth pinched.

"Samia—" Before I could get another word out she cut me off.

"No. I am very angry right now. I will say something I will regret. Goodbye, Cleo." And she stormed out.

"Bye, Samia," I said. But the door had already closed behind her.

Chapter 25

Mimi Comes to Dinner

Luc waved at me through his glass door to enter. He poured a glass of cabernet as I walked into his house.

"Hey," I said.

Luc walked to me with the glass of wine but held it to the side with one hand as he wrapped the other arm around my waist and pulled me toward him. He kissed me gently on the cheek and said softly in my ear, "Hey, you."

I leaned into the embrace for a moment, eyes closed. When I finally stepped back to smile at him, he cocked his head and looked quizzically at me as he handed me the glass of wine.

"Everything okay?" Luc asked.

Luc could read my emotions like no other man I had known. "I am now," I said.

"Want to talk about it?" he asked.

I walked over to see what was simmering in a pot on the stove. Tomato sauce. The scent of oregano, basil, and maybe a hint of lemon greeted me. I stepped away. "Samia isn't happy with me for helping Jon."

"Sorry. She has a temper, but she'll settle down."

I sipped my wine. "Whatever." I didn't want to admit how much her anger had hurt me. Samia had serious friend-potential. I was disappointed our friendship could end before it started. I missed my girlfriends in Hawaii, Rikki and Gina.

Luc picked up a wooden spoon and stirred the pot. With the other hand he lifted his wine glass. "I have an idea. Let's invite Mimi to dinner this week."

Was Luc reading my mind about wanting a friend? "Mimi?"

"You remember, Ginger's niece? She doesn't know many people in town, and I hear from Kyle that even though she lets him continue to live in Ginger's house, they aren't getting along."

"Really? What did he say?"

"Not a lot. Just that she was driving him crazy, and he couldn't wait for her to go back east." Luc sipped his wine. "What do you think? Should we have Mimi over?"

"That's a great idea." I waited for him to put the lid on the pot and put his wine glass down before I stepped up to lean against him as I stretched up to kiss him. Luc put a hand on each of my shoulders and held me back so he could peer into my eyes.

Whatever he saw there made him smile. He turned off the burner and led me by the hand to his bedroom.

****

Two days later I found myself back in Luc's kitchen. I put the final touches on a salad and prepared to slide some roasted potatoes back into the oven. Luc was on the patio grilling steaks. Another gorgeous sunny evening, it was crisp without being cold. I was loving early October in Santa Fe.

Mimi had been out on the patio, martini in hand, talking to Luc, but walked inside to join me. "Luc says I am supposed to tell you the steaks are three minutes away from being ready." Mimi laughed. "I got off easy.

You two are doing all the cooking and I just have to play messenger."

"Thanks, I'll give you another job if you want. Don't let me burn the potatoes; they need a few more minutes but they are close."

Mimi tapped her nose. "I can manage that. I love roasted potatoes and can smell when they are the perfect crispy golden brown."

"Then consider yourself a welcome member of this cooking team." I pulled out silverware to set the table. Nothing fancy, and with only three of us it only took a minute.

"How are you enjoying Santa Fe?" I asked.

"Better than I thought I would," Mimi said. "When I visited Aunt Ginger before, we went to her fancy parties or museums. Now that I am walking around and seeing the city on foot, I love it. I might even relocate here. With my business I travel a lot, but I can base it from anywhere."

"Nice," I said. "I love to travel. It's one of the things that attracted me to academics. We can travel in the summer and take sabbaticals every six years."

"That's right. I think someone told me you are here on sabbatical. I agree, I could never understand why Aunt Ginger, who had the money to live anywhere in the world, spent all her time here."

Mimi sipped her martini. "And that Center her Foundation funded," she said, exasperation in her voice. "Handing out money could be fun, but actually managing a Center to help people? Why she took on that headache I'll never know."

"Was it a headache for her?" I asked. "I know the Center has helped some traumatized women. Was her empathy giving her sleepless nights?"

"I don't know about that, but that partner of hers, that Samia-person, was a handful."

"I understand they disagreed on the scope, whether to narrow or broaden the women they would help. Is that what you mean?"

The corners of Mimi's mouth turned down. "There was that. But I think there was also some funny stuff going on with the books. And her files. She found stuff missing and Samia was the person most likely to have access to that stuff."

I frowned. I'd experienced Samia's temper firsthand, but she didn't seem dishonest. I had a hard time seeing her as a thief or embezzler. But maybe that was why she was so angry at Jon's whistleblowing? Could she be afraid of being outed? Before I could say anything, Mimi's nose twitched.

"The potatoes are ready," she sang out as Luc walked in the door with a plateful of steaks.

"Let's eat," I said.

Luc refreshed drinks as I pulled the potatoes out. A salad and a dish of sauteed asparagus were already on the table. We settled in and ate.

I had a mouthful of salad when Mimi picked up the conversation. "Luc, I was telling Cleo that before she died, Aunt Ginger thought there were some problems with the financial records at the Center." Mimi pointed her fork in Luc's direction. "She suspected Samia." Mimi speared a bite of steak and smiled before she popped it into her mouth.

Luc frowned and set down his fork. "Ginger never mentioned that to me. And I'm on the board of her Center. She should have told me her suspicions."

Mimi swallowed, washing the steak down with her glass of Pinot Noir.

"I guess maybe she didn't want Samia to get into trouble. You know, she thought she could redeem anybody. Like Kyle. I mean, seriously. What a mooch."

Luc and I exchanged glances.

"Kyle has worked hard on our project," Luc said, a crease in his brow. His gaze flicked to me again.

"Are you having problems with him?" I asked.

"Nothing I can't handle. I don't know why Aunt Ginger didn't boot him to the curb a long time ago, though."

"Let us know if you plan to boot him to the curb." Luc gave Mimi a twisted smile. "We need Kyle to finish the website for our project. I may need to prep a guest room." He looked at me and his smile grew warmer. "Or figure out some kind of housing for him."

My cheeks warmed.

Mimi winked at me. "I think it'll be fine. I'm not planning to move here yet—just staying long enough to wrap up Aunt Ginger's affairs." She sipped her wine. "And I guess I should cut Kyle some slack. He seems to be grieving my aunt. I didn't expect that." Mimi cocked her head. "I thought he was using her. But maybe he really loved her."

"I'm not surprised," I said. "I only met Ginger once, but I liked her very much. She seemed like an incredible woman."

"She was," Mimi said, and lifted her wine glass. "I propose a toast. To the late great, gorgeous Ginger, my doting aunt."

Luc and I lifted our glasses. "To Ginger."

Chapter 26

Dire Situation on the Big Island

"Hey, Rikki Tikki." My heart lightened at seeing my friend's name appear on my phone.

"Hey. I've got news on the volcano. It's not good."

My mood sank. "What happened?"

"You remember Kevin?"

A memory of a grinning Kevin telling me that "Rocks are on da road" and surfing conditions were primo in Hilo Bay, flashed through my mind.

"Of course. Is he okay?"

"He and his family lost their house."

"Oh no."

"Yeah. He lived in Leilani estates with his cousins, and a lot of houses there burned or were buried under lava."

"Poor Kevin. Have you talked to him?" Kevin and Rikki had dated for a while, years ago, and stayed friends after they parted ways.

"No, I haven't been able to track him down yet. I think he's staying at Mele's place, and, well, you know what a witch she can be."

"Right. Well, when you see him give him my… Tell him I'm sorry and if there is anything I can do, let me know."

"I will."

"Any word on Gina's cousin?" I asked.

"Yeah. Somebody sent a drone over the area. Her house is gone."

"Oh man."

"Yeah."

"How are you doing? This is turning into a slow-moving disaster. Are you okay?" I asked.

"I'm fine. It's crazy here in Hilo. We are safe and sound but we all know someone whose house is either gone or in danger. Everybody has someone couch surfing and is trying to stay upbeat for their sake. But man. It's tough to watch. And I don't know if you heard…but Kapoho Tidal pools were covered by lava."

I sucked up a big breath of air to stop a sob. Kapoho tidal pools were magical. Ben and I had spent many beautiful times there. I'd seen extravagantly colored fishes and snowflake eels. There was a pass between pools that had a wicked current when the tide changed. At the perfect moment you could swim full speed and stay in the same place, until the magic second, then be shot fast as lightning to the other tide pool, when the tide reached its tipping point. All that beauty, gone. I swallowed hard.

Rikki and I chatted a little longer, but I could tell her heart wasn't in it, and to be honest, mine wasn't either. She promised to tell me if she heard of any fundraising plans for Kevin's family or Gina's cousin and that we would talk soon.

I hung up my phone and watched the sun begin to set on the desert mountains. The juxtaposition of my two realities overwhelmed me. So many people I cared about were facing disaster on that lush, green, beautiful island I had called home for the last six years. Even those in

Hilo out of the path of the lava had unhealthy air to breathe. Geez, poor Gina. Bringing a baby into the world while this was happening. I hoped the poor air quality wouldn't affect the development of her little thumper.

And Ben. He wouldn't want to live with me when I returned. He had his pride, but there would be a major housing shortage. And so many of my students lived in Puna. With the lava covering the road it would keep a lot of them from attending classes. The department could switch to online courses. But if the lava burned down the power poles, they would have no power. Or internet. And for students from the mainland, I was sure most of their parents would want them to return home. If enrollment dropped too dramatically, the administration would have to consider downsizing. I had tenure, but I was the last person to receive it in the department. My job wouldn't be the first one cut, but it would be close to the top of the list.

I'd been weighing whether I wanted to go back permanently or only return for the required one semester. Now, would I have any reason to go back at all? Leaving Hawaii was one thing as a hypothetical. Now the choice could be taken away from me. It could be my reality whether I liked it or not. My gut twisted at the idea.

I should call Ben. He had to be stressed about finding a new place by next summer. We had broken up, but I still cared for him. Yet, the idea of calling him filled me with dread.

I'm being selfish. I steeled myself to call Ben. Our last call hadn't gone so well. But time has passed. Maybe we could get back to being friends.

He picked up on the first ring. "Cleo? Do you need something?"

"No, I just got to thinking. Rikki and Gina have been keeping me up to date on the lava. I feel guilty being so far away and not being able to help. Maybe I should come back early from my sabbatical. I could do some relief work or something. You wouldn't have to move out or anything, like I said before, but, I guess...well it would impact you if I was there. I thought I'd run it past you, first. I mean, do you think I could be of any help?" I cringed as I heard my voice creep up to a higher pitch. What was I afraid of? Hurting his feelings? Making him uncomfortable? It was *my* house.

"No. I don't know what you think you could do. They're having a hard enough time keeping looky-loo tourists out of the affected area. They don't need you here too."

I held the phone away from my ear and stared at it, stung by the harshness of his tone.

Ben couldn't see what I was doing and he continued without taking a breath. "What they need are places to crash until the lava stops flowing. I was planning on letting people stay in the guest bedroom and the office, but if you come back it would take a bed away from someone who needs it." He paused and his voice softened. "I know you want to help, and it's your house, so of course you can come back whenever you want to. But you're comfortable where you are, right? You won't be comfortable here. It will be crowded in the house and the vog is at dangerously high levels now. If you really want to help, send respirators and replacement filters. That's what we need. There aren't enough on the island and the vog is affecting more of the island than the lava."

Ben's reasoning made sense, but his response hurt me. I know I had broken up with him but he sounded like he didn't want me going back to my own house. I guess that made sense too. It would be uncomfortable. And he was right; the island needed temporary housing more than any skill I had.

"Okay. I'll stay away." I could be as blunt as him.

"Great. I gotta go, Cleo. One of those people I offered the room to is moving in tonight so I'm trying to clean it up and pack up some of the stuff that is in there to store under the house. Bye."

And before I could respond he hung up.

I tried to decide if I was angry or sad. Angry that he had invited strangers, at least I guessed they were strangers or he would have told me their names, right? Anyway, inviting strangers into our house without telling me. I would have said yes, of course, under these circumstances. But he could have asked. A tear slid down my cheek. What hurt was that he considered me an obstacle to his plans, rather than someone who could help. That's probably why we broke up. We were always on different trajectories. I wiped the tear away and decided I needed to do something. Anything but sit here and feel angry-sad. I surveyed my casita. Papers strewn across my table, books piled haphazardly and dirty mugs in the sink. I had spent so much time at Luc's house, the casita was in need of a good cleaning. Just what I needed. I stood up, took a deep breath, and started in the kitchen.

Chapter 27

Do You Ski?

"Cleo. I have a question for you."

I pulled my gaze from my laptop distracted with checking my statistical analysis. Luc's gorgeous brown and green streaked eyes were fixed on me. My concentration melted. He could ask me anything.

"I am an open book. What do you want to know?" I smiled at him.

Luc grinned. "Do you ski?"

"I have skied." Not well. But I've skied.

"But do you enjoy skiing?" he asked.

"I loved skiing," I said. "But, I'm not very good. I'm comfortable on greens and some blues, but petrified of black diamonds. I don't fall much, but let's just say my style is not what you would call elegant." I grinned. "But I have fun."

"Fabulous. I got an email from the local ski resort that they are opening early this year because they've had so much snow on the mountain."

I glanced out the window. We had a few flurries last week but it melted as soon as it hit the ground. The mountain was shrouded in clouds. I guess they were getting snow today. Luc's eye sparkled with excitement. "I guess you are a big skier if they notify you of season openings."

"I get a season pass every year. It's a great little ski mountain, privately owned and well-managed. It isn't as expensive as the ones run by big chains owned by multinational companies. I like to support them." Luc went back to his computer and typed and clicked grinning like a schoolboy. When he finished he looked at me. "I hope you don't mind, but I got you a pass too."

"No, no, wait."

Luc held up a hand. "No, you wait. I'm not going to go skiing and leave you behind, and a pass is cheaper if we go a lot. Not to mention, like I said, I like to support our local ski mountain. Please. I want to do this."

It was an expensive gift, and an uneasy feeling burbled up. I'd seen relationships crash and burn around expectations and assumptions related to big-ticket presents.

"But I don't have any gear," I said.

"My sister, Celia, left her old ski suit here when she came for a visit, before she was pregnant. You're about the same size, so I'm guessing it will fit you. She has a new one where she lives in Idaho and leaves this one here so she won't have to pack one when she comes to visit. And we can rent the skis and boots," Luc said.

"I'll rent the skis and boots," I said. "And if your sister is okay with it I'll borrow her ski suit. If not, I'll buy my own gear. I'd also like to pay you back for the season pass." I didn't know where I would find the money, but I didn't want to feel like I was mooching. Or for Luc to think I was in this relationship for his pricey gifts.

Luc's eyes softened and he reached for my hand. "Please, let me get the pass. We'll call it an early

Christmas present."

I started to protest but Luc pushed a strand of hair that had fallen loose behind my ear. He interrupted softly. "Please. You don't know how happy it makes me that you enjoy skiing. This is a gift I'm giving myself to have you with me on the slopes. If you don't want to go that's fine. But I don't want you staying behind because of the expense."

****

A few days later, I was decked out in Luc's sister's Spyder ski jumpsuit, and we made our way up the mountain. My ski suit was white with black zippers on the thighs and midriff and it fit like a glove, something a sex kitten in a James Bond movie would wear. Not something I would have picked out, but it was a guilty pleasure to wear.

I picked up my season pass and tucked it into a zippered pocket on my arm. My stomach gurgled. Excitement? Fear of breaking my neck? Fear of looking like an idiot? I haven't skied in six years. Not since before I moved to Hawaii.

We took the quad lift up to the midway point. The dry, cold air nipped at my chin and nose.

"Let's warm up on an easy green slope," Luc said.

I hopped off the lift, without falling, and stopped next to Luc at the top of our first slope to loop the poles on my wrist. This wasn't too bad.

We pushed off and the thrill of swooshing and gliding over gentle green and blue slopes rushed to my head. I had forgotten how much I loved skiing. I laughed out loud when I bobbled on a curve but managed to hold my edge. When I stabilized, I found Luc hanging behind in case I had trouble and watching me, a joyful smile on his face. I stopped abruptly, at the top of the next hill where two trails crossed, breathing hard and body bent at an awkward angle. I planted my poles to keep myself from sliding. I clumsily untangled my skis to realign them. Luc glided confidently to a stop inches from me.

"You're doing great. I thought you told me you weren't good at this." Luc's grin almost split his face.

"I'm fine on green and gentle blues. I know not to get in over my head. Most of the time." I laughed. "But thanks for getting me up here. I forgot how much I love it."

Luc leaned in and gave me a kiss, somehow managing to find my mouth between my goggles, turtleneck, and high-collared ski suit.

And wow. Just wow. How was everything so incredibly perfect with this guy?

"Ready to head back to the quad?" Luc asked, grin still in place.

I laughed. "You lead this time. I don't know where I am going."

He kept to easy slopes and we made it back happy and flushed to get on the lift again. It was a weekday, so no lines.

We drifted between blue spruce and fir trees, dripping with snow and Mardi gras beads that sparkled in the sunlight. The beauty and the quiet brought a tear to my eye. I leaned to rest my head on Luc's shoulder.

"Thank you," I said.

"Thank *you*," Luc responded.

I kissed him on the cheek. "You know, you don't have to stay down here on the green trails with me. You can go up to the top if you want. I don't want to hold you back. Go to the upper mountain and ride your black diamonds down. I've got my ski legs back and I can have fun by myself on these easy trails."

Luc put his gloved hand on my gloved hand. "I'm having a great time skiing with you today. Wherever you are comfortable skiing…that is where I want to be."

Wow. I didn't know if the endorphins from skiing were making my heart race or what, but I was falling hard for this guy.

The morning sparkled like glitter on marshmallows. The sheer joy of racing down the gentle slopes as Luc watched and smiled at me brought spontaneous laughter to my lips more than once. I don't know how many runs we made before Luc suggested we stop for lunch at the restaurant midway on the slope.

I ordered a tamale and Luc, a frito pie. We sat in the sun, James Taylor coming from the stereo system, eating our food and splitting a beer. I don't think I've ever been so in love with a day.

We decided on one more run before heading home. Back at the lodge, I left to turn in my skis and Luc to put his in his locker. When I found him, the smile had disappeared. His brows were drawn together, and his mouth a tight, straight line. He was holding his phone to his ear. He didn't seem to be aware of my presence, but I heard him say, "I'm on the mountain, but I'll get there as soon as I can."

We drove straight to the police station. Luc shed his ski jacket before we entered, and walked in wearing ski pants and a turtleneck. He mostly blended in with the crowd. I, on the other hand couldn't shed anything lest I be wearing only long underwear, so I walked in behind Luc wearing Celia's sex-kitten ski suit. A few heads swiveled toward me. I blushed, but didn't make eye contact with anyone. We found Jon fairly easily. He was in a back corner, standing in the doorway to a small room talking and gesticulating intensely with a dark-haired man wearing a blue suit. As we approached the man in the suit looked up at first Luc, then me. His eyes widened as they rested on me in my ski suit before he turned his attention back at Jon.

"*There* you are," Jon said. "I was wondering if I needed to call an uber."

"I told you we were on the mountain. We drove here as soon as we could." Luc extended his hand to the other man. "Hello, I'm Luc Bastien, a friend of Jon's. And this is Cleo Cooper. We were skiing when Jon called. Is there something we can help you with?"

The dark-haired man shook hands with me after Luc. "I'm special agent Joe Rivera. I'm investigating the death of Ginger Hanlon." His gaze shifted to Luc. "I brought—"

"He brought *me* in for questioning." Jon's voice trembled with rage. "He found some stupid email that *I* did *not* write that makes him think I killed Ginger. *Me*. A killer. I've never heard anything so ridiculous in my life." Jon jerked a hand in Luc's direction. "Tell him. I'm *not* a killer."

Before Luc could respond, Rivera spoke, "I know you came to pick up Mr. Suvorov, but I wonder if the two of you could answer just a few questions for me while you're here. As I said, I'm trying to solve a murder." Rivera's glance moved from Luc, to me, then back to Luc. "I won't keep you long." He flicked a glance in Jon's direction. "I realize your friend is anxious to leave. This will only take a moment." He ushered us into the small room behind him.

Jon fumed, but Luc entered the room. I followed.

"I'm not going to stand out here in the hallway, waiting," Jon said.

"I'm afraid you'll have to, Mr. Suvorov," Rivera said. "I want to ask them a few general questions. Alone."

Jon huffed and glared at us as Rivera closed the door slowly, but firmly in Jon's face. He waved toward two metal chairs on one side of a small table. A small dark woman in a blue suit sat on the other side, a small laptop in front of her. She angled the laptop so I couldn't see it.

"Please take a seat. I won't keep you long," Rivera said. He indicated the blue-suited woman. "This is Agent Rodriguez. She is assisting me while I am here." Rivera sat across from us and leaned back in his chair. He smiled, but his eyes were fixed on Luc. "I'm just trying to get the lay of the land here." Rivera's gaze flicked to me, "I understand from other witnesses that you haven't been here long, Ms. Cooper, but you have met the victim. Is that correct?"

"Yes."

Rivera pivoted to Luc. "But, Mr. Bastien, you have known Ms. Hanlon for some years."

"Yes," Luc said.

"Would you say that you and Ms. Hanlon were close?" Rivera's eyes slid briefly to me. "Close friends, I mean."

"Yes. Ginger and I were never romantically involved, but I admired her. We worked on several committees together over the years and became good friends." Luc's voice faltered. "I'm going to miss her."

Rivera leaned forward and interlaced his fingers before resting his hands on the table. "Can either of you think of anyone who would want to harm or kill Ms. Hanlon?"

Luc and I shook our heads.

"Ginger was a warm, gracious, intelligent woman. I don't know anyone who didn't like her," Luc said.

"That isn't the same answer I got from your friend out there." Rivera pointed his head at the door as he flipped through a notebook on the table in front of him. He stopped abruptly. "Here are Mr. Suvorov's thoughts—at the top of his list was Kyle Paige." Rivera watched Luc and me.

Luc scowled. "No, that's Jon's pettiness. The two were rivals, for art and Ginger's attention. But Kyle loved Ginger. Mimi was just telling us the other day that she didn't realize how much he loved her aunt until she saw him grieving for her. Right?"

"Yes, I heard her say that," I said.

"I take it from your response, you don't see Mr. Paige as a possible suspect. Is that correct, Mr. Bastien?"

Luc looked back at Rivera and shook his head. "No. I don't."

"Then I'll move to the next couple of names on Mr. Suvorov's list, Samia and Matias Keller."

"Really?" A muscle in Luc's jaw tightened. "And what was his rationale? Because Jon was fighting with them, they would take it out on Ginger?" Luc raised his hands in exasperation. "That is crazy. Matias and Ginger got along great. And Samia and Ginger were partners in the Hanlon non-profit Center. They were close friends."

Rivera read from his notes, "Samia Keller received a substantial inheritance and control of the non-profit Center. Suvorov says that Samia and Ginger had been fighting over that non-profit."

"Samia is not going to kill someone to get control over a non-profit. And the money didn't go to her personally; it went to the center."

I fidgeted in my chair remembering Mimi's allegations. Rivera watched me.

"Miss Cooper, is there something you want to contribute to the discussion?"

I glanced at Luc. His face told me nothing. Rivera lifted one eyebrow in question.

"I don't want to spread rumors," I said. "And I have no firsthand knowledge."

"I understand. We will carefully vet whatever you tell us. But if it could point us in the right direction..." Rivera said.

I had been holding my breath and slowly exhaled. "Well, someone told us that there may be some problem with the Center's financial record-keeping." I didn't want to give him Samia's name yet. No point in throwing around allegations if there were no financial irregularities. But even as I had that thought, Luc was shaking his head.

"I checked on that. There are no problems with the books. Mimi must have misunderstood."

"Who did you check with?" Rivera asked.

"Jon, he's the treasurer."

"Ah, perhaps I should also look at the Center's books." Rivera said as he scribbled on his notepad.

I cleared my throat. Rivera and Luc looked at me. "There might be someone else you want to consider. I don't have a last name, but Samia could give it to you."

Rivera's eyes tightened. "I'm listening."

"I was having lunch with Samia the other day when a man named Raul approached us. He works at the center and according to Samia is a nice guy. But he has a nephew who has gotten into some kind of trouble. Raul was pleading with Samia on behalf of his nephew. I saw the nephew, Manuel was his name I think. He looked angry."

"This is the center that helps abused women, correct?"

"Right," I said.

"And one of the ways they help these women is by supporting and encouraging them to bring charges against their abusers?"

"That is my understanding,"

Rivera nodded. "Thank you, Ms. Cooper. You have been helpful. Now I have another path to investigate in addition to Mr. Suvorov."

Rivera stood up and opened the door. Jon, whose anger had continued to simmer on a slow boil, overflowed. He stormed into the room, and pointed energetically at me. "Before you decide to charge me, you should be aware that Cleo has solved a murder case before." He glanced at me in my borrowed ski bunny suit and lost a little of his bravado.

"Well, okay, I know she looks like a bimbo in that, but Cleo is smarter than she looks."

What the…? I just gave the cops another suspect to focus on.

Rivera and I looked at each other with open mouths. I was about to splutter a defense of myself when Luc stood up and put his hand on Jon's shoulder.

His hand was gentle but there was steel in his voice. "Jon, I know you are upset, but so help me God, if you insult Cleo again, we will walk out and leave you here without a second thought. She has offered to help and you *will* treat her with respect if you want to receive that help."

"What's wrong with what I said? I said she was smart. I have faith that she will prove me innocent. Because I *am* innocent." Jon glanced at me again and his mouth twisted. "That is if she isn't too busy skiing."

Luc's mouth opened in a snarl, but I put a hand on his arm to stop him. "Is there anything else you need from us, Agent Rivera? If we're finished here, I think someone is getting cranky and maybe needs a nap."

We dropped Jon off at his place, but as we pulled away I noticed in the rearview mirror another car pulled into Jon's driveway as we were turning off his street. Hmm. Wonder who that could be? I asked Luc.

Luc sighed. "I don't know, and to be honest, I don't care. Jon is not my favorite person at the moment." He glanced at me. "What do you say we make dinner at my place tonight? I missed you last night."

I'd stayed at my casita last night. I'd worked through dinner and gone to bed early. "That sounds nice. Do you have anything we can make quick?" Our day of skiing had caught up with me. I was starving.

Luc dropped me off at my casita so I could peel off the ski-suit and take a quick shower. By the time I'd walked down to his house, my stomach growled like a mountain lion attempting escape. Luc greeted me at the door with a kiss and cracker with olive tapenade on it.

"Did you hear my stomach growling from up the road?" I laughed before popping the cracker in my mouth.

Luc grinned. "No. I assumed you must be as hungry as I am. I'm making spaghetti. I hope that's okay. I had homemade sauce in the freezer and just have to cook the pasta."

Luc stepped to the oven and pulled out garlic bread. I stirred the sauce and he poured the wine. Cooking with Luc was easy and natural. We anticipated each other's movements without awkwardness or clumsy missteps.

Dinner was ready in under ten minutes and we dug in. I was halfway through my pasta when Luc's phone rang. Luc grimaced and silenced his ringer and set it on a sideboard. A minute later it vibrated. "Ignore it. It's Jon and I do *not* want to talk to him right now."

We kept eating but the phone kept vibrating. As soon as the call went to voicemail, it would start again.

"Aargh. He is not going to give us a break. Let me just tell him to leave me alone and I'll call him in the morning." Luc reached for his phone and answered. "Jon—" Luc stopped abruptly. The frustration left his face. He winced. "Okay." Luc glanced up at me as he spoke. "Yes. I'll come bail you out. You can be a jerk, but I know you didn't kill anyone."

Chapter 28

A Busy Morning

A faint knocking broke through my sleep. I rolled over and found Luc still sleeping. He'd called me while he was waiting to arrange Jon's bail. Evidently, Kyle was in the car that had pulled up after we left. He had accused Jon of killing Ginger and the yelling had gotten so loud the neighbors had called the police. Jon and Kyle were both taken to the police department for creating a public disturbance, not arrested for murder. With both Jon and Kyle accusing the other of homicide, the police thought taking them both in and sorting it out was the wisest course of action.

I tried to wait up for Luc, but when I laid down to read, I must have fallen asleep.

I didn't wake up when he came in, but this morning, as I slowly woke up, I watched him as he slept. His thick lashes rested on his cheekbones, hair in reckless disarray. I wanted to kiss him, but I heard a knock at the front door. Another knock followed, louder this time. Someone was at the front door. I jumped up and pulled on Luc's robe before rushing downstairs to stop the knocking. Luc needed his sleep after the fiasco last night.

When I opened the door, Jon stood there, fist raised in a position to knock again. I was lucky not to get punched in the face. I checked my watch, 6:45.

"Jon, what are you doing here? I'm glad you aren't in jail, but for heaven's sake, you're pounding to wake the dead. Luc is still sleeping."

Jon smirked. "And it appears, you were sleeping with him, Chiquita. Not a problem. I brought coffee." And he lifted a brown paper bag with a label from Ohori Coffee Roasters. "Lead me to the coffee maker, oh my queen, and I will get started."

Jon gently pushed past me as my sleepy brain grappled with the situation. "Didn't Luc tell you I was coming this morning?"

"I didn't get a chance to tell her."

Jon and I both turned as Luc's voice preceded him down the stairs. I was wrapped in his robe, so he had pulled on a sweatshirt and jeans. Luc smiled at me. "You look better in that robe than I do." He kissed me on the forehead. "Sorry about the surprise visit but you were asleep when I came home. You're welcome to join us…"

"You *have* to join us," Jon called from the kitchen. "You're the only one of us with any experience with a murder investigation. I came over to pick your brain more than Luc's."

Luc gave me a half-smile.

I sighed. "You make sure Jon makes the coffee right, and I'll run up and throw on some clothes."

As I climbed the stairs I could hear Jon. "Make the coffee right? *Make* the *coffee* right? Does Cleo know who she's dealing with here?"

Once upstairs, I pulled on the jeans and turtleneck that I'd worn last night. Luc and I weren't to the stage where I left clothes here. But it was a chilly morning; he'd pulled out a sweater and left it on the bed still folded. Had Luc left it out for me to wear? Or had he pulled two out by mistake? I shivered and heard Jon's voice from downstairs.

"Where is that woman? I didn't bring Ohori's coffee with me for just any reason. I expect some detection work out of her."

I grabbed the sweater and pulled it over my head. I ran my hands over my sweatered arms. It was cashmere-soft and comfortably large. First his robe, now his sweater; wearing Luc's clothes was becoming a thing. I flicked my fingers. I'd think about that later. I needed to get downstairs. The sooner we started, the sooner Jon would leave. I hoped.

The coffee was ready and when Jon saw me step off the bottom step he poured it into my favorite mug. Luc must have told him which one I usually used. Jon held the mug up and politely asked me, "Sugar? Milk?" Jon grimaced. "Luc only has 1% milk; don't blame me for that."

"One sugar, and a generous splash of milk; 1% is fine," I didn't mention Luc bought the 1% milk for me.

Jon meticulously followed my instructions, glancing at me for approval after he added the splash of milk. I smiled, and he stirred the mixture before handing it to me.

His eyes tightened as I took the mug and swallowed my first sip. I closed my eyes in ecstasy. It was perfect. Strong, but smooth, not too bitter, not too sweet. Maybe Jon had some redeeming characteristics after all.

I opened my eyes and found Jon observing me intently.

"The best coffee I've ever had. Thank you."

Jon's lips twitched and he gave me a little nod, his face relaxing. "Well, you weren't to know, I guess. But

152

I take coffee seriously."

"I can tell." I took another sip.

"And don't worry, I don't judge. I am tolerant of people who adulterate their coffee with milk and sugar," Jon said as he walked to the table.

I choked on my swallow of his fantastic coffee. Luc patted my back and tried to hide his smile.

"I can whip up some breakfast while you two brainstorm at the table." Luc looked at me as he spoke with a lifted eyebrow, changing the statement to a question.

"Sure, but you can still be part of the conversation." Luc's house had an open plan with one large space for the kitchen, dining, and living area.

At the dining table, Jon opened his laptop. I pulled over a pad of paper and a pen that Luc must have left on the table while I was dressing.

"So you've done this before, Cleo. Where do we start?" Jon's voice was quiet.

He sounded scared. I took a deep breath, and instead of explaining that I was not a trained investigator, I jumped in. "We start with who has a motive. Who gains from Ginger's death?"

"Do you mean money?" Jon asked. "That would have to be Mimi. She gains most of the money and property."

Jon bobbed his chin toward Luc. "And of course Luc for his Institute. And Samia for her control of the Hanlon Foundation and the Center." Jon typed on his laptop. "In fact, Samia not only benefits from the continued influx of money for her Center, but she now has total control. She and Ginger had been butting heads on the direction and focus of their Center. Now Samia doesn't have to compromise."

I'd been jotting down Jon's ideas. But I paused next to Samia's name. I didn't want to mention Mimi's accusation of Samia and the books in front of Jon. But I wanted to confirm what Luc had told me. "Speaking of the Center, Luc said you are on the Board of Directors, is that right?"

"Yes, I'm the Treasurer." Jon continued typing notes into his computer without looking up.

"Does the Center have enough funding? Any money shortages that risk having to cut back on services?" I asked.

"No, of course not. Ginger was a co-director with Samia. If they needed money, the Hanlon Foundation poured a new donation into it. I kept an eye on the books to make sure things weren't sloppy, and they weren't. Ginger and Samia were excellent at record-keeping. As well as Sandra, who ran the office."

Well that doesn't fit with what Mimi said. One of them is either wrong or lying.

A memory flashed in my head of Jon and Mimi in what appeared to be an intimate moment on the Plaza the other day. If they were close wouldn't Mimi have told Jon about Samia and the books? Funny he didn't mention it. Is he hiding a relationship with Mimi and deflecting our attention from her by blaming Samia? Or did I imagine what I saw?

"Jon, I'm curious, how well do you know Mimi?" I asked.

"Mimi? She's fun. I've met her on some of her previous trips to visit Ginger. I played tour guide one time, at her request. Mimi is a lot of laughs, and sometimes she calls me if she needs something when she is in town. But beyond that, we don't keep in contact. We aren't close friends or anything."

Hmm. Do I believe him? "Okay, let's keep going. We can't forget you and Kyle."

Jon shook his head. "I didn't forget. But consider this…Yes, we got a bequest, but probably we would have gotten that anyway if Ginger was alive. And maybe more. She was generous to her friends, especially those of us seriously working at our art."

I tapped my pen on the pad. "Okay. Fair assessment. But we need to spread our concept of motives further. Not just who gains by her death but let's flip the question around. Who has something to lose by Ginger being alive?"

Jon scowled. "That's a false differentiation. By definition, if someone gains something by a person's death, then they lose something by them being alive."

Luc carried a tray with a bowl of blueberries and a plate of sliced cheese and nuts to the table. "Not necessarily. For instance, you gain a painting and support for a show by Ginger's death, but weren't you already getting support for a show? And don't you think she would have gifted you with even more support if she had stayed alive? You gained by her death in the short run, but you also probably lost future support from her death."

But, if Jon and Mimi were secretly dating, he could have access to even more money if he married Mimi after Ginger's death. I needed to find out once and for all if they were a thing. Jon had given me his answer. I should approach Mimi and see how she responds.

"And don't forget Kyle," I said. "He will lose his cushy digs now that Ginger is gone. I have the impression Mimi isn't going to let him stay there any longer than she has to."

"Good point," Jon said.

"So who might need to stop Ginger?" I asked.

"Certainly any guy who had assaulted one of the women in her program," Jon said.

"I'm working on that," I said. "I've done a lot of research projects with confidential data. The University ethics boards have strict rules on how we handle it. So I offered to set up a blind screen. All personal identification will be separated from the pertinent details of the case. I will keep the coding system that can connect those names to the data in a locked, password-protected file. But I'm curious, from your roles on the Board, do either of you know of any threats that have been made against Ginger or the Center?" I asked.

Jon shook his head.

Luc shook his head too, but then stopped and lifted his chin. "Samia might know," he said. "And what about that guy you mentioned to the FBI agent? The one who ran into you and Samia at lunch?"

Jon jerked his eyes back to me. "What? Who are you talking about?"

"I don't know any more than what I told Agent Rivera. Raul—the man that approached our table—he seemed nice. But his nephew gave us the stink eye the entire time Raul was talking to Samia."

Jon scowled. "Stink eye?"

"An angry, pissed-off look." I shrugged. "It's a Hawaii thing. But I know Samia was planning to dig through the files before…" I glanced from Luc to Jon. Samia was a private person and not fond of Jon. I didn't think she'd want us sharing her personal history or struggles with him. "…Before that call. It kind of distracted her."

"What call?" Jon asked.

Of course, he wouldn't let anything slip by. "Nothing related to this," I said. "I think the person with the biggest motive is Mimi. She inherits a huge pile of money. She'll be a wealthy woman for someone her age."

Jon grinned. "She'll be a wealthy woman for any age."

"I don't see it," Luc said. "She already had a career and supported herself. She didn't seem like the kind of person who could kill someone."

Killers came in all shapes, sizes, ages, and genders. Jon caught my eye and smirked as if he had read my cynical mind.

"Okay," I said. "Let's keep thinking of motives. You guys might remember more after you mull it over. But we also need to think about *means*. Who *could* have killed Ginger?"

Jon twisted his napkin. "I haven't a clue. But that lets Mimi off. She was still on the East Coast when Ginger was killed." He frowned. "How does a person send Ginger, who was not a stupid woman, to a deserted road with bad directions and then damage her car and escape without anyone knowing?" He dropped the napkin on the table and brought his index finger up to his chin, slowly rubbing it. "Unless…" He pursed his lips and paused. "…the only thing that makes sense is if someone damaged it slightly, a slow air leak or oil line or something. That could explain how they weren't found at the scene. He, or she, was never at the scene."

"That makes sense," I said. "And Kyle told me the

FBI found sabotage to Ginger's car. But that begs the question, who would know how to sabotage a car?"

Luc's face saddened and he glanced at Jon. "It wouldn't, in fact, have to be car experience, would it?"

Jon's face fell. "Damn."

"What?" I asked.

Jon glowered, so Luc answered me. "Jon works with a lot of automobile parts in his art. His sculptures move. That, and with his PhDs in both mechanical engineering and nuclear physics, the police are likely to believe he would know how to sabotage a car."

Jon stuck his chin out. "Yeah, maybe so, but what about Matias and Samia? They are robotics engineers. They work on military robots to be used in wartime, so they'd have to know how machines work in a desert...and what *stops* a machine from working in the desert. They both also have knowledge and tools to sabotage a car."

"And then there's Kyle," I said. Luc and Jon stared at me.

"Kyle?" Jon looked at me as if I was crazy. "What does he know other than websites? Certainly not art. He pretends to be an artist but he isn't." Jon snorted and smiled smugly as if he enjoyed the opportunity to insult Kyle, even if he wasn't there to hear it.

I picked up my coffee cup but answered before drinking. "Kyle mentioned that he used to work as a car mechanic as a kid. He hated it so he moved on to website design. I don't know how long he worked in that garage, but he has at least some car mechanic experience."

"There is also the distinct possibility that a person would not need any expertise to damage the car." Luc glanced between me and Jon. "With enough money, you can hire anyone to do anything, and then quietly disappear."

I sighed. Luc was right. We were in over our heads. Ginger was uber-wealthy. There was a serious amount of money at stake. I sat up straight. "Wait, you're right. So we can't rule Mimi out. She has money and knows how to hire the right person for the right job."

Jon stared at me for a moment, then shook his head. "How would she have known Ginger was going into the Sonoran Desert. I didn't even know that. I thought she was heading up to Navajo country. Ginger wouldn't have died of heat exhaustion up there. Hell, Mimi probably didn't know Ginger was going out of town at all. Ginger only decided to go at the last minute, and she and Mimi didn't keep in super close touch. I think Mimi just made the annual visit each year to secure her place in the will. Her uncle Roger, Ginger's late husband was loaded and left most of it to Ginger.

"But your thought is a good one, Cleo. Who else had knowledge of Ginger's trip and has access to that kind of money?" A puckish grin appeared on Jon's face. "Ah, of course, Luc, you knew about the trip and have access to your uber-wealthy uncle. We need to add Luc to the suspect list, Cleo. Welcome to the club, Luc." Jon laughed.

Luc's uncle? Uber-wealthy? Luc hadn't mentioned that to me. What else don't I know?

Luc rolled his eyes. "You're getting punchy, Jon. I think that's enough brainstorming for today."

"Yeah," I said. "Keep those questions in mind, though. Who had a motive? And who had means and knowledge of Ginger's plans, that we haven't thought of yet? We don't want to count anyone out this early in our effort to clear your name, Jon."

Serious, and not snarky for once, Jon agreed and stood to leave.

No sooner had he carried his bag of remaining precious coffee beans with him out the door, when both Luc's and my phone dinged. Luc was closer to his and picked it up to read the message.

"It's Samia," he said. "She's in the neighborhood and wondered if she can stop by to chat with us."

I had reached my phone by then. "She sent the text to me, too. How did she know I'd be here?" I asked.

Luc gave me a shy, little-boy smile. "I think she knows I'm crazy about you." He looked at me out of the corner of his eye. His smile became very grown up.

My cheeks warmed even as I took an involuntary step toward him. "And I guess she has a pretty big hunch I'm just as crazy about you." Luc kissed me and my heart raced. Before I could reach a hand up to the nape of his neck he backed away a step and held up his phone and waggled it at me.

"What should I tell Samia?" he asked. I surveyed our dirty coffee cups and tattered napkins, twisted into shreds during the discussion.

"Tell her to come on over. I can have this cleared away before she gets here," I said.

I rinsed the last coffee mug and put it on the drainer to dry when I saw, through the kitchen window, Samia pull into the driveway. I dried my hands while Luc met her at the door.

Samia walked in all smiles carrying a foil-covered tray. "I brought dark chocolate pinon brownies to apologize for dropping in practically unannounced."

Luc and I looked at each other and shared a smile.

"Thank you, Samia. That is kind of you. I'm going to get fat, though." Luc patted his flat stomach. "Jon just left and we've been having coffee and a light breakfast."

"Jon? What was he doing here?" Samia pushed past Luc angrily and set the tray on the counter with more force than needed.

Luc grimaced. Resentment on his face. The same resentment that twisted my stomach.

"Samia, you are my friend," Luc said. "But so is Jon. I don't expect that you two will get along now, knowing what is going on at the lab. But you have to respect my right to maintain my friendship with him. Don't make me choose between you."

The fire in Samia's eyes flared up, then died. She pouted.

"I won't make you choose, but you have some stupid friends." Samia glanced at me. "And I mean Jon, not Cleo."

I smiled. "Thanks for that clarification. What did you bring again? Luc may be full but I'm not." I'd been concentrating on making notes and lists, and forgot to eat during our meeting with Jon.

I made another pot of coffee. Unfortunately, without Jon's magic coffee beans, it lacked the perfection of his pot, but I managed some darned good coffee. I lifted the foil off Samia's tray and arranged the brownies on a plate. I carried them, along with the barely touched cheese and nut platter to a coffee table in the center of one of the seating arrangements in Luc's large living room. Luc and Samia were sitting across from each other, Luc's mouth a firm line. Samia sat ramrod straight, perched on the edge of the cushion on a plush leather couch. It couldn't have been easy to balance there. Her chin was in the air and her mouth in the same firm line as Luc's.

"Samia, your text said you wanted to stop by to talk." I poured three coffees and added milk and sugar to mine. I was going to be wired after this, but I had the feeling I was going to need caffeine for this conversation. I sipped my coffee. "Anything in particular you want to discuss?"

Samia's eyes lost their haughtiness. "I received a text. The threats have always been phone calls before. This is the first text." She studied her hands holding the coffee cup as if wondering how it had gotten there.

Luc leaned forward. "Matias is back, though. Right? I mean you weren't home alone again, were you?"

"Matias had to leave yesterday for a short trip. He will be back tomorrow. But there is not anything he can do." Samia lifted her eyes to Luc and then me. "It feels strange. The text, it was always phone calls before, and when I received one of those calls then I stopped picking up if I did not recognize the number. How can I not pick up a text? They just pop up." Samia lifted her arm and jangled her wrist. Bracelets rattled but I also saw a smartwatch. "Here on my watch. It vibrates and I check to see if I need steps for the hour and *die, bitch die* scrolls on my wrist."

"Can we track the sender?" I asked.

Samia shook her head. "Matias tried. I called him when I got it. He called some people he knows at the Defense Department who tried to trace it for him. It was a burner phone."

"I guess everybody texts more these days…but it seems odd that after years of telephone calls to deliver threats, they now would turn to texting." I bit my lower lip as I struggled to decipher what that meant. Then it hit me. "These messages are coming from a different source."

Samia sat up straighter. "I think you are right." She faced Luc. "Do not get mad. I am not asking you to pick sides. But does it not seem strange? Ginger is murdered, and the police think Jon is the killer, and then when I defend Matias at the Institute and think Jon is the killer, I receive threats again? In English. I told you I have not had any in years. Now, two in a week using different methods."

Luc sat back in his chair and Samia leaned forward. "You have to admit it. You cannot blame me for thinking Jon is behind this. He killed Ginger, he is trying to drag Matias down, and now me." Samia pointed at Luc. "How do you explain that?"

"Exactly what time did you get the text?" I asked.

"Early this morning," she said. "Around 6:30 I think, but I can check. Why?"

I looked at Luc. "Jon didn't get here until 6:45."

Luc frowned. "It's not Jon. I've known him for years. He would never do something as cowardly as sending an anonymous text. If he wanted to threaten someone he would sign his name in big bold letters." Luc scooted his chair back. "It wasn't him. I think, most likely, it's one of your Saudi relations who have graduated to texting."

Samia shifted her gaze from Luc to me. "But you think it could be him, do you not, Cleo? He killed Ginger and now he is threatening me."

"I don't know, Samia. I trust Luc's opinion, but it's a possibility. Although…how would he know to make those threats? Does he know your past?"

Samia pursed her lips.

"And I guess I don't see a clear motive, either for Ginger's murder or your threats. Why are you so sure it's him?" I asked.

"He is out to get me and Matias. Maybe he is racist."

"But that doesn't explain Ginger," I said.

"Ginger and our Center help native women. Maybe he is against that."

"Wait." Luc's voice was sharp as broken glass. "Samia, I don't appreciate you hurling unfounded accusations about my friend. I've known him for over twenty years. Jon is not racist. You are being unfair. I want to help you defend yourself against these threatening texts, but it's irresponsible of you to accuse Jon of being racist without a grain of evidence. And you don't have any."

Samia stood up, chin stuck out. "I know what I know, and if you want to be blinded by old friendships and not see it. That is up to you Luc. But I am disappointed that you will not even consider it. I will leave now."

Back straight, Samia walked to the front door and opened it. I trailed after her, stunned at the brusque end of the discussion. Luc glared at Samia's back.

As she passed through the door, Samia said over her shoulder, "Goodbye, Cleo. I will be in touch with *you*."

I mumbled goodbye and closed the door behind her. Samia's accusations and response were over-sized for the situation. I didn't know Jon as well as Luc, but I hadn't heard a racist word or seen a racist deed from him. Cocky? Arrogant? Equal-opportunity obnoxious? Yes. What else could be driving Samia's accusations? She left in such a hurry I didn't have a chance to ask her about the Center's books. Could she be hiding something? Is that why she was so intent on pushing attention in other directions?

Chapter 29

Family Relations

The next afternoon Luc and I strolled the sidewalks of downtown Santa Fe. A cornflower blue sky kissed the creamy adobe of buildings that lined the streets. We had meandered on the shady sidewalk between Alameda and the trickling Santa Fe River, then crossed over to the Plaza. After sitting in front of our laptops most of the day, the walk helped us work up an appetite for dinner and we decided to eat downtown since we were already there. Luc pulled out his phone to make a dinner reservation but hesitated when he saw the screen.

"Just a second," he said. "My uncle texted." As he unlocked the phone and read the text, I peered into the window of Lucchese Bootmakers. I loved their boots, but I would never wear them once I left Santa Fe. Too heavy to pack and definitely not Hawaii-style. Not to mention they were pricey. Mimi might be able to afford them, but not me.

"My uncle is coming to visit. And my sister and her baby." Luc smiled. "Celia had a baby boy and Enzo is flying over to meet him. When he called to tell her, she suggested we meet up here. She loves Santa Fe, and I haven't met her baby yet either. Apparently, you are going to get to meet the crazy side of my family."

I managed a weak smile. *Crazy side?*

Luc laughed at my expression. "Crazy is probably the wrong word. Enzo is great, he just… well, he comes up with big, bold ideas, and goes after them with gusto. More often than not he is a success, but when the ideas are bad, they really bust." Luc's smile grew and he put an arm around my shoulder as we walked. "My parents and other uncles are more serious and practical. Not Enzo. But I have to admit, he is my favorite uncle. I'm glad you're going to get a chance to meet him. And you're going to love Celia. Everybody does." Luc kissed the top of my head and we headed in the direction of our restaurant.

We hadn't made it more than a block when we ran into Kyle.

"What a coincidence," I said.

"Not really, I only live a couple of blocks from here," he said.

"That's right. When we were at your place for the dinner party we parked on the other side from town. I'd forgotten you lived close to the Plaza."

Kyle's face was tense.

"How are you doing?" I asked.

Kyle shrugged.

"It's good that you came outside to walk. It's a beautiful day," Luc said.

Kyle frowned. "I left to get away from that FBI guy."

"Agent Rivera? Was he questioning you?" Luc asked

"No, not me today. He wanted to talk to Teresa, of all people."

"Teresa, Ginger's cook?" Luc asked.

"Yep. Did you know her brother is that guy who

works at Ginger's…I guess now it's Samia's Center?"

"No, but it makes sense. Ginger thought highly of Teresa. Of course she would ask her for a recommendation for a reliable, trustworthy handyman."

"Are you talking about Raul? Is that the handyman you mean?" I asked.

"Yeah, I think that's his name."

"Raul, who has the nephew, Manuel?"

Kyle looked at me like I was crazy. "Right, Teresa's son. Manuel is Raul's nephew. What's the big deal with Teresa's family history?"

I bit my lip. "Probably nothing, I didn't realize that Manuel, Teresa, and Raul were all related." My mind whirled. Teresa may need to be added to our list of suspects. Or maybe the Federal Agent was way ahead of me. Perhaps we could leave that to him.

****

I woke early, shaken from a bad dream by the eerie yips, howls, and soul-wrenching screams of the pack of coyotes that lived nearby. The full moon was like a spotlight on my face, but even after closing the cracked window and curtain on my side of the bed, I couldn't get back to sleep. My hand groped around on the nearby chair for the robe I'd tossed off the night before and I slipped my feet into thick wool socks. By the light of my phone, I trod as quietly as possible down Luc's circular stairway, closing the bedroom door behind so as not to awaken him.

I made a pot of coffee and opened my laptop for a quick glance at my email. No late-night lava updates from Rikki or Gina. Santa Fe was four hours later than Hilo, so any morning updates wouldn't come until lunchtime. I closed my computer and stood, stretched my legs, and poured myself a cup of coffee. In that little time that had passed since I crept downstairs, the moon had set and Luc's floor-to-ceiling east windows were full of the first shades of morning light. I sipped my coffee and watched the world wake up. A Steller's jay landed on a pinon branch that hung over the adobe wall of the courtyard. The flashy blue bird, with his dazzling black plume that bobbed and danced as he hunted for seeds, reminded me of an enthusiastic drum major from my high school band.

As I watched the birds gather around, drawn by Luc's bird feeders, my mind revisited the dream I'd had last night. I was back in Hilo with Suki, my dog that died last year. In the dream, she was alive but surrounded by lava. I couldn't get to her and I couldn't find a way to get her out. Ben was on the other side of the lava flow too, but he calmly watched it without any apparent worry. In my dream, I was at first mad at him for not caring about the dire situation for my dog, and then guilty because I was more worried about Suki than him.

I stretched my neck and rolled my shoulders to chase the dream away.

Luc's sister would arrive tomorrow, with her new baby. I was eager for the visit. Ben's sister and I had never developed the rapport I had hoped to have with her. Maybe it would be different with Celia. And being around Celia's baby would be good practice for me as a future Auntie to Gina's baby when I was back in Hawaii.

I heard a noise behind me and found Luc. He smiled as he approached. When he reached me, he stood behind and wrapped his arms around me interlacing his fingers across my stomach. We stood there, content with the physical connection, and watched the birds.

After a few minutes, Luc kissed my ear and moved away toward the coffee pot. He was already dressed and ready for the day. "Can I ask a favor?"

"Sure. What is it?"

Luc laughed, "Be careful. You should ask 'what is it?' before promising to do it."

I rolled my eyes. "Right. Like you are going to ask me to do something revolting. What is this dastardly deed you need me to do?"

"We-e-ell. As you know, my sister gets here tomorrow."

"Sure."

"And she is bringing her eight-month old baby."

I raised my eyebrows. "And?"

"I was talking to Celia last night, and according to her, there are all kinds of equipment I need to have here for the baby. And I am swamped with meetings today."

"And you want me to shop for baby stuff?" I smiled. What a fun favor.

Luc winced. "Yes. Do you mind?"

"Mind? It'll be great. Is Celia bringing anything with her and the baby, or do we need to get a crib and everything?" I asked.

"I don't know. I'll text her for a list. Thank you so much, Cleo. I have an incredibly busy day but I didn't want to be sexist expecting you to do the shopping for my family."

I laughed. "No problem. I'm caught up on my section of the grant. And it should be fun. Just let me know what Celia needs." After my bad night, maybe today was taking a turn for the better. It would be a joy shopping for baby stuff.

Luc texted his sister immediately and wrote out a list

of what she wanted while I ate some breakfast. I started back upstairs to brush my teeth and get dressed and get ready for the baby shopping when Luc called out to me while he was packing his briefcase.

"Thanks again, Cleo. I'm hopeless with baby stuff. They are cute, but so much work. Not sure why anyone wants to have one."

My foot faltered on the step and I twisted around to ask Luc if he really meant that. But he was closing the door behind him on the way to his car.

****

I found everything on the list, but the joy had been sucked out of the activity. Last year, I had thought Ben and I would have a child. *But when that relationship ended...and Luc and I have been so great together... I guess in the back of my mind in that picture of a happy couple with a baby, I had slipped Luc into the father role.* Except he doesn't want a child. We hadn't discussed kids. It was too early in the relationship for that. But...

I wanted a child.

At least I thought I did.

Here's what I told my girlfriends when they struggled with relationship issues. A person had to make a choice between two realities, not a fantasy and a reality, not a hope and a reality. I needed to choose between a life with Luc and no baby, or a life without Luc, and raising a baby, by myself. Neither reality appealed to me.

I flicked the fingers of my hand that wasn't on the steering wheel. I was almost to Ginger's, now Samia's Center. I had called her for advice on baby cribs. She told me the Institute kept a couple on hand for clients. None were in use at the moment, so she suggested I borrow one of those for the couple of nights Celia would be in town.

I pulled into the parking lot and noticed two pick-up trucks. An older, well-kept white one and a red one that had been used and abused. I didn't see Samia's Lexus, but she had promised to leave word with Sandra that I was coming by for one of the portable cribs.

I entered and found a woman seated at a wooden desk to my right reading a document. A short, round woman, she had dark hair and wore glasses. She lifted her head as I opened the door and squinted at me. She gave me a quick smile. "You're Cleo, right?"

"Right," I said. "And you must be Sandra?"

"Yes. Samia told me you'd be coming. The crib is in a storage closet. I'll go get it."

"Let me help you with it."

Before I could take a step she raised a hand and waved me off. "Wait here, I'll be right back with it."

She stood and walked down a hall. She opened a door near the end, and as it closed behind her two men exited one of the doors she had passed. They walked toward me. Actually, they were probably heading to the front door I'd just entered, and currently blocked. I stepped to the side and closer to Sandra's desk to get out of their way. Waves of anger emanated from the older man, his face a thundercloud. The younger man stuck his chin out, mouth thin and tight, but his eyes winced with worry. As they approached I recognized one of them.

"You're Raul? Right." The older of the two men paused. His scowl became a challenge as he stared at me. "Do I know you?"

"I was having lunch with Samia when you stopped at our table the other day…" I glanced at the second man and realized it was Manuel, Raul's nephew, Teresa's son. And Manuel was glaring at me every bit as angrily as he had at the restaurant. He had silky dark hair, large dark eyes, and almond-colored skin. He was a handsome man with a proud set to his mouth. If he didn't appear enraged, I might have found him attractive.

I looked back at Raul and saw a hint of recognition, and suspicion. "Yes. I remember. Is there something I can help you with?" His tone was polite but reluctant.

I focused my attention on Raul and ignored the angry young man next to him. "I wanted to express my condolences. I understand you and your sister were close to Ms. Hanlon. I know she relied on you. Her death must have been a shock. I'm sorry."

Manuel stepped closer to me, forcing me to bring my eyes back to him. "Why are you sorry?" His words were bitter. "Did you kill her? You didn't even know Miss Ginger. You didn't grow up in her house, and you haven't lost a job like my mom. What the hell do you have to be sorry about?"

I opened my mouth to respond, but I didn't know what to say. Before I had formed words, Raul put a hand on his nephew's shoulder. "Manuel, that is enough. The lady was extending a courtesy. Go home. You've done what you came here to do; now go home." After one more acidic glance in my direction Manuel moved toward the door.

"*Adios Tio, hasta luego.*" Manuel managed to inject anger into the harmless phrase.

The door closed behind Manuel and Raul turned back at me. His shoulders slumped and he appeared worn-out. "*Gracias* for your kind words. I apologize for my nephew. He has had a difficult life, but he is a good boy. My sister raised him well." Raul shrugged his shoulders. "Kids. I know he'll grow out of this anger. I only hope it's sooner rather than later."

A door in the hallway opened and Sandra struggled to maneuver a folded crib through the opening. Raul hurried over to help and easily lifted it and carried it to the desk.

"Thanks, Raul. That was heavier than I remembered." Sandra pushed a stray hair that had escaped her bun out of her face and sat down at her desk. "Do you mind putting that in Cleo's car? Samia said she could borrow it."

Raul lifted the crib again, and I followed him when Sandra asked, "I thought I heard another voice out here when I was digging this out of the closet. Did someone else come by?"

Raul busied himself with readjusting the crib, so I responded. "It was Raul's nephew. He just left."

Raul froze and Sandra bolted up straight in her chair.

"Manuel was here? Raul? Is this true? You know what Ginger and Samia's policy is." She scowled.

"I know the policy. He came by to see if I needed a ride home, but I sent him away," Raul mumbled. Head bent, he lifted the crib and walked out the front door.

I glanced at Sandra. Her eyes narrowed as she watched the door close behind Raul.

"Thanks," I said. "I'll get this back to you as soon as Celia's baby goes home."

"Sure," Sandra said. But her eyes were not on me. She was reaching for her telephone and her mind seemed to be on other things.

I rushed out the door to open the trunk for Raul. After the dark interior of the reception area, I squinted in the bright sunlight. Raul stood with the crib behind my car and I hurried over to unlock the trunk. The white pick-up was parked nearby, but the red beat-up truck was gone. That must be Manuel's truck.

I thanked Raul, but he too appeared distracted and waved vaguely at me before turning to walk back to the building.

Chapter 30

Celia

Luc's sister floated into the room on a cloud of happiness…if it's possible to float with a 25-pound baby in your arms. Dark curls surrounded sparkling eyes and her large mouth seemed to never still as it bubbled between laughter, cooing, and chatter with Luc.

For his part, Luc appeared delighted as he struggled to maneuver Celia's six bags into the room.

They were speaking rapidly in French, but Celia stopped mid-sentence when she saw me. She composed herself, smiled at me, and handed the baby to Luc as he set the last bag down. With arms outstretched, Celia put a hand on each of my shoulders and studied my face, before letting another burble of laughter slip out.

"I can't believe I'm finally getting to meet you, Cleo. You look exactly like I thought you would."

Before I could respond she embraced me in a bear hug and kissed me on both cheeks.

The difference between Celia and Ben's sister, Kerri, was like night and day. Ben and Kerri had grown up with an abusive father when they were young and a stiff, walking on eggshells atmosphere pervaded our house whenever Kerri visited. Not that Ben's sister wasn't interesting to talk to…there was just never this sense of relaxed happiness. This delight merely being in the presence of each other. One day maybe they would feel this sense of joy with family. I had it when I went home to see my parents, but I could never replicate it with Ben and Kerri.

Enough of that. I brought myself back to the happy present.

Celia and I chatted. She truly was a delight.

Luc, who was still holding the baby, interrupted. "I'll take these suitcases to your room, Celia, then get us all some drinks and we can sit on the patio. If one of you would take Tonio?"

"I'd love to hold him," I said.

Celia beamed. "Of course, Cleo. What's the matter, Luc? Scared of little Tonio?"

Luc rolled his eyes and stepped toward me so I could scoop little Tonio into my arms. I kissed Tonio's little forehead and breathed in the sweet baby smell. His big brown eyes widened and a gurgle greeted me.

Celia followed Luc to her room to set down her purse and the baby bag and together they moved into the kitchen, catching Luc up on her husband's activities.

I watched the little peanut in my arms with awe. So many expressions on his young face, and he was amazingly comfortable with me, a stranger. *Maybe he can tell I have a major crush on him. I can see a little Luc in that smile. I wonder what our baby would look like if Luc and I had...*I sucked in a quick breath. *Don't go there Cleo.*

Celia and Luc joined me on the patio, Luc carrying a tray of glasses and a pitcher of lemonade, Celia holding the door for him, then closing it behind him. Little Tonio saw his mom and waved his arms saying, "enh, enh, enh."

"He has been an angel, but I think he wants his mom now." I smiled and lifted him into Celia's outstretched arms. As soon as she had him settled, he grabbed a fist full of her hair as if to say, *I'm not letting you sneak away again.*

Luc's phone rang. He picked it up and checked the caller. "Sorry, I need to take this, but it shouldn't take long. Is that okay?" He stood up, his eyes on me.

"Sure. Celia and I can get to know each other. Go." I lifted a hand to wave him off.

Luc went back into the house. "Hi, yeah, I'm here. I'm glad we were able to connect..." floated out to us before he closed the door behind him.

Celia gently disentangled the baby's fingers from her hair, her smile beatific. She lifted her gaze to mine.

"You probably think I'm crazy coming this far with a baby to visit my uncle." Celia's smile moved to me. "But my uncle never had any children of his own. My mother tells me, as a young man, he was desperately in love with a woman training to become a pilot. They had plans to marry and have a large family. But weeks before the wedding, they had a big fight over whether she should continue her career after the babies were born. Enzo's fiancée drove off in a fury and a few days later was involved in a major crash in Beaune. The crash was horrific and it took them weeks to identify her as one of the dead and then only because of her car. The fire was so intense she couldn't be identified. Enzo was heartbroken."

I poured us lemonade and set her glass out of reach of the baby. "That's tragic."

Celia sighed. She gazed down at her baby and kissed him on the top of his head, before turning somber eyes back to me.

"After his fiancée's death, Enzo became a playboy. He had a string of girlfriends and lovers, but never considered marriage, or children, again. He doted on me and Luc, visiting often when we were children. Always bringing us presents. He taught us to ski and swim and we each received a graduation trip with him when we finished lycee, the equivalent of high school in Switzerland."

"Wow, what a gift," I said. "Where did you go?"

Celia laughed. "I was eighteen. I chose New York. He took me shopping. We hit Nolita and Williamsburg and caught a couple of Broadway shows. I loved it, but Luc was much more adventurous."

"Where did he go?" I asked.

"Patagonia."

I heard the door open and watched Luc approach us on the patio.

"Luc, do you remember your graduation trip to Patagonia with Uncle Enzo? I was telling Cleo about it."

Luc's smile broadened, "Of course." He kissed me on the head, then his sister while extending a finger to allow the baby to grasp it. "Uncle Enzo was great. I thought of myself as an adventurous explorer, the next Indiana Jones. Enzo gave that to me. No fancy hotels like he would normally book. We camped on the steppes and cooked over a fire we made ourselves. We didn't have access to a shower or bathroom for a week. And, well, he made it an adventure." A smaller, but endearing smile took over his face.

"He gave us credit for his recreational empire," Celia said. The baby fussed a little and Celia stood up and tenderly jogged him up and down as she paced around the patio. "He says he had so much fun on our trips," Celia tilted her head toward Luc, "and by that I think he means your trip to Patagonia. He says that gave him the idea to arrange adventure travel."

"I look forward to meeting him," I said. And I meant it. Meeting Celia gave me a window into Luc that I hadn't seen before, but hoped was there. His love of family. Their uncle Enzo sounded like a fascinating character. My shoulders released a tightness I hadn't realized was there. I think I was more anxious about meeting Luc's family than I realized. After meeting Celia and hearing the entertaining Enzo stories, I could relax and enjoy their visit.

Celia raised a hand to stifle a yawn. "Sorry," she said. "Baby and I had to get up early to catch this flight. If you don't mind, I think I'll put him down for a nap and maybe catch a quick nap myself." She blew kisses to Luc then me, and with a drowsy smile went to her room.

As her door closed, my phone rang. Samia. Luc was gathering our glasses to carry them back inside, so I hit the green button on my phone. "Hi, Samia, what's up?"

"I am glad I caught you. I know Luc's family landed in town today. I would not bother you but this is important." Samia's voice was heavy.

"Go ahead, I have a few minutes."

"I just found out that Manuel, Raul's nephew was here at the center yesterday. Sandra, our receptionist, told me you were here at the same time."

"Yes, Manuel was leaving while I waited for Sandra to bring the crib out."

"Did you see which room they were in?" Samia asked. She sounded tense.

I tried to visualize the scene in my mind. "I think

so," I said. "Why does it matter?"

But it sounded like Samia had her hand covering her phone and I heard her muffled voice talking to someone else. I waited and listened, my curiosity aroused. I couldn't make out words but the person she was talking with sounded like a man.

"I hate to ask you this, Cleo…" Samia's voice came back clearly on the line. "But that federal agent is here, and he thinks it would be best if you come to the center now. It will not take long, but he wants you to show him which room Manuel was in and ask you a few questions."

"Right now?" I asked as Luc returned to the patio and watched me.

"Please. I would not ask but the agent thinks it might be important."

"Okay, sure. I think I have a little free time, and you promise it won't take long?"

"Promise."

I hung up and looked at Luc. "I have to go out for about an hour. The Federal agent is at Samia's Center, and he wants to ask me a few questions."

Luc's face grew serious. "I'll drive you. Let me get my keys." And he stood. I put a hand on his arm to stop him.

"No worries. I should be back soon. You should stay here in case Celia or the baby wake up. I'll be fine."

Luc kissed me on my forehead. "Are you sure you don't want me there?"

I savored his touch for a second then stood up. "I've got this."

I arrived at the center within fifteen minutes. Two cars were parked in the lot, Samia's Lexus and a Ford

Taurus. I entered the building and found Samia and the Federal agent I'd met the other day, Joe Rivera.

They had been sitting in the waiting area clutching cardboard cups of what was probably coffee.

"Hi," I said. "How can I help?"

Samia gave me a nervous smile. Rivera spoke. "Thanks for coming down, Ms. Cooper.

"Of course, I could have just told you over the phone, but Samia said it was important."

"It is. Memory can be place dependent. Of course, you are a psychologist so you know that, I expect."

I did. In psychology, we called it context-dependent learning but it's the same thing. A person is more likely to remember things more clearly, and in more detail, if they either return to the place it occurred or visualize it in their minds. I remind my students of that before each test. If they can't quite remember something they studied, I tell them to picture the location where they studied it.

I smiled. "Right. Well, Raul and Manuel came out of that door." I pointed to the door I had seen them exit.

Samia frowned. Rivera's face remained placid, but his voice lowered a notch. "You are sure it was that door?"

"Yes," I said.

"Did you hear them say anything as they left?"

"No, they seemed tense. Raul angry. Manuel angry and maybe worried." I shrugged. "That was just my impression anyway. I don't really know."

Rivera tapped something into his tablet. "Were they carrying anything? Anything in their hands?"

I thought back. "No."

"No briefcase or backpack? No folder, newspaper,

envelope?"

"No."

Rivera took a deep breath. "Did they speak to you when they saw you? I believe you told me you had met them before?"

"Right. They seemed distracted, but when I recognized Raul I said hello and expressed my condolences for Ginger's death."

"And his response?"

"Raul was polite and respectful. Manuel was… bitter. He seemed to resent my intrusion."

Rivera noted something on his tablet and looked back up at me. "Thank you, Ms. Cooper. I appreciate your cooperation. If I have any further questions I will be in touch. And if you think of anything else, here is my card."

I entered his number into my contacts, because I'm terrible at keeping track of cards, and turned to Samia. There were lines around her eyes I had not noticed before. I lifted an eyebrow in question. She shook her head. "Go back to Luc and his family."

She didn't have to tell me twice.

Chapter 31

Enzo

A man I judged to be in his fifties entered the hotel restaurant. He was tall, dark-haired with hints of silver glinting at his temples. His eyes roved the room, but settled on Luc, before flashing over to me. His eyebrows drew together as he stopped and placed his hand on the back of a tall, elegant woman, who had moved up to stand beside him. I guessed her to be twenty years younger than him. He only needed to lean down a few inches to whisper in her ear. Her gaze moved to our table, but it rested on Luc and stayed there as the man and woman crossed the room to join us.

"Uncle Enzo, I didn't know you were bringing Anya." Luc stood up to exchange kisses on the cheek with the impossibly thin woman who must be Anya, before shaking his uncle's hand with both of his. Luc's delight at seeing his uncle made me smile.

"Anya is integral to the project I want to propose to you." Enzo gave a Gallic shrug before he contemplated me. "And I didn't know you were bringing this lovely lady." Enzo took my hand, bowing his head to kiss my knuckles that rested on two of his outstretched fingers.

"This is Cleo. She is working with me on that project I mentioned." Luc placed a hand on my back. "She's on sabbatical from Hawaii, but if I get the project going I hope she'll come back to stay." Luc winked at me with an enigmatic smile that made my stomach flip. "But, Anya, Uncle, please sit down."

Enzo glanced around the room. "Where are your sister and the baby?"

Luc held up a hand. "As we were walking out the door, Tonio started shrieking. Celia sends her regrets and promises to introduce her son to you tomorrow. She thinks he's overtired after the trip and maybe had an upset tummy or something. Believe me, the noise that baby was making…we couldn't have heard each other talk." Luc shook his head. "I'm sure he will be better tomorrow, and Celia is excited to see you."

"Babies can be like that. I don't want her to worry. I have a surprise for the boy. I can wait until it arrives." Enzo smiled to himself.

A waiter appeared to take drink orders for all of us. Once he had left, Anya finally spoke, *"Quelle langue parlerons-nous?"*

Everyone looked at me.

"English, I think," Enzo said. "We are in America now, after all."

Anya rolled her eyes.

"Cleo knows a few Hawaiian words, but not much French…yet." Luc winked at me again and grinned.

Anya watched Luc, then glanced at me, and smirked. "How nice."

Enzo leaned toward me and spoke loud enough that everyone at our table, and probably the table next to ours could hear, "Anya speaks…How many languages is it, my dear? Five or six?"

Anya shrugged and her lovely brows drew together. "Does it matter, Enzo?"

Enzo laughed a deep, hearty laugh. "I guess not, my dear. I think you have one or two more than Luc and me, but you're right. No need to remind us of family weaknesses." Enzo laughed again and clapped a hand on my shoulder to include me in the joke. Although perhaps he intended to make me the joke.

"Uncle Enzo." Luc's voice held a note of warning. "Play nice."

"Wha-a-a-t?" Enzo spread his hands wide and leaned back. "I want to get to know your Cleo, and I thought she would want to get to know us."

Luc shook his head. "Cleo, my uncle can be a bit full of himself sometimes. Please ignore him when he gets like this. I promise there is a much better side to him that I hope you will be seeing soon." Luc raised his eyebrows and glared at Enzo.

"*Bien sur*," Enzo said, turning to me. "I had no wish to offend, my dear. Please let me try again…"

Enzo was nothing but charming after that. He refused to speak of his surprise for baby Tonio, or the project he wanted to propose to Luc. But he was entertaining. He told me funny stories of Luc and Celia as children. He told flattering stories of Anya and her accomplishments. He did all this while watching me like a hawk.

Chapter 32

Voggy Days and Surprises

"Hey, Rikki Tikki. What's happening, girl?" I was still a little hyped after meeting first Celia, then Enzo and Anya. I felt like I'd ridden a roller coaster and had called to get Rikki's take on the situation. Luc and I had stayed for drinks and appetizers then left to let all the travelers get to sleep early. I told him to drop me off at my casita, so I could talk to Rikki in private.

I heard a cough on the other end of the line. "Hey, Cleo, what's up?" The normal lilt to Rikki's voice was missing, her voice raspy.

"Are you okay? You sound like you are coming down with a cold?" My mood shifted to concern.

"It's not a cold. It's the vog. It's been awful. At record levels." I heard Rikki cough again.

"You aren't down in Puna, are you? I hope you didn't go down to see the lava."

"No. The trade winds aren't blowing and the vog slides down the mountain to settle in Hilo." Rikki cleared her throat with a rattle.

"You should get out of the vog. I'm worried about you, Riks."

"Where am I going to go?" Irritation crept into her voice. She must be feeling terrible. "You know what it's like here. Nobody has air conditioning, so the windows are always open. All the restaurants are open-air. Maybe you don't remember because your office at the University was air-conditioned, but outside of the University, the mall, and the hospital, AC is hard to find. There is nowhere to get out of this without leaving the island."

She was right. I had forgotten. Voggy days used to give me a cough and made my skin itch, but I'd stay later at the office and that gave my lungs a break. But the vog in those days was nowhere near the level it was now with the active eruption. And Rikki and Gina didn't have air-conditioned offices, or homes.

I spoke quietly, "Go to the mall. You sound bad, sweetie. I know you hate the mall, but…I'm worried about you."

Rikki gave a raspy sigh. "I'm okay. Gina has me drinking detox tea by the gallon, and my mom sent me a gas mask, but I gave it to Gina because of the baby. I know you're worried. Just like my parents. But you haven't been gone that long. You know what it's like here. The locals take everything in stride. 'If Pele wants to visit, she is welcome in my house.' I can't tell you how many times I've heard that lately. They don't want their house overrun by lava, but there is nothing to be done so why stress out. I don't want to freak out when the locals handle things so calmly."

I took a deep breath. "I get it." I took another deep breath, thankful for the fresh, clean desert air. "So other than the vog, what's up with you?"

Rikki's raspy voice grew gentle. "Not much is happening with me. But there have been some significant changes around here lately."

"Other than Gina's pregnancy?" I asked.

"Yeah. I don't mean Gina."

"Who?" My curiosity was piqued.

"Well, you know the lava covered the roads to Puna, and put some of the neighborhoods there in danger. Right?"

"Oh no, did somebody else we know lose their home?"

"No. But, you know that because of the lava a lot of people had to move to Hilo, that there is a major housing shortage. Right?"

"What's up Rikki?"

"Ben offered one of the spare rooms in your house to a Chemistry professor who is here for one year, and whose rented house was in the direct path of the lava."

"Okay, Ben is a nice guy. I would expect that," I said. The silence that followed changed my curiosity into a sick feeling in the pit of my stomach. "Tell me about this visiting Chemistry professor."

"Well, she's only here for a year."

SHE? Ben invited a woman into MY house. I took a deep breath. Okay, he is a nice guy, she was in need, new to the area, and didn't have family and friends around. It's the kind of thing Ben would do.

Rikki rushed on, "At least that's how long her contract is. I guess she could get rehired for next year. But who knows. Right? She could be gone before you get back."

"Come on, you are talking way too fast. What's up other than that she is a visiting professor and Ben has her in the guest room during this emergency?"

Another long pause from Rikki.

"Rikki?" *What didn't Rikki want to tell me?*

"I'm not exactly sure she is sleeping in the guest

room," Rikki said in a quiet voice.

And POW! I sucked air in after feeling that gut punch. Air is good. Air helped me think. I broke up with Ben. I am sleeping with Luc. Ben has every right to find someone new. Why I didn't see this coming I don't know. But I was gobsmacked. I tried to shake it off so Rikki didn't feel guilty breaking the news to me.

"Wow, okay. So Ben is with someone." I struggled to keep my voice from shaking or cracking. "That's good. No, I'm happy for Ben. I'm glad he's moving on." I clamped my mouth tightly shut to stop myself from babbling.

"Really?" Rikki sounded skeptical.

I smiled at my friend's voice. "No. But I will be. Thanks for breaking it to me, Rikki."

"That's what friends are for," she said.

"Yes. And I'm lucky to have such good friends."

We said our goodbyes and hung up. I opened my computer and immediately ordered Rikki a gas mask and a dozen filters.

Friends can do more than gently break bad news.

Chapter 33

Another Dinner Party

"The horizon is on fire." I soaked in the sunset, unfolding through Luc's western wall of windows. The pinon trees stood out as lacy black ghosts, backlit with day-glo fluorescent orange. Luc followed to stand behind me.

"Be careful what you say," Luc whispered into my ear. "A lot of the people relocating to Santa Fe are from California. Running away from wildfires."

"I didn't realize."

He kissed my cheek and took my hand. I think I first started falling in love with Luc during a sunset he showed me on my first visit to Santa Fe. Something stirred in my heart as I remembered the moment, and regretted we had guests.

"Well, aren't you two just the little lovebirds." I turned toward the elegant, silky voice and found a straight-lipped, one eyebrow raised Anya. My hand still enclosed in Luc's suddenly felt awkward.

"Just admiring the sunset. It's fabulous tonight," I said.

Luc squeezed my hand. "But we should get back to our guests. I need to check the prime rib."

Anya smirked. "Of course, Lucas." She spun on her heel so her back was to us, walked to lay a hand on

Enzo's shoulder, and whispered something in his ear. Enzo frowned for a split second, then forced a smile and a laugh to respond to something Celia had said to him. He then glanced at Luc and me as we made our way past him and Celia toward the kitchen. The frown reappeared but was gone so quickly I would have thought I imagined it if I hadn't seen it twice in a matter of minutes.

I spent last night at my casita to give Luc time alone with his family. Enzo, Anya, Luc, and Celia had breakfast at Enzo's hotel and spent the day exploring Santa Fe together. I didn't join them until this evening to help Luc prepare dinner. He had planned a dinner party to give his family a chance to meet some of his Santa Fe friends. His family knew Jon, so of course he was invited. But Luc wanted them to meet Samia and Matias. We vacillated on whether to invite Kyle because of the rancor between him and Jon. But Luc planned to invite Mimi since she didn't know anyone else in town, and he didn't want Kyle to feel abandoned by Ginger's friends now that she was gone. It was a calculated risk, but it was Luc's party.

In the kitchen, Luc checked the temperature of the prime rib while I assembled a dish of charred peppers with ricotta, walnuts, and cucumbers. A thought flashed through my head that in my old life, Ben and I had never entertained like this. We invited our friends over to grill whatever fish Ben or one of our guests had caught, and salad a la Cleo. But Luc had culinary skills. His friends and family had high expectations.

"Luc, I just saw on my app that your mountain is getting snow tonight," Enzo called from the other side of the great room. "We should all go skiing tomorrow."

Luc was pulling the prime rib out of the oven, and

after setting it on the counter, glanced at me with a question in his eye. I grinned and flashed him a thumb's up.

"Sounds great," Luc said.

Mimi squealed with delight and clapped her hands. Excited voices rose, as the group planned to meet up and determine who needed to borrow equipment.

Luc and I brought the food to the table as everyone sat. It was casual, no seating charts. I went back for another bottle of wine. When I reached the table, I found the only chair left was at the end of the table opposite Luc and between Enzo and Anya with Matias and Kyle seated on the other side of them.

I inwardly groaned at the prospect of dinner conversation with chilly Anya and overpowering Enzo.

Before I sat, I offered wine to those around me as Luc did at his end of the table. Enzo and Kyle accepted my offer but Matias and Anya still had glasses half full and declined. Okay, nothing else to do but sit...between two people that I had a distinct impression didn't like me.

We passed food around and I tried to engage Anya in conversation first, as she was slightly less intimidating than Enzo. But Anya studiously turned her back on me to engage Kyle in a discussion on painting techniques.

Steeling myself I peeked at Enzo. He stared at me as he lifted a forkful of roast to his mouth.

I took a deep breath and took this bull by the horns. "Enzo, it has been great to meet you after hearing so much about you from Luc. But I get the feeling, well...I don't think you like me. And I'm not sure why."

I broke my gaze with him, with some effort, and took a generous swallow of the heavenly wine Luc had chosen for the evening.

When I glanced back, Enzo was smiling at me. Perhaps the first genuine smile I had received from him.

He lifted his glass toward me. "I admire a woman who meets a challenge head on."

Anya's back flinched and straightened, though she didn't turn in our direction.

"Am I wrong?" I asked Enzo.

"A little bit." Enzo held a thumb and forefinger a half-inch apart. "It is not you, *mia cara*. It is the temptation of you." And Enzo smiled an enormous smile. "I miss my nephew tremendously. I miss Celia also." Enzo gave a gallic shrug. "But with a bambino, she is a lost cause. I will never pull her back to Europe with her husband and baby. Luc, I thought would return. Until he met you." Enzo's smile disappeared. "I want him to come home."

Enzo's face softened. "I'm getting older. Celia and Luc are my family. I want them closer. You, I think. You also know the importance of family, yes?"

A picture of my parents flashed in my head. "Yes."

"Your family is here?" Enzo asked.

"Not in New Mexico, but on the East Coast," I said.

"Then you understand. Having an ocean between parent and child..." the eyebrows lifted again, "that is not good, yes?"

I nodded slowly. "Yes, it has been nice to be just a couple of states away instead of an ocean and a continent away from my parents. I get it."

I heard Luc laugh at something Mimi had said and both Enzo and I glanced in his direction. He must have felt our eyes on him and turned to us. His large happy smile became quizzical.

I sent Luc a gentle smile and winked. His uncle was

plotting against us, but I didn't want to spoil Luc's evening.

I looked at Enzo again. "You want Luc to live closer to you, just like my parents want me to live closer to them." I paused. "But don't you think the decision of where Luc chooses to live is up to him?" Luc and I were in the early days of our relationship, but I felt a surprising urge to protect it.

Before Enzo could answer Jon's voice inserted itself.

"Ha. You are such an idiot, Kyle. Tell him, Matias. Tell Kyle what an algorithm is. And that his hands are *not* one." Jon's chuckle drew the eyes of everyone at the table.

Matias and Kyle sat, red-faced next to each other and across from Jon and Mimi.

"Jon, you are such an ass." Matias' voice was severe. "You go out of your way to humiliate and belittle people. You throw verbal darts in an effort to destroy a person with a thousand cuts." Matias took a deep breath before continuing in a softer, but no less intense tone. "Kyle is an artist. Why in the world should he need to know the definition of an algorithm."

Kyle's face was beet red.

Jon laughed again. "I'm not saying he necessarily should know what it means but he shouldn't use a word he doesn't know. Kyle, what was it you were telling Anya?"

"Nothing. Shut up, Jon," Kyle spit out between tight lips.

Anya sighed, looked at Enzo with a raised eyebrow, and picked up her glass of wine for a drink.

Luc, at the other end of the table, sucked in a deep

breath. "Come on, Jon. Let up on Kyle. He is a guest in my home. Don't pick a fight."

Samia laid her hand on Matias' which rested on the table.

But Mimi, who sat on the other side of Jon, leaned toward him and in an overly loud whisper said, "Yeah, leave it, Jon. I heard what he said, and he clearly doesn't know what he's talking about. Hands can't be algorithms for his art. But he's an idiot and he can't help that. No need to make him feel worse." She shot a mocking smile at Kyle.

Kyle jumped up from the table. "Screw you, Mimi." He glanced at Luc darkly. "Thanks for the invitation to go skiing tomorrow. But if those two are going, I'm not. Dinner was great but I'm suddenly sick of the company." Kyle threw his napkin on the table and stormed out the front door. Luc and I both stood to follow him, but I raised a hand to stop him. I had it, and I was closer to the front door. Luc smiled his thanks and sat down.

I caught Kyle as he was opening his car door. "Kyle, wait."

He stopped at the sound of his name and paused, the door open a couple inches but not farther.

"I'm sorry, Kyle. That was awful of Jon. He was a jerk. If anyone should leave it should be him."

Kyle looked blankly at his hand holding the car door open. "You're helping him get off for Ginger's murder. Why are you doing that?" His anger seemed to have been replaced by sadness.

"I'm not helping Jon. I'm helping Ginger. I want the police to find who killed her. If it's Jon, I'll turn him in, but if it isn't…maybe when he isn't under the pressure of being a murder suspect he will mellow. Please come back inside. If Jon doesn't shut up, we'll ask him to leave."

"Thanks, Cleo, but I don't think so. It wasn't just Jon."

"No? Oh, of course, you're still grieving for Ginger."

Kyle's eyes jerked to mine. "Right." He stared intensely at me. "Everyone else seems to be moving on, especially that Mimi." His lips curled up in distaste. "It's hell living with her. Ginger was so easy to get along with, so laid back, but Mimi is a bitch. I hope she changes her mind and leaves soon."

"Mimi decided to stay? I hadn't heard that."

"Unfortunately. Anyway. I'm going home and plan to curl up with a nice bottle of tequila. Thanks again for the invite, and hope I didn't ruin your party." Kyle attempted an unsuccessful smile and opened his car door enough to climb in. He closed the door and gave me just enough time to step away before he drove off.

I walked slowly back into the house. Mimi's cruelty toward Kyle at the table, and his description of her, didn't fit with my initial impression of Mimi. I had seen her as a charming, inoffensive, bon vivant. Maybe I should reassess that.

As I returned to my seat, Enzo dramatically stood up to pull my chair out for me and waved his arm to indicate I should sit.

I complied.

Enzo sat back down next to me. He and the other guests were well along in their meal but I had barely touched mine. I forked a blistered pepper and swirled it in the ricotta before lifting it into my mouth.

"You were successful in stopping the young man

from leaving?" Enzo asked.

I shook my head, still chewing.

Enzo lifted his glass to me again. "Please forgive me *mio cara*, but as much as I admire you, I hope you are just as unsuccessful in stopping Luc from leaving."

He sipped from his raised glass then topped off my glass, which I had barely touched.

Time to change that situation.

The rest of the evening went by in a blur. Maybe because I was tired, and maybe because I kept drinking the wine Enzo kept pouring. Anya spent an inordinate amount of time hanging on Luc. Jon circled them both. Enzo explained to me the three of them had grown up together.

After dinner when we moved to the seating areas, I spent most of the time talking with Matias, Samia, and Mimi. The topic swung to gun violence in the U.S. New Mexico was a gun friendly state.

"So I can go shooting while I'm here?" Mimi asked. "Uncle Roger took me to target practice when I was a kid. I loved it."

Matias smiled. "I'll take you. I go shooting occasionally at my gun club. I've tried to get Samia to learn…"

Samia shook her head. "I hate guns."

"But target practice is like golf. It's about improving your precision," Mimi said.

"Exactly," Enzo said. "In Switzerland gun clubs are family gatherings. There is nothing sinister about them and we have no mass shootings. Luc, Anya, and Jon all learned to shoot at the club."

Enzo flirted outrageously with Mimi. And me. Jon whispered to me that it wasn't personal. Enzo liked to flirt with any unattached women. Evidently Enzo considered me unattached.

We ooed and ahhed at Samia's desert before I got up to make coffee. Jon stopped me halfway to the coffee maker.

"Please, Cleo, let me."

"You're a guest. I can make good coffee, too," I said.

Jon rolled his eyes, "First of all you *know* I make the best coffee you've ever tasted."

He had me there.

When I didn't object, he continued. "And, I need to redeem myself for being such a jerk at your first dinner party with Luc." He spoke so softly I had to lean in to hear. "Please. Let me make it up to you."

I gave him a tired smile. "Okay. I have to admit you make better coffee than anyone I know. Can I help you?"

Jon waved me away and I went to stand next to Luc. Anya was on the other side chatting to Luc in French, but when I approached he put his arm around me and pulled me in. He kissed the side of my forehead and whispered in my ear, "Thanks for putting up with my crazy family and friends. You're the best."

A goofy smile must have slipped onto my face. Anya's eyes narrowed.

Celia chose that moment to walk up and kiss me on the other cheek. There was a smile in her eyes as she glanced from Anya to Enzo. "Trial by fire, but you appear unscathed." Celia laughed and pulled Anya away. "Come on, tell me what all the fashionistas are wearing in Milan these days. As soon as I shed a couple more baby pounds I'm going to be ready to roll."

I smiled at Celia and reveled in the feeling of warm

security I felt standing there with Luc's arm around my neck and shoulder.

Luc spoke softly. "I know Enzo and Anya are giving you a hard time. I'm sorry. They are protective of me. They will grow to accept you in time. Celia already loves you, they will soon, too." I received another butterfly kiss on the ear.

"It's okay, and I get where Enzo is coming from. But Anya, I'm not sure why she feels the need to protect you. Is there a history there?"

"She had it rough growing up. My parents and Enzo took her in when she needed it." Luc gave a low, sexy chuckle. "Speaking of Enzo, he seems to be hitting it off with Mimi. Look at those two." Luc removed his arm to stand behind me and gently spun me to face Enzo and Mimi.

Enzo stood close to Mimi's right shoulder, his mouth inches away from her ear as he whispered something. Mimi's eyes widened then a bubbling laugh burst from her mouth. She lightly poked Enzo on the shoulder.

Enzo staggered back and raised both hands to where Mimi had poked him. But his eyes sparkled, and his laugh was infectious.

Mimi and Enzo were irrepressible and fed off each other's energy.

"Coffee is served," came a pronouncement from the kitchen. I went back to help Jon deliver individual espressos to Luc, Anya, Samia, and Matias, café Americanos to Enzo and Celia, and cappuccinos for Mimi and me. Jon kept an espresso for himself.

We murmured our thanks to Jon. Samia sighed. "I hate to admit it, Jon, but you make a perfect coffee."

Jon shook his head. "Thank you, Samia, but even my coffee can't compare to the coconut cream pie you made tonight. Brava, Samia." Jon slow-clapped melodramatically in her direction.

My mouth almost fell open. Jon and Samia were conversing like grown adults. Speaking without spitting. Complimenting the other without choking. Maybe there was hope for the world.

We sipped our coffees and made plans for skiing tomorrow. Enzo, Mimi, and Anya would buy gear at a shop in town. Celia assured me she couldn't fit in the suit she had left here, that I had been using. She had borrowed a ski-suit from a friend that forgave her those few baby pounds and brought it just in case. Everybody else was set and we decided to meet at Luc's the next morning and carpool together.

Chapter 34

"I Love to Ski"

The snowfall intensified as we drove up the mountain.

"You get better snow here than we do," Celia said.

Celia and I were on the back bench of Enzo's gigantic 4-wheel drive SUV rental. Luc had found a highly recommended babysitter so Baby Tonio stayed home while his Mama scored a snow day.

"Where do you ski near Boise?" I asked.

"Bogus Basin. It's nice but we don't have the base that Santa Fe has this year. Must be the elevation. Have you skied in powder before?" Celia asked.

"Nothing like this," I said. I gazed out the window at the cantaloupe-sized clumps of snow weighing down the branches of fir trees lining the winding road. The drifts were also getting higher. The snowbank on my side of the road blocked the view of the trees on one curve.

"Powder is fun, but it can be exhausting if you aren't used to it," Celia said. "Remember to round out your turns or you might end up doing a face-plant." Celia had a sparkle in her eye and a smile kept driving up the corners of her mouth. She was itchy to ski these conditions, visible in her constant small movements.

Trepidation seized me at her warning. But her exuberance was contagious.

"Tell me about Bogus. I didn't expect there to be a ski resort so close to Boise."

"I'm not sure you can call Bogus a resort. It's a non-profit ski mountain. The lodge has food and a tiny ski shop with not much in it. It's also pretty weak on signage. But most of the people who ski there are locals. We don't need the signs and the only thing we need a ski shop for is to replace a lost glove."

"I've never heard of a non-profit ski mountain."

"Not surprising. There are only five in the country. It's not fancy but it skis like a big mountain. The lifts are fast and modern, and the ski passes are cheap."

We made it up the mountain and I buckled into my rented boots and carried my skis, following Luc and Celia to a quad lift. Enzo, Anya, Jon, and Mimi were in line ahead of us, Matias and Samia behind. I didn't think it was possible but it was snowing even harder now than on the drive up. We piled on the lift, which zipped us up the mountain. At the top we had accumulated enough snow on the ride up that we needed to shake off a thick layer of powder after we unloaded. The slope was foggy and hazy. I felt clumsy and even more awkward than usual in the deep, and getting deeper, powder. Luc was patient and stopped and waited for me every hundred feet or so. But I didn't catch sight of Celia again until Luc and I made it to the bottom of the run and the lift line that would take us to the top of the mountain. The rest of our group was already on their way up.

"I don't want to slow you guys down," I said after we boarded the lift.

"That's okay; I don't mind waiting for you," said Luc.

"Great, that's so sweet of you. I'll take Luc to a run

that will challenge us," Celia said at the same time.

I laughed as Luc looked back and forth between me and Celia.

"I'm not leaving Cleo alone on these slopes with the snow coming down like this."

"I'll be fine," I said. "In fact, probably safer because I won't be trying to over-terrain myself keeping up with you two." By the time we'd ridden to the top I'd convinced him to go enjoy skiing with his sister and we could meet up in an hour.

Celia and Luc headed in the direction of a black diamond trail while I decided to take the nice and easy green Santa Fe trail. After a couple more runs down easy trails I wound up at the restaurant midway up the slope. I stopped in for a hot drink and waited for the snow to slow down. Powder was nice and soft to land on when I fell, but the heavy snow made the terrain difficult to see. I fell more than usual. Perfect time to recharge and hope the snow slacked off.

I bought a cup of hot cider and a bag of M&Ms and found an open seat near a window where I could watch for Luc or Celia. I enjoyed my runs but the break felt good. The deep powder and baby moguls had jellified my knees. Living in Hawaii for five years had impacted my skiing. I was never great at it. Luc, Celia, and everyone else were head and shoulders better than me on the slopes. My parents had scrounged enough money once every other year to send me on a ski trip with our local church group.

We didn't have the money for lessons, so I learned by watching my friends—bad habits as well as good. I'd developed a love for it. My affection for the sparkly snow and the quiet of the trails between the trees was fueled by the heart-thumping adrenalin of fear when I would almost lose control, not an infrequent occurrence.

Luc and Celia were like sleek angels, floating over the snowy terrain. I felt myself falling for Luc. The way he checked in with me before committing to an action, our talks, our well, I have to admit it the sex was amazing. Would I ever fit into his world? Today I didn't want to hold him back. His boyish joy when his sister suggested a challenging black diamond slope made me giggle. I loved seeing him happy.

But now my cider was finished and an empty candy wrapper sat in front of me.

If Luc and I stayed together would this be my new role? The watcher, the waiter, the cheerleader. Did I want that for myself? Or would his guilt drive him to curtail his exuberant fun? Did I want that for him?

I shook my head to get rid of the questions that floated in my brain. Time to get back on the slope, doing something I loved.

I glided back on to the nearby trail. I couldn't believe it was snowing harder. If I was going to practice in this deep powder, I had better stick to easy green trails until the snow lightened up and my visibility wasn't impacted.

I took a long green trail. It was nice and flattish so I wouldn't lose control. A good thing because several steep black trails crossed it, and the better-than-me skiers came barreling down the mountain. I stopped at the tree line before I crossed the black trails to check for downhill traffic. On the second crossroads, there was a snowboarder stopped halfway up the slope above me. The person was dressed all in black. It was hard to tell if it was a he or she when a person was covered from head to toe with gear, especially in this crazy snowstorm. They seemed to be waiting for someone, so I pushed off to continue on my green trail. I was almost to the next tree line, feeling firmly in control, when—

"Oof." I was clipped from behind.

It felt like someone had carved over the back of my skis and shoved me. My boots came out of the bindings and I stumbled into a tree. I had been skiing slowly and the deep snow softened my fall but when I landed against the tree it took my breath away. I wore goggles and a helmet, so avoided eye gouges or too many face scratches from the branches.

I extricated myself from the tree as quickly as I could to see who had crashed into me, and if they were okay. I expected an apologetic teenager spread-eagled in the snow. Instead, the only person in sight was the back of the black-clad snowboarder, navigating undisturbed through the moguls below. The snowboarder had to have seen me crash. I couldn't believe they would keep going without checking if I was hurt.

I was shaky as I snapped my boots back onto the skis and cautiously continued down the mountain on my green slope. At the bottom I checked the time. Thirty minutes before I was supposed to meet Luc. I took a deep breath. *Is the snow getting lighter? Maybe. Do I want to be cautious or courageous?*

I rolled my shoulders. *I'll make one more run before I meet up with Luc.* I'd thread the needle by coming down the easy slope again.

I skied into the singles line on the left and joined with another couple who were lined up to ride the quad lift. As I twisted around to grab the armrest and sit down, out of the corner of my eye I caught a glimpse of the black-suited snowboarder who had bumped me, waiting in line. At least I thought it was the same snowboarder. With the lift coming in fast I only got a quick glimpse. After we were seated and riding up I tried to turn around and check again. I thought it was the same person, but couldn't be sure. Our chair moved up the cable and the snowboarder was still in line.

The snow grew thicker.

The woman I rode with complimented me on my ski suit. I thanked her but told her it was borrowed.

She laughed. "That person must be a good friend. Those ski suits go for ten thousand dollars."

My stomach flipped. I hoped I hadn't torn anything when I crashed into the tree. I'd hate to damage Celia's suit. Especially now that I knew it would take me years to save up to replace it.

As we off-loaded the lift we wished each other a good run. They glided to more challenging trails, while I stuck to the easier path I'd taken last time. I was having a good run, despite the snowfall becoming fierce again. I learned to navigate the powder but Celia was right— my thighs burned. I came to the place on a green trail where the black trails cross. I stopped at the tree line where the snowboarder had crashed into me. No one upslope, as best as I could tell in the snow. I skied across with no problems. At the next crossing with a black trail, I scrutinized the upslope again. Was that someone at the top of the trail standing near the opposite tree line? I couldn't tell with the low visibility. I waited to be sure.

And I waited. No movement from the shape. And no let-up in the snow. Flakes swirled with a fury in the wind gusts.

I couldn't stay up here forever. I had the heebie-jeebies from my crash on my last run and my mind could be spooked by the threat of another collision. The shape up the hill was probably a tree branch or young sapling.

I skied across, feeling silly about my hesitancy. But halfway across a movement upslope caught my eye. The black-suited snowboarder was flying full-speed directly at me. Again. And closing in fast.

"Hey, watch it!" My yell was muffled by my neck gaiter but I skied as fast as I could, desperate to avoid another smash-up. But I had less momentum on my flatter trail than the snowboarder had on the steeper downhill slope heading straight for me.

Wham.

A hard push from the snowboarder bowled me over again. This time there was no tree to stop my fall. My shoulder screamed as I tumbled and rolled ten feet down the black slope before I could stop myself. My heart pounded and my hands trembled as I dug an edge into the snow to prevent sliding further. I peered at the impossibly steep black slope and struggled to suppress a wave of panic. I took a deep breath and assessed my situation. Magically, my bindings hadn't released. Thank God, or I would have fallen a lot farther. I caught my breath and looked up. Once again, the snowboarder had skied off without offering to help. I shivered uncontrollably, adrenalin spiking. I couldn't believe this crash was unintentional. The visibility was bad, but I saw that person barreling down on me. That idiot must have seen me.

My heart thudded in my ears as I tested my legs and arms. Nothing broken. I took another deep breath to steady myself. I was on a dangerously steep slope. How to get to the bottom without killing myself? I spread my back, arms, and poles flat against the snow to create drag in case I started to slip down the side of the mountain. I tightened my stomach muscles and managed to lift my lower leg with ski attached so it was perpendicular to the slope, next to my upper leg.

Okay. Now if I stood up and lost control, I wouldn't ski downhill at seventy miles an hour and kill myself. I could zig-zag, skiing horizontally, and after a hundred turns, maybe make it down safely.

Once I was sure I had everything in the right place I pushed up. *Okay, I'm standing.*

Uh oh,

I hadn't gotten as perpendicular as I needed and my skis slid faster than I could control. My heart raced as I skied toward the trees that lined the slope. Crashing into them at this speed could be deadly. I was going much too fast and couldn't turn my skis. Terrified, I tipped uphill, in an intentional fall.

Thud.

I hugged the snow.

Lying on the slope, safe. Standing on the slope, scary-out-of-control. But that was only because the skis ran away with me. What if I took my skis off?

I used my poles to push the back lever that would release a ski. It took a couple of tries. My hands wouldn't cooperate in the cold, but I managed it.

As soon as my boot was released I lifted my leg, and the damn ski started running again on its own. Heart racing, I captured it with one desperate grab before it was out of reach. Damn it all to hell. This was not going as planned.

In for a penny, in for a pound, as my mother would say. I maneuvered my free ski uphill so I could lie on it while I worked on releasing the other ski. I grabbed it quickly this time, not giving it a chance to slide away.

I took another deep breath. Okay. If I walked to the trees, they would give me something to hang on to as I fumbled my way down tree by tree to an easier trail. I used one arm to hold my skis and one pole and using the other pole pushed myself up and took my first step.

At least that's what I tried to do. My pole sank deep in the snow, just like my booted leg. This damn powder had been coming down since last night. I sank up to my thigh in the snow. Plan B was not working either. I swallowed a freakout that was building in my throat. An old news report of some movie star who had died skiing into a tree flashed in my head.

No. I am not going to lose it. I couldn't ski. I couldn't walk. But I'd been okay spread-eagled on the slope. Maybe if I could somehow unearth my booted leg out of this drift, I could crawl to the trees.

It took some time, but it worked. Inch by inch splayed on the snow, skis uphill from me under one arm, poles downhill in my other hand. Spread out as much as possible I crawled to the tree line. When I reached the first tree I hugged it. Maybe a tear slipped out before I laughed out loud. *Lucky nobody was around to video that.*

I could figure this out. I wasn't going to let one jerk ruin skiing for me. Hanging onto the tree, I peered through the surrounding pocket of forest. There was another slope heading downhill fifteen trees away, and maybe it was my imagination, but it didn't appear as steep as the one that almost killed me. Skis in one hand, poles in the other I scooted on my butt, lurching from tree to tree to the next slope.

Yes. This one I could manage. After some clumsy maneuvering I clicked my skis back on. A panic grew in my chest, but I swallowed it.

"You love to ski, Cleo," I said aloud. *I love to ski. I love to ski. I love to ski!*

I pushed off onto a blue slope. I was tired, but my body responded and I turned smoothly. A mixture of relief and elation filled me at being in control of my skis and the slope.

"I *do* love to ski," I said, joyful as I swooshed to the rendezvous.

Sometime during my crawl through the trees, the snow had stopped, and as I took my skis off and left them on the rack, the sun broke through the clouds and the freshly fallen powder sparkled. I found Luc, Celia, and the rest of the group gathered around a large outdoor picnic table, close to the slope. Some had food, but all had a drink in hand.

Luc stood up as I approached. Celia, who had been sitting next to her brother, scooted over making room for me. Luc kissed my cheek and one hand on each shoulder inspected me.

"Are you okay? Did you have fun? You're a bit flushed."

"I'm fine. I had fun," I lied. My shoulder was screaming at me. But I'd be damned if I'd show weakness with Enzo and Anya watching me. And as if on cue…

"How was the baby slope?" Anya asked.

Samia rolled her eyes. "That was a blue she just came down, Anya. Not all of us grew up in the mountains."

I smiled at Samia and ignored Anya. I sat in the

space between Luc and Celia.

"I had a yard sale," said Mimi, who sat across from me in her iced-pink ski jacket. "Looks like you did too. There's snow inside your collar."

"What's a yard sale?" I brushed the snow out of the top of my ski suit.

"When you crash so bad your gear gets spread out across the slope like junk at a yard sale." Mimi laughed. "Mine was epic. What about yours?"

I grinned at Mimi's youthful ebullience. "Not particularly epic. Somebody just crashed me into a tree." I tried to laugh. I would tell Luc later, but right now I was exhausted from my ordeal. I didn't have the energy to explain, in front of Anya and Enzo, how I'd crawled off the slope. "I hope I didn't damage your ski suit, Celia." I glanced down, hoping I wouldn't find any rips.

Celia waved me off. "Don't worry, that's part of skiing. There are always idiots on the slope who think they are better than they are. And honestly, I don't know if I'll ever fit back into that thing again." She smiled and nudged her shoulder into mine. "I'm just glad you get out there and ski," she said. "My favorite memories are of our family ski trips. I can't wait until Tonio is old enough to get out on the slopes with us."

"Here, here." Enzo raised his drink in Celia's direction.

Anya followed by raising her drink in my direction. "And if Cleo is still around, she can hang out with him on the bunny slopes…at least for a week or two before he's catching up with Celia on the black slopes."

Protests came from around the table as Anya aimed an unkind smile at me before she brought her glass back to her lips, her eyes never leaving mine.

Chapter 35

Apres-ski

Most of us stopped for an early dinner on the way home from the ski mountain. Mimi and Jon were the exceptions. Jon offered to drop Mimi off, doubtless so he could worm an invitation inside and gloat to Kyle about spending the day skiing. Celia also decided to catch a ride with them. She wanted to go home and get Tonio from the baby-sitter. Mama Bear had been separated from her Baby Bear as long as she could tolerate it. She and Tonio would take an Uber to meet us at Cowgirl, a kid-friendly restaurant with good food.

Celia and Tonio arrived at Cowgirl shortly after the rest of us, and we were seated between two large tables with children. The kids at the neighboring table flocked to Celia and the baby. It was noisy and I let those with louder voices, Enzo, Matias, and Samia do most of the talking as they argued playfully about the last World Cup Final. My mind drifted back to the black-suited snowboarder who seemed to have it in for me on the slope. The more I replayed it, the more convinced I became that it must have been a man. But who could want to hurt me? Almost everyone I knew in Santa Fe was in our group on the mountain, and none of them wore black.

I bit my lip in concentration which caught Luc's

attention. He lifted an eyebrow at me. I smiled and mouthed to him it was nothing. *But was it?* The snowboarder that ran over me was probably just a jerk trying to show off, then was embarrassed when he crashed into me and skedaddled out of there. But twice? Why not twice? Idiots don't learn from their mistakes. But the second time wasn't a mistake. He ran into me intentionally. Maybe he was one of those jerks who liked to frighten women.

The waitress approached with our food. Celia settled Tonio into a highchair, and the smell of chili peppers and melted cheese piqued my appetite. My stomach lurched awake at the scent. I pushed my dark thoughts away and chowed down.

By the time I had eaten so much I thought I might burst out of Celia's ski suit, the large tables next to us had emptied. The baby fussed and yawned. Enzo offered to take him and Celia back to the house. Luc said he would carry Tonio for a tired Celia and Anya said she was going too. That filled up Enzo's car. Samia and Matias offered to drop me off, if I wouldn't mind if they had a coffee first.

"A coffee? I never mind waiting for a coffee. I think I'll get one too."

The restaurant had quieted significantly, and I appreciated the chance to talk with Samia and Matias. I hadn't spent much time with Samia's husband, but with every interaction, I liked him more. We ordered our coffees and Matias asked me about the investigation into Ginger's death. Samia had told him I was helping Jon. Unlike Samia though, Matias didn't appear angered by it.

"I know you and Jon don't get along. Are you upset

that I'm investigating other possible suspects?" I asked.

Matias smiled and put his arm around Samia's shoulders. "I disagree with my lovely wife. I don't think Jon killed Ginger. I'm furious at how he has dragged the Lab through the mud. But no. Jon Suvorov is not a killer." Matias pulled his arm back from around Samia as he saw the waitress approach with our three coffees. "Now torture." Matias barked a laugh. "Jon would excel at torture, even if he could never actually kill a person."

Samia shook her head as the waitress set our coffees down and left. "You always see the best in people, Matias. You are too good. Jon has a dark side you refuse to acknowledge."

Matias sipped his coffee. "Oh, I see his dark side." He glanced in my direction. "Cleo has seen me lose my temper, when I was angry with Jon. We all have a dark side. That doesn't mean we have a black soul. And I don't think Jon's soul is black."

"Then who do you think killed Ginger?" I asked.

Matias glanced at his wife before answering me. "I think it's someone connected to one of the women Ginger and Samia have helped. What were you telling me the other day about Raul's nephew? Didn't you have to call security on him because he made threats to a client, and the Center, the week before Ginger was killed?"

This was news.

"Really, Samia? Why didn't you tell me someone had threatened Ginger? Did you tell the FBI guy?"

Samia wrapped her hands around her cup and stared at it. She didn't respond.

Matias put a hand on his wife's forearm. "Samia feels terrible that Raul's nephew, Manuel might be the killer. She feels responsible because Ginger wanted Raul to take a leave of absence because of the connection between him and Manuel. Ginger said Manuel was a troubled soul. She had known him as a boy, but as a man he had become a stranger. But not to Teresa and Raul. They were still close with him. Ginger was concerned Raul might have a conflict of interest."

"And I talked her out of it." Samia cut in, her eyes full of tears she didn't let fall. "I do not know if Manuel killed her, but he can be cruel and has harmed a woman in the past. A woman Ginger was helping. She was right. I should not have given him a second chance because he was Raul's nephew." Samia looked up at me. "Do you not see, I need it to be Jon. It would solve all our problems. It would relieve my guilt that Manuel might have been the killer, and it would solve Matias' problems at the Lab. I need it to be Jon."

"You know life doesn't work that way. Right? Someone isn't guilty just because we want them to be."

"I know. It just seems like sometimes... sometimes things *should* work out the way I want them to."

Matias patted his wife's hand. His eyes slid from her face to mine. "Samia has had to deal with challenges and make choices no one should have to make. I think she is to be admired because she still has hope that things can work out the way they should."

Samia sighed. "Cleo knows my past. I told her."

His eyes widened. "You did?"

"She came over with Luc, that time when you were on the plane home and I received one of those calls. Remember, I told you I had called Luc so I wouldn't have to be alone?"

"Ah, right."

Samia looked at me. "Did I tell you I got another one this week?"

"Oh no, that's terrible."

Samia shrugged. "Let us discuss happier things than murder or death threats."

"Fair enough, an excellent idea, my love. We should make some plans to go skiing again with Luc and Cleo after his family has gone home."

Samia smiled, "Sure, and Cleo, you have to tell me where you found that ski suit. It is to die for."

Chapter 36

Joe Rivera at Work

Joe Rivera leaned back in his chair, closed his laptop, and stretched his arms out in front of himself. His eyes were blurry from reading files on the screen. The coded files that the psychologist set up protected victim confidentiality and were online. There were original hard copies with handwritten notes, but he had agreed to avoid those unless he, the director of the center, or that psychologist found something suspicious in the coded files first. He suspected they might be able to recognize something dodgy from casual references to people easier than he would.

The only thing I'll find in these files are people with a record, or an obvious motive, or both. Like that fellow the psychologist put me on to, Manuel Martinez.

Rivera's mind drifted back to that psychologist, Cleo Cooper. When she walked in to the station wearing that va-va-va-voom ski outfit, he took her for an airheaded snow bunny. One of those high society types…all show but no substance.

But she surprised me. She thinks for herself and picks up on things most people don't notice. Rivera shook his head. *I've been at this job long enough to know I shouldn't judge a book by its cover.*

Rivera tapped the middle finger of his right hand on

the desk as he stared off into space. *But then again, sometimes the cover describes exactly what is in a book.*

He studied the list of names he had written on the legal pad. Right there at the top was Manuel Martinez. But Rivera knew it was too soon in this case to narrow down to one suspect. He went slowly through his list, noting possible motives, means, and opportunities. When he finished, he went back over his list and drew a line between the fourth and fifth name.

Yes, I'd bet that the murderer is one of these top four. Two men and two women.

That is where he would focus his time. He looked again at five and six and decided to draw a line after six. Those two were also a possibility but his gut was telling him otherwise. He knew it wasn't smart to rely too heavily on instinct, so he would keep his mind open until the case was closed. *But I have to start somewhere, and it makes sense to begin with these four.*

Joe eyed his watch. Those phone records should be here today or tomorrow. They might help confirm his hunches.

Perhaps a coffee was in order. One thing he liked on this assignment was the temporary office they let him use at the center. Full of light with an excellent coffee machine in the break room next door.

As he sipped his drink Joe saw a dark-haired woman walk by the window outside. She wore her long straight black hair tied back in a ponytail, just like his M. E. A smile curled his lips. He had better get back to work. The sooner he solved this case the sooner he could get home and ask her out to dinner.

Chapter 37

A Family Hike

We were hiking the La Tierra trails, a system of hikes, bikes, and bridle paths three miles from town, Luc, Celia, with baby Tonio in a carrier, his back strapped against Celia's chest, so he could watch the trail ahead. Enzo and Anya had joined us. It was a spectacular day, a robin's egg blue sky, golden chamisa still in bloom peeking out between juniper and pinon trees. There had been one other car at the trailhead, but we were unlikely to cross paths with its occupants. With over ten miles of trails, the area felt remote despite its proximity to Santa Fe. The remote feeling matched the cell service.

"*Mannaggia.* I still can't pull up a signal," Enzo said as he clenched his fist around his phone when we stopped for a break.

"What do you need that's so important, Uncle? Why can't you just enjoy nature and your little grand nephew." Celia was next to Enzo and unstrapped the baby and sat him on her lap facing her uncle.

Enzo looked up from his phone and grinned at the cherub. "But it is for you and Tonio, Cara, that I need to check my messages. I have a surprise for you and the *bambino* that I need to pick up before we all leave. I need to check that the arrangements are running smoothly and the package will arrive as scheduled."

Celia's mouth broadened into a large grin before she kissed the top of her baby's head. She waved a hand in Enzo's direction. "A surprise for us? Then by all means, make all the calls you want." She laughed and looked sideways at Luc. "Do you know what it is? I'm sure Anya knows, but she'll never tell."

"Haven't a clue," Luc said.

Anya sighed and gave a one-shouldered shrug of indifference. "It's Enzo's surprise. I won't ruin it for him." Her voice flat, she unscrewed her water bottle to take a drink.

"Of course she won't," Enzo said as he shoved the phone back into his pocket. "No signal at all. Where the hell are we?"

"We're only two or three miles from home, but there are large dead spots in this area. People come here to get away from their phones and enjoy nature. If you need to go back to the house to make your calls, we can," Luc said.

"No, no. The surprise can wait. I'll call when we get back to town or your house. I'm with my family in nature." Enzo spread his arms expansively. "This happens less and less often now that you two are grown. I don't want to shorten our outing by a minute. Are we rested? Shall we hike on?"

Celia strapped baby Tonio into his carrier, and Luc asked, "Celia, you probably need a break. Do you want me to carry Tonio?"

"Oh, let me," I said. "I need to practice being an auntie. One of my best friends in Hawaii is having a baby."

Celia smiled. She handed Tonio and the carrier to me and helped me strap it on. The baby added a level of challenge to the trail as Tonio kicked his legs out from time to time, throwing off my balance as we climbed up and down the hilly path. But not more than I could handle, and being able to kiss the baby's head and smell his sweet baby scent was worth it.

Celia and Anya walked ahead chatting about old friends. Tonio and I were behind them. Luc and Enzo walked side by side behind us. I couldn't see them, with my eyes on the trail, but I clearly heard their voices.

"*Nipote*, I miss having you close. I wasn't worried when you first moved here, but I thought you'd be back in Europe by now. Don't you miss it?" Enzo asked.

"Of course. And I miss you, too. Our camping trips, your dinner parties." I heard the sound of a hand clapping a back. "Some of the greatest memories of my younger years were with you."

"Then come home, my boy." Enzo's voice boomed with enthusiasm. "What is stopping you?"

"My career, for one thing. I'm doing well here. I have backers here who appreciate my research," Luc said.

"*Zut alors*, Luc. I have connections. You know that. You have an institute here. I can help you set up an institute there. You can grow it so there are two locations. I know globalism is not popular with politicians these days, but with academics and people who support them, I think globalism is always valued."

"Thanks, Uncle Enzo. I appreciate the offer. And you might be right, but there are other issues too...." Luc's voice died out and it took every ounce of my willpower to not spin around to see the expression on his face, or ask him what, or who, were the other issues.

Enzo sighed. "I know, I know." I detected sadness

in his voice.

"I will definitely consider it, Uncle. It is generous of you to offer, and a good idea. Maybe… But… I don't know. I'll think about it, and we can talk more after that. Okay?"

"Yes, yes. It's just…*nipote,* there will always be *issues* for you, and your poor old Uncle Enzo won't be around forever. I know you don't want to leave your *issue* here, but I promise there will be beautiful *issues* in Eur—"

"*Basta.* Enough, Enzo." Luc's voice was gentle but firm. "You have made a proposal. I have said I will think about it and then we can talk again. I am an adult now and I will make my own decisions."

For once, Enzo wisely kept his mouth shut.

Chapter 38

A Moment

After our hike we met back at Luc's house. Celia was tired, and when she put Tonio down for his nap, decided she would take one too. Enzo finally connected on his phone call, which he made outside so we couldn't hear. I filled a tray with glasses of water and a bowl of chips and salsa.

Enzo walked back into the room beaming. "*Perfetto*. It was complicated but everything worked out beautifully. I will need to take a quick trip into Albuquerque to pick up the surprise, but I should be back with it before dinner. Come, Anya, I know this is not your cup of tea, but I need you for this errand."

Anya did not appear pleased. She glumly stood up to follow Enzo. She waved goodbye to Luc, ignoring me. They were out the door before taking a single chip or drink of water.

"I don't have a good feeling about this surprise," Luc said.

"Why is that?" I reached for a chip and dipped it into the salsa.

"Enzo loves to make grand surprise gestures. Sometimes they are a hit, and sometimes a miss."

"A miss? Like what?" I popped the loaded chip into my mouth. *Zing.* The salsa was nice and spicy.

Luc reached for a chip. "There was the time he decided his girlfriend was such a good cook, he would buy her a restaurant since she didn't get an accounting job she wanted. The girlfriend took it as a lack of faith in her professional abilities as an accountant, and an effort to put his little woman back into the kitchen. She broke it off and Enzo was stuck with a restaurant he didn't want to run."

"Yikes," I said.

Luc, who had just put a chip in his mouth, nodded as he chewed.

"It appears that he recovered from the financial hit. He seems to live a comfortable lifestyle now," I said.

Luc swallowed. "Yes, Uncle Enzo always lands on his feet. He found a buyer quickly for the restaurant, made a profit on the deal, and the buyer, who was a beautiful woman, became Enzo's new girlfriend."

I raised my eyebrows. "So Enzo had a little woman back in the kitchen, after all."

Luc shrugged. "Let's not discuss Enzo. We have a little time alone…let's add a couple of glasses of wine to this tray and take it upstairs to the terrace off my bedroom. We can talk in private without being interrupted by Celia if she wakes up."

Settled on the terrace, I sipped a glass of chardonnay and sighed at the peace and quiet. I genuinely liked Celia and her baby, and even Enzo was winning me over with his blunt enthusiasm for life. But they were loud, gregarious, and exhausting. I luxuriated in the chance to sit here next to Luc and relax as we soaked up the northern New Mexico mountains.

I felt Luc's gaze and turned my head to smile at him.

His eyes searched my face. "Are you happy here,

Cleo? I mean, do you like it here?"

The question was unexpected, but I was so relaxed and tired from our hike that I didn't expend energy processing where it was coming from.

"What's not to like?" I asked, and with my right hand still holding my wineglass I gestured toward the Jemez mountains. "Thanks again for inviting me here for sabbatical."

Luc gazed at the countryside, forehead scrunched, and slowly bobbed his head. He stopped. "I guess, what I'm wondering...I know your home is Hawaii, a paradise. But...would you ever consider leaving it? To move here? Or Europe?"

I almost dropped my glass of wine.

Luc's gaze shifted from the mountains to me.

I need to say something. But what? He didn't say anything about a relationship. Does that mean this is job related? Is he referring to work? But we're sleeping together. I can't ignore that. But Luc has a reputation as a player. And he's never talked commitment. Okay, Cleo, play it cool. You got this.

"I love Hawaii. It's an amazing place." I put my glass of wine down and hoped Luc didn't see my hands shaking. "But, I also love to travel. And that is really hard to do from the middle of the Pacific Ocean."

Luc observed me closely. I shifted my eyes to a scrub jay that had landed on a branch not far from us.

"I guess I didn't expect to live there forever. I still love it, and I'm not tired of it. I could live there happily for years. But, when adventure calls..." I chuckled awkwardly and took a deep breath. "When adventure calls, I usually come running." The bird flew off as I spoke, and I looked back at Luc.

The furrow was gone from his brow, and he grinned. "That's good to hear," he said. "That's very good to hear." He picked up my hand and brought it to his lips, leaving a fiery kiss that sent shivers up my arm.

A half a second later, a baby shrieked, and Celia's voice came up the stairs. "Luc? Luc? I need some extra towels, Tonio has made a mess."

Luc gave me an apologetic glance. "On my way, Celia."

Before letting go of my hand he turned it over and kissed the inside of my wrist. My insides tightened. In a good way. Luc gave me a reluctant smile and went to help his sister clean up a messy baby.

I probably should have followed to help, but I needed a moment to think.

Things with Luc were good, better than good. Fabulous. But we hadn't been together long. In my experience, relationships started with a honeymoon period before reality set in. All the idiosyncrasies that I found endearing in the beginning became annoying after the initial glow wore off. Were Luc and I still glowing? I thought of that kiss on the inside of my wrist. Yes, my cheeks were probably glowing. But, I *really* liked Luc. It wasn't only the sexual attraction. We had a lot of interests in common, and we talked things through. That's what Momma always told me. I should find someone I could talk over my problems with...not just the problems of the world, but the problems we had with each other. Ben and I never had that. We could discuss the world, but not what was happening between us. I tried, but he wasn't open to it. He shut it down.

Luc and I have great discussions and debates. But, wow. I realized that I'd never even tried to talk about our relationship with Luc. He'd brought it up. Initially he asked where I stood with Ben when I first arrived, then mentioned that he didn't want kids. And now, asking if I could be happy leaving Hawaii. I was the one who either let the subject drop or gave vague answers. I sat up straight in my chair. This time *I'm* the closed-off person of the relationship.

Huh. Didn't see that one coming.

I needed to reflect on what I should have said to Luc. I guess I wanted to give it a try with him. But for all my love of adventure...I needed to be able to pay my own way. I didn't want to be financially dependent on any man. It would be impossible to make the jump here without a job. Luc had mentioned that if one of the grants we are writing hits, I'd have a job if I wanted it. That was by no means a sure thing.

From my perch on the upstairs patio, another Tonio shriek roused me from my deep thoughts. I loaded our glasses back on the tray and carried it downstairs to join the chaos that was Luc's family.

Chapter 39

Enzo's Surprise

After pushing baby Tonio in his stroller up and down Luc's dead end dirt road, Celia managed to get the baby back to sleep. We sat on the western patio bundled up. The air was cold but it felt good in the warm, just-getting-ready-to-go-down sun. We each had a glass of wine and talked quietly of projects, plans, and the purpose of one's life.

"I always thought I'd take three to six months off with the baby, then go back to work full time, but now he's eight months, and I'm still home. I love my job. That's the only reason I was ready for a baby now, because I have the freedom to take off and then go back. But now that Tonio is here…I'm wondering if I would be a terrible mother going back to work."

"I don't think it makes you a terrible mother if you want to go back to work," I said. 'Is there any chance it doesn't have to be an either or situation? Could you go back part time?"

"Part-time would be hard for me. I'm an all-in kind of person," Celia said.

I could believe that of Celia. Her effervescent joy of life would require a lot of energy.

A spotted towhee landed on a forsythia bush three feet from Celia's chair. He observed us until Luc spoke, and the bird flew off.

"Don't reject the idea so fast, Celia. I think Cleo's idea is a good option. You don't have to think about the job in its totality. Pick a smaller part of the job that wouldn't take forty hours of your week, but maybe ten or twenty. You could do that to the best of your abilities and be all in, but not be away from home or the baby full time. It's your life, but there are a lot of possibilities."

The sound of tires crunching came from the direction of the front of the house. The courtyard wall blocked our view, but it had to be Enzo and Anya, back from picking up the surprise.

"We're back here, Enzo," Luc called in a loud voice.

"Is Celia with you?" Enzo asked over the courtyard wall.

"Here, you take it. It's your surprise." Anya's voice was urgent. We still couldn't see them.

"I would be most happy to." Enzo's voice boomed. "Celia, close your eyes."

Celia laughed and closed her eyes. "Uncle Enzo, what are you up to?"

The courtyard gate opened and a ball of black and white fur bounced through it with a leash trailing behind.

She, or he, was the cutest thing I'd ever seen. It took every ounce of my self-restraint to resist cuddling the adorable creature. But this was Celia's surprise, so I pressed my palms together to resist enticing the puppy to me. The youngster gamboled up to each of us, sniffed, licked, twisted in a circle, and moved on to the next person, making the circuit several times.

Celia petted the fluffball with a frown on her face. How was that possible? The cutest puppy in the world wiggled at her feet. The pup moved on to Luc, who grinned and scooped it up in his arms to let the puppy lick his face.

"Enzo? Why did you bring a puppy to Luc's house?" Celia, straight-faced with a tight mouth, spoke in a calm, firm voice.

"Why, Celia, this is your surprise. An Old English Sheepdog puppy, the perfect companion for your boy as he grows." Enzo's eyes shone as his smile grew.

Celia sighed. Her brow furrowed but her mouth softened. "Uncle Enzo, you don't surprise someone with a puppy. Especially when that someone already has an eight-month-old baby that depends on that someone for his every need. I don't have time to care for a puppy right now. In a couple years maybe, but not now while Tonio is a baby."

Enzo's face fell. "But he is a baby boy. And all boys need a dog." He appeared genuinely confused. Enzo extended an open palm in Celia's general direction. "You know the Robert Benchley quote, 'Every boy should have two things,' " Enzo clenched that palm into a loose fist before he extended his thumb from the closed fist. " 'A dog.' " Enzo unrolled his index finger. " 'And a mother who lets him have one.' " He extended his fingers in Celia's direction.

Anya had followed behind the puppy and Enzo. Her hair and clothes disheveled, she positioned herself so that Enzo stood between her and the puppy. That must have been an interesting ride in the car from Albuquerque if Anya had puppy duty while Enzo drove.

"I warned you, Enzo. Not everyone is a dog person. I warned you not to ship the puppy over here without talking to Celia first," Anya said.

"It is too late now. We are not flying her back," Enzo

said

"Where did she come from?" I asked.

Enzo's eyes never left the puppy as it romped back and forth between each of us, a quizzical expression on his face. "From my breeder. She had a litter from my dog's sister that she said was especially good. And was the perfect age to fly when I was coming over. I had planned to deliver it to you in Boise. I was going to surprise you there, Celia. But when you wanted to come here, I had to work fast to change the puppy's travel arrangements."

Enzo observed Celia, his face somber. "It never occurred to me that you would not want her. You have always loved my dogs."

Luc stood up from his chair and offered it to Enzo or Anya. He crouched down next to me and extended his hand, with wiggling fingers toward the puppy. "Uncle Enzo has had at least one Old English Sheepdog as long as I can remember. They are great dogs," he said to me and picked up the puppy.

She squirmed in delight, licking the underside of Luc's chin.

Celia sighed heavily. "Of course I loved your dogs, and one day I would love for you to bring Tonio and me a puppy. But the timing, Uncle Enzo." She shook her head sadly. "I have my hands full with Tonio, and I was hoping to go back to work soon." She glanced at me quickly. "At least part-time. How can I swing that with a puppy that will need loads of attention?"

Anya smirked. "Why doesn't Luc take the puppy? He seems to enjoy that fidgeting mess." She raised a delicate eyebrow as the puppy's licking became more emphatic when Luc rubbed her belly.

"Whoa." Luc expressed an alarm I didn't quite believe. "Leave me out of this." Then he found a new area to scratch that sent the puppy into a state of ecstatic wiggling. "This is between Uncle Enzo and Celia. We're just innocent bystanders over here, aren't we? Aren't we? Yes we are." He sat cross-legged on the ground and spoke the words to the puppy, who appeared to have fallen head over heels in love with Luc.

Chapter 40

The Files

"I'll take this pile," Mimi said. During the ski trip she had offered to help Samia and me go through the coded files of reported rape and abuse cases that Ginger had been handling. I had worked with Samia to disguise the identity of the victims with numbers to keep the records confidential. The files were prepped, and with Luc's family on their way home, we were ready to dive into the files. Samia, Mimi, and I had taken over the conference room of the Hanlon Foundation office, spread around a large table.

"I'll take the one on the top." Samia snatched the top file, glancing at me out of the corner of her eye.

Mimi handed the second folder in the pile to me, then pulled the next folder toward herself. "Remind me what we're looking for?"

"We're searching for a perpetrator who might have a means, motive, or both, to kill Ginger. Maybe an incident that's old and the guy thought he had gotten away with it, but Ginger convinced the victim to report it in the last weeks before her death. Or a rapist whose case was getting ready to go to court and has threatened the victim or Ginger. Or someone who thought Ginger's death would scare the victim into dropping charges. Basically, anybody who benefits from Ginger's death.

All of these cases—" I waved my hand in the direction of the table full of folders in front of us. "—involve a man who has been accused of a violent act toward a woman. We have to find which ones, if any, gain something by Ginger's death."

"Okay," Mimi said, as she leafed quickly through her folder.

How could she read that fast? I hoped she realized this was important.

I focused on the folder I had in front of me. My heart ached for the woman in this case. A tear leaked down my cheek and I wiped it away surreptitiously. I glanced up to see if anyone noticed. Samia was engrossed in her file, Mimi texting, her folder already closed. Samia or I should go back over the folders Mimi examined. Her offer to help was nice, but I didn't think she gave it the attention needed.

An hour later Samia's phone rang. As she reached for her phone, I closed the folder I had finished and stretched my neck. Comparing our stacks, Samia and I had worked our way through a dozen cases each. Mimi had left to go to the break room. She'd done that frequently, messing with her phone. She had only completed four folders. I reminded myself to slip them into my to-do pile when she left. I peeked at Samia, to see why I hadn't heard a word out of her since she answered the call.

Samia's face was pale and her hands trembled. Silent tears rolled down her cheeks as she stared into the middle distance.

Oh, no, another threatening call? Or has something terrible happened to Matias? A car accident? Whatever it was she needed help.

"Samia, what is it?"

She jerked her head up wide-eyed, blinked, and dropped her phone on the table. She pushed her chair back as if the phone was a snake coiling to strike.

I grabbed Samia's phone. "Hello, who is this?"

Click. The caller disconnected.

Samia lifted a shaking hand to rub her temple, then curled forward hugging herself. To see this strong, confident woman so shattered, hurt my heart. I laid her phone on the worktable and kneeled next to her chair. Samia turned her huge liquid eyes to me.

"Who was that? What did they say?"

"He, I don't know who it was, but he said they were tired of waiting for me to come to my senses and return to Saudi. They said they were coming after me, and they would kill Matias first, and I would have to watch them do it."

I took Samia's hand. "We have to call the police. This is a clear threat. From what you've told me and what I've read in the news, if the Saudi government is involved, they follow through on their threats."

Samia sat back and intertwined her fingers. She blinked away tears and tilted her head with a furrowed brow.

"Except, something was wrong," Samia said.

"Everything about that call was wrong. They have no right to threaten you, or Matias. This is outrageous."

Samia shook her head a fraction of a centimeter, "No, I mean, as I think about it, I do not think it was the Saudis. It did not sound like any of the other threats I have received over the years."

"How so?"

"For one thing, the person used a voice changer to

disguise his voice. The Saudis usually have a friend or family member call me. Or someone who says they are a friend of a friend. This person claimed to be working directly for the Crown Prince, MBS." Samia shook her head again, with more force. "The Crown Prince would never allow a threat to be traced back directly to himself. For all he knew, I could have recorded that message. But that is not all…" Samia straightened in her chair and unlaced her hands. "The threat itself was…blunt. So unequivocal."

Samia tapped the tabletop three times as she spoke. "That is not their style. MBS received such bad press after Kashioggi was murdered, he does not want to be viewed internationally as a thug. MBS would not want more bad publicity over crimes like these. He prefers trickery and heavy-handed persuasion. This caller did not give me an out this time. There was no come home on your own, or come for a visit to your parents, or to the Saudi embassy to discuss the situation. No, this person said it was decided and there was nothing I could do to stop it. That is not how the Crown Prince or his government would issue a threat unless they already had me in custody. Matias has connections with the Department of Defense. They have to know that. They have to know he and I will get protection now."

"What's up, chicas?" Mimi asked as she walked back into the conference room. Samia and I looked at each other.

"Nothing." Samia straightened her files. "Cleo and I were thinking we should take a break. Are you up for a walk around downtown, Mimi?"

I followed Samia's lead and stacked my files. "The office is within walking distance of a lot of shops and restaurants. You should come. It will be a nice break," I said.

Mimi glanced at her phone. "Okay, yeah. I might not come back afterwards, though, if that's okay. I've got some work of my own to do."

"Of course," Samia said.

Mimi grabbed her backpack as we were collecting our bags. "There's a shop I've been trying to find. The art director at one of my last gigs told me about it. Maybe you guys can help me find it?"

"Of course. What is it called?" Samia asked.

Mimi showed us the text from the art director.

Samia and I burst out laughing. Mimi looked confused before Samia explained. "This is one of the most famous shops in town. Totally unique; you can walk into most of the great houses here in town and find pieces from there."

"What does it have?" Mimi asked.

The three of us walked out the door.

Once Mimi was in the hall, I said, "I forgot something. You two go on. I'll meet you there. It's only a couple blocks away."

Samia tossed me her key to the conference room. "Do not forget to lock up. Even coded, those files are confidential. You can return my key when you catch up."

I agreed, and we waved goodbye as Samia explained the treasures of the very special shop to Mimi while they walked down the hall and out the door.

I unlocked the conference room and moved to Mimi's folders. I didn't want to be hyper-critical, but my research projects with students had taught me that non-academics often didn't screen data as closely as someone with years of experience. Mimi had flipped through those files quickly. She could easily have missed a threat or a compromising situation. I had seen Samia's laser-focus on the files before her phone call, but I wanted to take a second run at Mimi's to double-check she hadn't missed something important. I had a hunch that if Jon wasn't the murderer, then the answer of who had killed Ginger would be found in one of these folders.

I had a plan to avoid hurting Mimi's feelings, or give her the impression I doubted her competency. Even though I did on this issue. I pulled four folders from my finished stack that I had dismissed as no motive or opportunity, I traded them out with Mimi's four finished folders.

But, as I picked up Mimi's finished folders, there were only three. Hmm, I must have miscounted. Possibly caused by my guilty conscience about second-guessing a person's competency. My plan had gone smoothly though. Mimi appeared so bored, I doubted she would volunteer again. But Samia and I could knock the rest out after lunch. If Samia was up for it after that phone call.

I locked the door behind me and texted Samia that I was on the way. She texted back that they were wandering through the courtyards, and I could find them there.

A couple minutes later, I arrived. I loved this place. The owner had deep roots in Central Asia and the Middle East and had been salvaging artifacts from old buildings that were destined for destruction. Articles were rescued from temples and old compounds that were being destroyed to make room for new modern structures that had indoor plumbing and air conditioning. Inside the store were rugs, pottery, and newer pieces from artists. But their courtyard area captivated me.

A fifteen-foot-tall elephant statue greeted me at the entrance. The store took up an entire block with generous outdoor grounds with rows and stacks of doors, pillars, and statues from Kashmir, Pakistan, and India. I considered texting Samia to find her and Mimi, but instead indulged myself in a few minutes of wandering through the tiny passageways. Surrounded by exotic antiquities, I studied artifacts piled and stacked that towered above me, like books in an overflowing used bookstore.

I admired a set of pillars with animals carved into the design. Panthers and snakes stalked birds and rabbits who played hide and seek around the curve of the twenty-foot-tall pillar. A few steps farther and I found a section of heavy teak doors carved with human figures. I examined them more closely and laughed when I realized the scenes were people performing acts from the Kama Sutra.

Who would install that in their home? I guess maybe a bedroom, in a house with no kids? I chuckled. To each his own.

Was that a noise?

I glanced around. No one. Maybe a bird? Or a rat?

Ugh.

This narrow path was a problem. If I confronted a rat I would need to maneuver.

But when I found a cross path I was faced with dead ends to the left and straight ahead.

I turned right.

That path also quickly narrowed. I hesitated, but images of a lurking rat kept me moving.

The thick, teak doors on either side were tall and stacked haphazardly. Leaves cluttered the ground.

Probably few customers ventured this far back. I sucked up my courage to go back the same way I'd come, when I heard the shuffling sound again. It came from about five feet away on the other side of the stacked doors. It sounded heavier than a rat.

"Samia? Mimi?"

Grunting and creaking answered me.

The lament of tons of wooden slabs sliding and resisting displacement crescendoed. The sound assaulted my ears.

A door in front of me repositioned from leaning away to standing erect. Its thickness would crush me if it tipped over. If this avalanche of heavy shifting wooden caught me, I'd be dead.

Stepping back, my foot caught on an errant two by four that had shifted with the doors.

I twisted and landed on my butt, thrusting my arms overhead to deflect the doors that continued falling toward me.

I tasted dust and squeezed my eyes shut to block particulates.

Holding my breath, I was deafened by the press of thousands of pounds of ancient wood moaning and groaning.

The cacophony stopped after hours, but was likely only seconds. I opened my eyes.

The doors had shifted dramatically, but because the path was narrow, and I'd fallen to the ground, I had survived in a tunnel of leaning doors. The displaced doors tipped onto the doors on the other side of the path. When I fell, it saved me from being crushed.

Wood creaked around me. The doors could shift again.

The danger was not past. If I dislodged the wrong door I could yet be crushed.

I crawled, so as not to disturb any door that was holding the others back. Especially the Kama Sutra doors. I wouldn't want to be found buried under those.

My pants collected dirt and spiderwebs as I crawled ten feet before I reached the cross path I'd used on my way in. The doors and pillars along here were not disturbed. I stood up and walked warily searching for the path out of the maze of artifacts. I made it to the large entryway patio on the side of the main building as Samia and Mimi exited it.

"There she is," Mimi called out, waving at me.

"What was that noise?" Samia asked. "We came out to see what happened. It sounded like a car had crashed into the wooden structures out here."

Two men rushed past Samia and Mimi toward the maze of doors and pillars. One of them stopped in front of me.

"Are you okay?" he asked.

The dust, dirt, and splinters in my hair must have clued him in that I'd been caught in the collapse.

"Yeah." I was a bit shaky but he looked so concerned I didn't want to worry him.

"It sounds like a stack of doors collapsed. That has never happened before. I can't believe it. I'll find out who stacked them and see what caused it. We check this area regularly to be sure a client never gets hurt." He examined my face closely. 'You are sure you're okay?"

"Yes, I'm fine. It startled me, but I'm fine."

"I found it. Back here," a voice called from the depths of the maze.

"Go," I said. "And be careful; the collapsed path

looked precarious."

The frown deepened on the man's face. "If you are sure you are okay…"

"I'm fine," I said.

"I'm coming; don't move. Wait until I reach you," he yelled to his co-worker before he entered the maze himself.

Mimi approached with a rueful expression on her face. "What did you *do*? I mean, I'm a klutz, but I didn't think anyone could cause a crash that loud."

Samia frowned at Mimi, who laughed and held up her hands in surrender. "Just kidding. Seriously, I was just kidding."

Samia gave a quick head shake. "What do you say we go grab some lunch? Unless you want to shop more, Mimi?"

"No, I'm ready to go, but I need to run an errand, so I can't do lunch. And I can't go back to the Foundation this afternoon. Do you mind if I bail?"

"No problem."

Mimi hitched her backpack over her shoulder again and waved as she headed to the Foundation to pick up her car.

"How about you, Samia?"

"I think we could both use a little food after the last couple of hours, and may I be so bold as to suggest a glass of wine with our lunch. We have both received a fright."

Damn, I trembled from the shock of almost getting crushed by doors carved with people having sex in a hundred different positions. Perhaps a little alcohol was in order.

We walked toward Terracotta Wine Bistro, but less

than a block away ran into Kyle, Luc, and Jon talking on a corner.

Luc and Kyle had a meeting earlier to discuss the website for Luc's Institute, but I didn't know Jon would be there. Luc kissed me on the cheek and pulled a dried leaf out of my hair. He smiled. "Are you okay? You look like you fell into a ditch or something?"

I brushed off what dust I could from my pants and sleeves. "Close, but not exactly. I'll tell you about it tonight."

"Do you want to join us?" Samia asked.

Kyle declined, saying he needed to get back to work.

"I'd love to take you up on that offer," Luc said. "What do you think, Jon?"

"You people may have time to waste, but I don't. Luc, you agreed to meet with me so we could plan…" he glanced at Samia first, then me. "To plan. But, first you are late and leave me waiting, then we run into Kyle, and that is fifteen minutes of my life I'll never get back. And now you want me to go watch you make goo-goo eyes at Cleo. No thanks. I need your help on this, and you promised."

I blushed at the "goo-goo" eyes bit. Samia appeared amused.

Luc sighed in resignation, "Raincheck? I did promise Jon to help him with something. I realized when I got to Jon's office I'd left my phone at Kyle's place. He agreed to meet me here so I wouldn't have to walk all the way back. Jon got impatient waiting in his office and came to find me. So he's right; we are behind schedule."

"No problem. Have a good meeting."

Jon and Luc walked toward the Plaza and Samia and I walked the few blocks to the Bistro. We managed to get a table and ordered. While we waited for the food, Samia told me some of the history of the shop we had visited.

When the wine arrived, Samia lifted hers in my direction and we clinked glasses. "To us, two strong women surviving death threats," she said and took a drink.

"Wait, what? I know *you* got a death threat. But I didn't." I took a late drink of my wine. I've been told it's bad luck to not drink after you clink to a toast.

Samia looked at me like a mother looks at a teenager who still believes in the tooth fairy.

"Cleo, dear. Mine was an overt threat, and not from the Saudis, I tell you. But you almost getting crushed was a veiled threat. Someone wanted to tell you that you are not safe anywhere. Believe me, I have received those too." Samia took another, deeper, drink of her wine.

"Samia. I'm sorry that you received that awful phone call this morning and that you've received all those threats in the past. Truly, you don't deserve it, and I wish I could make them stop. But..." I hesitated. I didn't want to offend Samia. "I think what happened to me in that courtyard was an accident. The wind, or an animal, or sloppy placement. That maze is like a house of cards."

Samia shook her head vigorously. "No. You do not know that store like I do. Matias and I have been clients for years. They know what they are doing. They are professionals and would never put their clients in danger. They have ninety-year-olds who totter through those doors and pillars. That would be a lawsuit waiting to happen. They are too smart for that. I tell you, that was no accident. Somebody is out to get you, Cleo. But why?"

"I really don't think..." An image of a black-suited, black-helmeted snowboarder flashed in my mind. Could Samia be right?

"What?" Samia asked. "You have remembered something. I can see it on your face. Tell me."

I didn't like her demanding tone, but I believed she wanted to help.

Our food arrived, and as we ate, I told Samia of the two events where the same snowboarder had pushed or knocked me onto steep trails way above my level of expertise. To her credit, Samia listened quietly and intently without comment.

I finished my story, and we ate in silence for a few minutes before she gently spoke.

"I think someone is trying to scare you off." Samia broke off a piece of bread and chewed it slowly. I ate the last bite of my grilled peach-parmesan-pecan salad.

I kept my voice low and calm. "Samia, I don't see how I've been in Santa Fe long enough to make any enemies. Except maybe Luc's uncle and Anya, but they have already left the country."

Samia swallowed her bread and gave a tentative smile. "I would also suggest that someone, not the Saudis, are trying to throw me off my game. If you remember the first time you and Luc came over, I told you that wasn't their normal format. And then today..."

Aah. "You think it's Jon."

"Well, if the shoe fits. Both of these incidents happened after he was accused of killing Ginger. You have been digging into the facts, and I have been loudly accusing him. He just told us he was alone this morning waiting for Luc when I received my threatening call, and you were almost crushed." Samia shrugged with, in my opinion, overconfidence.

"Okay, Samia, he was alone when you got your call, but I don't think it is clear that he wasn't with Luc when the doors fell on me. Let's say these threats…" I used two fingers of both hands to make air quotes when I said the word threats. I wasn't completely convinced my threats weren't accidents. "… all occurred after Ginger's death."

"Okay, let us say that."

"Even your own husband doesn't think it's Jon. There are other possible suspects."

Samia frowned, "Who?"

I held up a thumb. "First, Raul's nephew, Manuel. They were at your offices the morning I picked up the crib. Maybe Raul saw us there today and guessed what we were doing. Or Teresa. Did you hear that the FBI wanted to talk to her? She can't have been happy that Ginger was investigating her son. Raul could have made the call to you, or called his nephew to have him call you."

Samia's mouth pursed. "By the way, I grabbed Manuel's folder off the top so Mimi wouldn't see it. I do not want her to fire Teresa before we even find out if her son did anything wrong." She took a sip of her wine and continued. "I don't think Raul has a voice synthesizer, but Jon could get one easily."

"Anyone can buy one online or get an app for their phone. But there is also Kyle. He would know how to change his voice, and we'll have to check with Luc on timing, but he may have been alone for both your phone call and the incident with the crashing doors."

"But what is his motive?" Samia asked.

"Well, the police always look at the husband or

boyfriend first when a woman is murdered."

"But he lost the most of anyone by her death. He was living the high life with Ginger while she footed all his bills." Samia leaned forward and glanced around before lowering the volume of her voice. "And despite Ginger's support of his art, Kyle is a terrible artist. He has neither skill nor creativity. Although I would never admit it to Jon, that is one opinion I share with him. Kyle does not have the talent to make it as an artist." She leaned back in her chair. "And on the ski mountain when you were harassed, Kyle was not even there. Jon was."

"Yeah, but Jon wasn't dressed all in black. Unless you think he had time to change in between his runs with you guys and when I was pushed down the slopes. And isn't it possible Kyle was on the mountain and just didn't tell any of us?" I asked.

"Who else?"

I thought for a minute. "Okay, if you want motives, how about Mimi? She has become a very rich woman since Ginger died."

"But she was not even in the state when Ginger was killed," Samia said. "And she was with us going through the files when I received the call."

"But she wasn't in the room with us when the call came," I said.

"The voice was disguised, but it definitely sounded like a man. Could an app change the sex of a voice?"

"I think so," I said. "But the snowboarder who pushed me was a man, and wasn't Mimi with you when the doors crashed on me?"

Samia frowned. "She left to make a phone call. We ran into each other in the doorway, both of us coming out to see what caused the noise. She came from inside the building though." Samia shook her head. "But, if you are sure it was a man who pushed you on the ski slope…"

"I'm not as sure as you that the snowboarder was tied up in this," I said. "For me the fact that Mimi was out of the state when it happened and she didn't know Ginger's plans to go into the desert are what disqualify her."

A thought came to me as Samia took her last drink of wine and seemed lost in concentration. Samia gained complete control over the Center and the well-endowed Hanlon Foundation as a result of Ginger's death. And there had been a difference of opinion on which direction to take the charity. I had witnessed Samia's strong feelings on that. She also fiercely pushed the idea of Jon being the killer. That narrative cleared her if she was the killer as well as removing a major annoyance for her husband.

Samia caught me staring at her. She raised an eyebrow in question.

"Uh, did you want another glass of wine?" It was the only thing I could think of to say.

"No, we should get back to work. If you're ready, I'll get the check."

I watched Samia lift her hand with grace and purpose. I wanted to think of Samia as a friend. But an uneasy question settled into my brain. How well did I really know her?

Chapter 41

More News from Hawaii

I looked up from my laptop and rubbed my eyes. Miraculously, the puppy continued sleeping at my feet. Luc and I had agreed to keep the puppy until it could be resolved where she would live permanently. I decided that waking her up and taking her for a pee walk in the yard might be a good idea for both of us. I bundled the little black and white fluff ball in my arms so we wouldn't have any accidents before we made it out the door. It was a good thing I did because after setting her down, she didn't walk five steps before she stopped to relieve herself. I told her what a good girl she was and continued our stroll around Luc's gravel driveway. It was an elongated figure eight that stretched three sides of his house. Perfect length for a puppy walk. My phone rang and I smiled when the caller's name popped up.

"Hey, Rikki. What's up, girl?"

"It's rough here. The vog is terrible. It's like pea soup. You picked a good time to go on sabbatical."

A pang of guilt speared my chest. In all the hustle and bustle of entertaining Luc's family, my friends in Hawaii suffered.

"The vog hasn't let up yet?"

"No sign of it. And more vents have opened up. Everybody that can get out of Puna, is getting out. Which reminds me..." Rikki's voice dropped. "You are planning on coming back, aren't you, Cleo?"

I thought of my recent conversation with Luc. I might not stay in Hawaii forever, especially if a grant hit, but I was required by contract to go back for a semester.

"Yes, but why are you asking?"

"Apparently, Ben and his new woman are getting serious. They were seen at Cronie's, behaving...well...affectionate."

Ben? *Affectionate in public?* I struggled to keep my voice normal. "Ben's a good guy. I'm not surprised he found a new girlfriend." But that he'd display his affection in public...that was a surprise.

Out of the corner of my eye, I noticed the puppy wandering onto the neighbor's property. "Hey, Odette, come back, come on, come here." A sing-song timber crept into my voice automatically when I talked to dogs or babies, and was especially prevalent with a baby-dog.

"Who are you talking to?" Rikki asked.

"We're taking care of a puppy, Odette, and she wandered—"

Rikki cut me off. "A puppy. You and Luc are serious, then. Moving in is the first step and puppies are the second. Why didn't you tell me?"

"She isn't ours. We're just puppy-sitting for a while. Luc's uncle brought her for Luc's sister. But Celia has a new baby and doesn't think she has time for a puppy, too. Luc offered to raise the puppy until Celia is ready, or at least until we get the puppy over the house-training, chewing, destructive age."

"Uh-huh, like you're going to be able to give a puppy back after that. Right. I know you, Cleo Cooper."

"I will. I'll have to go back to Hawaii and leave her

here with Luc in a couple of months anyway. You know how hard it is to bring a puppy into the state. I couldn't bring her with me."

"And it might be even more complicated now, with Ben and his new woman."

"What do you mean?" I asked. I braced myself. Of course, Ben was building a new life without me.

"They've been looking for a place together. But there's nothing available. One of the most heavily populated sections of the island has been covered with lava and all those people need at least temporary housing until Pele goes back to sleep. Everybody has somebody sleeping in any extra room, basement, or couch they have. It's going to be a tight fit if they can't find another place."

I hadn't thought of that. What if Ben couldn't find a new place to move into when I needed to go back at the end of my sabbatical? There was a chance Ben and I would have to share the house temporarily. But while he was living with a new girlfriend? *Ugh*.

My phone vibrated. Jon was calling. "Rikki, another call is coming in. Let me tell him I'll call him back, hang on."

"No, I have to head to work; I just wanted to update you on the Ben situation. Better to hear it from a friend. Go answer your call. We'll talk again soon."

Rikki hung up and I answered Jon.

"Took you long enough to answer." Jon sounded irritated.

"I was on another call. What do you want, Jon?" The baby sheepdog wandered off again. She meandered slowly so I let her go and followed behind. I'd probably lose my cell phone connection if we roamed too far from the house, but it was only Jon. I wasn't in the mood for his attitude.

"Mimi called me. Rivera, that FBI guy came by to talk with Teresa. Alone. He didn't want Mimi in the room."

"So why did Mimi call you?" I asked.

"She and I have become friends," Jon said.

Hmm, that was interesting. I needed to explore possible implications of that friendship later. "Did Mimi want you to call a lawyer for Teresa?"

"No, she called to say I may be off the hook. Teresa or someone in her family may be the main suspect now."

That made sense. When I found out Raul was Teresa's brother, and Manuel was her son, that moved all three up on my personal suspect list.

"Well, it is good news for you if the FBI is looking at other suspects. I agree with her on that," I said. Though I wasn't sure Jon was exonerated yet. Rivera could be confirming details related to Jon's relationship with Ginger, for all we knew. But it didn't do anybody any good to get Jon riled up.

"That's why I'm calling you. Since you have been willing to help my case, I wanted to update you. But don't give up yet. I may still need you. Teresa would never kill Ginger. She was devoted to her boss; so was Raul, for that matter."

We said our goodbyes and I reflected on Jon's words. Teresa was devoted to her boss. But would her devotion withstand Ginger working against Teresa's son? Something else to ponder. But I needed to round up Odette and get back to work. My data wasn't going to analyze itself.

Chapter 42

Little Sisters

Gina and I were saying goodbye when Luc walked into the room. I ended the call, but my thoughts were on my friend in Hawaii. Gina enjoyed her pregnancy, but worried about her baby. The vog was thick on the Big Island and one of her cousins had lost his house to the lava so he and his wife and baby had moved into Gina's basement. Her mother had already moved into Gina's guestroom. She had lived a half mile away in one of the first neighborhoods overtaken by lava.

I realized Luc had spoken. "Sorry, what did you say?"

Luc smiled. "You were a thousand miles away. What's on your mind?"

"Gina gave me an update on the lava. Another fissure opened up. That makes twenty fissures. Almost two thousand acres have been covered in lava. And it's still flowing. If more fissures open, more homes could be destroyed."

Luc enveloped me with his arms. "These are dark times, between lava flows on the Big Island, Ginger's murder, Samia's threatening calls, and Jon under suspicion." Luc kissed the top of my head. "I'm glad you are here. I'm selfish, I know, but at least I don't have to worry about whether the lava is heading toward you.

I immersed myself in the sensation of Luc's arms.

"It's also lucky for me that you're here to help me figure out how to get Jon off the police suspect list."

I gently pushed away from his chest and looked in his eyes. I wanted him to know I meant this kindly.

"I know Jon is your friend and you're sure he is innocent, but don't you have even a shadow of a doubt that he could've killed Ginger? Isn't the most important thing that we get to the truth?" I asked.

Luc stepped back and took my hand to lead me to his long, low, leather couch. We sat next to each other. "Isn't someone innocent until proven guilty? What makes you think Jon is the killer?" He spoke without anger or condescension.

"For one, the email sending her to the wrong place was sent from his email address."

"But anyone with moderate computer skills can hack an email address or fake a user address. That's how scammers make so much money," Luc said. "What's his motive?"

"There's the money he inherited." I shrugged. "But I know he didn't need her money and several other people received as large, or larger bequests." I laid a finger on Luc's knee, nestled next to mine. "Including you. I know this. But I don't think money is the motivator here. Samia and I are going through the files at the charity. Past violence is related to future violence and aggression. I think we are going to find that Ginger encouraged one of her clients to press charges of assault or rape on her perpetrator. If so, that violent perpetrator may have feared that all the financial backing of the Hanlon Foundation could bring the law down on him. And he would want to stop that. I believe we will find

Ginger's killer in those files."

"So you believe Jon is innocent."

"Maybe. But maybe not. He shows a lot of disrespect to women and men alike. He thinks he's better than most of us. Maybe he was sure that some young woman would see him as the God he thinks he is…and she didn't. It could have been a misunderstanding that he refused to recognize or acknowledge. And I think, if that happened, Jon would not want that misunderstanding to come to light."

Luc's mouth turned down, his jaw tightened. "No. Cleo, I can't believe that. I know Jon's past. It's not possible."

"I don't know his past, but frankly, there's enough circumstantial evidence which points to Jon to make me wonder if I'll find a profile fitting him in those files. You seem convinced though. What is in his past that exculpates him?" I asked.

Luc ran the fingers of his hand through his hair and stared at the floor. "It's not a pretty story. Are you sure you want to hear it?"

"If we're going to figure out who killed Ginger, I think I need to know Jon's background."

Luc studied me for a long moment. "Jon's father was a Russian scientist, a member of the Russian Academy of Science. He split his time between Moscow and Geneva. Jon traveled with him and went to school in both Switzerland and Russia. When Jon was eight his mother died while giving birth to Jon's little sister. The sister survived. An aunt helped raise Jon and his baby sister until his father moved with both of his children to the U.S. Jon was twelve at the time. The aunt stayed in Russia, and Jon took over the role of main caretaker and protector of his younger sibling."

Luc's face relaxed and the corner of his mouth slowly lifted up. "Svetla was this cheerful, funny kid who idolized her older brother. She followed Jon around like a puppy. And he doted on her as long as she behaved. But if she acted up, all he had to do was look sternly at her, and she would mend her ways. I know, usually older brothers don't like their kid sisters, but it's one of the things that Jon and I had in common. We both loved our little sisters and we let them hang out with us. Celia was a few years older than Svetla but they were great friends until Svetla had to go back to Russia." Luc frowned.

"Why did she have to go back?" I asked.

"The Russian government decided they needed Jon's father to return home." Luc's face darkened. "Jon was allowed to stay here in boarding school. My parents were also working here in the States at the time and they promised Jon's father they would keep an eye out for him. But Jon's father and aunt decided Svetla was too young. She had to go back to Moscow with her father."

Luc's eyes sought mine. "You sure you want to hear the rest of this story? It's not a happy one."

"Yes."

Luc winced but continued. "Jon finished high school here, then college and then grad school. He and Svetla only saw each other on school breaks, but they talked and texted and stayed in close touch. I guess it was Jon's second year of grad school." Luc rubbed his chin. "Svetla was eighteen. Jon called me and asked me to have Celia reach out to her. Svetla had cut off contact with Jon and wasn't returning his calls. He had no idea why." Luc shook his head.

"Of course, Celia called. She and Svetla had not

stayed in close contact, but had been good friends before Svetla moved away." Luc's scowl deepened. "Evidently, she needed a woman to talk to. Celia told me that after a little hesitation, the story had poured out of Svetla. At an important dinner honoring her father, a senior member of the Politburo had dragged her into an empty room and raped her. Afterwards he told her that if she reported him, the Politburo officer would make sure her father lost his job and apartment and any rights to leave the country." Luc's face lost its color. "And it didn't stop at that. This monster had taken a fancy to Svetla and invited her and her father to more events. Always at large private homes, with empty bedrooms."

Luc's mouth twisted. "After the second time she was raped, Svetla told her aunt and asked her what to do. This aunt told her not to speak about it or the family would lose everything."

"Poor Svetla. She must have felt trapped." I placed a hand on Luc's knee. "What did she do? What could she do?"

Luc took a deep breath. "She killed herself."

Tears welled into my eyes. I raised my fingers to my mouth.

Luc appeared lost in his thoughts. "Celia was devastated. She had encouraged Svetla to speak out and promised not to tell anyone until Svetla had spoken with her father. But instead of telling her father, Svetla took poison the morning before the next event where she would see her rapist. When she heard the news, Celia told me, I told Jon, Jon told his father, who confronted the aunt, who tearfully confirmed it." Luc rubbed his forehead. "All too late to help Svetla. Celia still feels guilty, as if she had spoken out sooner, things might have been different. Jon was angry and blamed her for years, but his father convinced him to forgive."

A ghost of a smile flitted across Luc's face. "I hope you meet Jon's father one day. He is an interesting guy."

I blinked away my unshed tears. "I hope so too."

"I know Kyle told you Jon's father was a Russian spy. What he didn't make clear, and maybe because he didn't know…but Jon's father spied on the Russians for the USA. When he found out what Svetla had gone through and why she hadn't told him, he considered calling the police. But he realized nothing would happen to that senior official. Instead, his father decided to work to bring down the entire corrupt Russian leadership. Dr. Suvorov was a high-ranking scientist who designed weapons for Russia. On a trip to a conference in Europe he approached a U.S. scholar he had known. It was complicated, but for the next ten years he supplied them with golden intelligence. At some point the U.S. became aware he had been compromised and pulled him out. Again, not easy, but he made it and has been living in upstate New York on a farm ever since."

I was stunned. I needed to process. I wasn't sure Jon's tragic story got him off the hook. But I had a lot of information to sift through.

Puppy had been sleeping, curled up under the coffee table. She stretched and yawned. The emotionally charged energy in the room must have woken her. She stood and took a few clumsy steps and collapsed on the floor at our feet, her chin on my toes and one hind leg thrown across Luc's foot. Thank heaven for puppies, fluffy, bright spots in a dark world.

Chapter 43

A Snowy Day

The mountain has had snow for a month but today we were gifted with our first snowfall at Luc's house. I had worked diligently all morning on data analysis, but now I closed my computer with a barely suppressed excitement.

I loved to shovel snow. I've adored it ever since I was a kid in Virginia. We didn't get much. We lived too close to the coast. I would beg my father to let me shovel it in the morning. But he was always up before me and had the front walk cleared before I wiped the sleep out of my eyes. When I wailed that I'd wanted to do it, he would laugh and say, "Well, sleepyhead, the world won't wait for you if you spend your mornings in bed." My only opportunities to shovel were weekends when it snowed during the day. I loved the untouched blanket of pristine white and then watched my bold stripes appear as I cleared a path. I was an artist, the shovel my brush. If I had lived somewhere with frequent, deep snowfalls, I doubtless would have grown bored with it. But it never snowed in Hilo, and many years had passed since I'd gotten to shovel the frozen, white glitter.

I raced to pull on snow boots and my jacket. I scooped up Odette to bring her with me and went in search of Luc's snow shovel. She had never seen snow and loved it. She ran around in circles, jumped in the air, and tried to eat it. I kept her out with me while I shoveled until I noticed her walking gingerly. I examined her paws and found tiny snowballs hardening between the pads of her feet. I carried her inside and left her to sleep in the kitchen while the snowballs melted.

I hoped to have the driveway cleared before Luc returned. He was working at the office and planned to pick up groceries and coffee on his way home. I shoveled for an hour and made satisfying progress. I set the snow shovel perpendicular to the ground with one elbow resting on it and surveyed my work.

The snow had stopped and the little bits that I had missed, melted. I'd made a path from a parking spot to the front door. This deserved a coffee. I leaned the shovel against a nearby pinon tree, close to the next area I wanted to tackle. My father would be disappointed in me. He didn't believe in leaving good tools out in the weather. But it was heavy with a wooden handle and metal scoop, and I didn't relish carrying it to the outdoor closet on the other side of the house and back again. My father would never know, and Luc wouldn't care. More likely he'd be surprised that I had so much of the driveway cleared. I left the shovel under the tree and returned to the house to collect my car keys. Luc could be hours, and I wanted a coffee now. Puppy slept peacefully so I left her gated in the kitchen.

As I drove out of the freshly plowed road, headed toward my favorite coffee shop, I noticed a beat-up red pickup truck parked at the vacant house next door. It pulled out behind me to follow me off our dead-end street. Probably a worker doing repairs, who had waited until our road was plowed to leave. Tano Road had been cleared and even Camino de las Montoyas was plowed, so I took the shortcut. The red pickup also turned onto Camino de las Montoyas.

He was probably going for coffee, too. We were in a coffee caravan. I chuckled.

But as we passed the long driveways and approached the La Tierra trail system, the red pickup accelerated up to my bumper. I frowned. Has this guy been drinking? Why was he tailgating me? I glanced back to see the driver, but the road twisted through that area. My car skidded a bit as the road curved on the top of a hill. I had inadvertently sped up as the red truck approached. My tires gripped the road again. I hadn't seen the driver's face, but the license plate was from Mexico.

My neck snapped back and my head hit the headrest. What the hell?

"He hit me," I yelled.

Had he slipped on the road too? I regained control of my car and risked a glance in the mirror.

The red truck sped up again.

That bump was no accident.

What should I do?

I couldn't safely drive any faster on this twisty, icy road, but there was a maniac behind me. I didn't know if he was drunk or what. My neck snapped back again.

Dammit. He hit me again

I accelerated. I wasn't going to let him do it a third time.

The red truck stuck close and hit my bumper at the wrong moment...and...I was off the road, bouncing over a drainage ditch, blowing through chamisa bushes and coming to rest ten feet away.

I slammed my fist on to the steering wheel. Then dug into my purse and pulled out my cell phone. No signal. I got out of the car to see if I would be able to drive back onto the road.

The red truck pulled off the road too. The driver had parked carefully and would be able to drive away, whereas I couldn't. Did the driver feel guilty? Would he offer help now that he had created this situation?

A man exited the driver's side wearing a black ski mask. A chill ran down my spine. My anger mutated to fear when I saw the rifle in his hand.

I ran.

I dashed as fast as I could through the deep snow, stumbling over unseen rocks. I heard him chasing, crashing through stubby juniper trees to take a short cut to reach me.

I heard an "oof." I hoped he fell.

I kept running.

I had crashed next to the La Tierra Trail system. The snow had intensified. I stayed on the main path, where other hikers had already left tracks. I didn't want him following my footprints in the fresh snow so I ran until I'd passed several forks in the trail where earlier hikers had veered off. Then I peeled off the trail at a rocky area, carefully jumping from one boulder to another to avoid leaving tracks my pursuer could follow.

I dug deep to try and pick up my pace. My arms raised to protect my face from juniper and pinon branches. I stumbled on a prickly pear cactus but managed to stay on my feet.

After I thought I had put some distance between us I stopped behind one of the larger juniper trees to see if he was still following me. My heart raced and chest heaved, but I closed my mouth to try and breathe quietly so I could hear him if he was close.

All I heard was the sound of the wind in the trees and a few crows cawing nearby. Probably at me. I gently pushed a branch a little to the side. I couldn't see the rifle-carrying ski-masked man, but from my elevation I could see the red truck, parked where he had climbed out of it. Out there somewhere, he still searched for me.

I couldn't stay here. It was cold and he had a gun. He'd eventually find me. Especially if he followed the sound of those crows.

I needed to move. More quietly, which would be slower, but it would put distance between me and the crows. My mind raced.

How far was I from Luc's house? By road, probably four miles, but if I cut through the woods I could shave a mile off that. But I'd hit rougher terrain.

I pushed the branch down again. The red pickup hadn't moved. I'd stick to the woods with scrub trees and arroyos. And hope I didn't run into a den of coyotes. At least the heavy snow covered my tracks.

My legs told me I had run for hours but likely it was less than half that. Covered with scratches and my clothes torn, I stopped behind a bushy juniper tree for a quick rest. I couldn't hear anyone behind me. I listened for a couple of minutes to be sure and then peeked around the tree. I no longer saw the red truck or my car but the snow had let up and my recent tracks in the snow were visible. No other hikers had come in this direction. I would keep moving. But first I tried again to call Luc to let him know what happened.

No signal. Damn.

I jogged at this point, exhausted and relying on

adrenalin. But my mind struggled to identify the person who rammed my car and chased me. He wore a black face mask. But I recognized the way he moved.

My jogging slowed as my brain went into overdrive. The person who had tried to push me down the ski slope moved the same way. Samia was right. That person deliberately tried to hurt me. And now apparently he wanted to kill me. Both wore the same black ski mask, had the same height and build. He didn't wear the bulky snowboard jacket today, but everything else was identical. And the way he moved...I'd seen that another time too.

Think, Cleo.

I stopped in my tracks.

I knew my pursuer.

I started running again. I needed to warn Luc.

Chapter 44

Do I Stay or Do I Go Now

An hour later…I think…it felt like I'd been running all day. My thighs burned and my heart almost burst out of my chest from adrenalin and racing up and down ravines and washes that gave me the shortest path to Luc's house. I approached from the side, a shortcut through a neighbor's property. Luc was talking to someone I couldn't see.

"Did you borrow that truck from Teresa's son?"

When Kyle answered, my heart sank.

"No, it belongs to a worker at the construction site next door to my house. I told him I needed to haul something and offered the guy fifty bucks, if I could borrow his truck for a couple of hours while he's working."

I rested behind Luc's propane tank to catch my breath and check my phone. Finally, a signal. I must have caught Luc's Wi-Fi.

I texted the Special Agent explaining Kyle was the killer, he had come after me with a gun and was now at Luc's house. Then I texted Luc.

—*Kyle killed Ginger… BE CAREFUL*—

I scrutinized the neighboring houses. There were only a few, and all of them had empty driveways. No one appeared to be at home. Should I run back up the street and knock on doors hoping to find someone? I could wait in safety and call the police again.

No. Luc needs me. I'm not running away.

That thought brought back a flood of memories. I ran from the killer last year in Hawaii. I ran when a relationship with a man didn't work. I ran from my small town in Virginia. And I've been running from Kyle for the last hour. I've always run. I sucked in a deep breath.

I don't want to run away from life. I want to face it. Luc wouldn't leave me alone with a killer, and I'm not leaving him.

Luc continued to casually talk with Kyle. I texted him to get away from Kyle. I heard his phone ping as my message arrived, but he hadn't pulled it out. I moved around to the back of the house and checked if any doors were open. If Luc and I could get inside before Kyle realized we were on to him we had a chance.

Nothing was open. Damn. Luc was standing in front of the only unlocked door.

I texted him again:

—*I'm in the back of the house, PLEASE find an excuse to go inside and lock Kyle out. Then let me in a back door.*—

I peeked around the corner, and heard his phone ding again. This time he pulled his phone out. Great.

Damn, I didn't call 911. I'm an idiot. I wanted as many cops here as possible. I called 911, and whispered Luc's address and the situation. But as they were telling me to stay on the line, I heard Kyle's voice again.

"Who keeps texting you? Is that Cleo?"

I peeked around the corner again. Luc stood stiffly, the phone still in his hand and his eyes on Kyle.

"No," Luc said. "It's a work call."

Luc was a terrible liar. Something I liked in a boyfriend, but right now it could get him killed.

"I think that *was* Cleo," Kyle said. He opened the door to the truck and then closed it before he stepped into view. He had the rifle in his hand.

"I like you, Luc. I was hoping I wasn't going to have to do this."

I moved in Kyle's direction. Quietly I creeped behind a courtyard wall and scratched my hand on the rough stucco, leaving a trail of blood. I had almost circled the house when I saw the snow shovel I'd left out. A lifetime ago I'd happily shoveled snow, and there it remained, leaning against the pinon tree, five feet behind Kyle.

"Did you come to shoot rabbits? Cleo won't like that. She leaves carrots out for them." Luc spoke too fast and moved in the opposite direction of me. He didn't head toward the door. He was trying to lead Kyle away from me.

Kyle took a few quick steps toward Luc. "I'm not an idiot," he said. "I know Cleo texted you that I tried to chase her down. And don't worry, I'll get her for sticking her nose in Ginger's files. But now I have to get rid of you and destroy your phone."

I crept the last few steps to the shovel. Which end to hit him with? The wooden handle could maybe knock him down and I could grab the gun. Or the large metal scoop…but that could kill him. I didn't want to be a killer.

"Wait a minute." Kyle stopped. "Cleo's already here, isn't she?" He scanned left and right, but couldn't look directly behind without exposing his back to Luc.

"No," Luc said. "She texted me to come pick her up,

but she's not here."

Kyle laughed. Luc, God love him, was a truly, terrible liar.

Kyle raised his voice. "Cleo, if you don't come out, I'm going to shoot Luc right in front of you." He slowly raised his rifle.

I raised the shovel and with a couple of running steps slammed the metal scoop of the snow shovel down on Kyle's head with all my might.

Kyle crumpled, face first from the force of my clobbering him from behind. I waited, shovel poised for another whack at him. But Kyle didn't move.

Oh my God, have I killed him? Have I killed a person? Someone with whom I've had coffee and conversations? Is Kyle dead? Because of me?

I quivered.

Luc dashed forward and grabbed the fallen rifle before checking Kyle's pulse. A copper scent invaded my nose as I stared, hypnotized by Kyle's blond hair darkening as the blood streamed into it.

"He's alive," Luc said.

I almost collapsed to my knees. Luc moved quickly to support me, still holding the rifle.

He held me tight and spoke calmly. "Cleo, there's rope in the shed over there. In the closet where you found the snow shovel. Go get it and bring it here, please. We need to tie him up. He could come to any minute."

Luc took the shovel out of my hand. I dropped it like it was scalding hot as he grasped it.

"Go get the rope, Cleo." Luc spoke gently and tilted his head in the direction of the outdoor closet.

Without the snow shovel in my hands my brain could process again. "Right. Rope. We need to tie him up."

I rushed to the shed and found the rope. I returned in a flash. Luc held the gun on Kyle while I tied his hands behind his back. When that was done, I decided better safe than sorry and tied his ankles together. Then one of Kyle's fingers twitched and I thought, what the hell, and tied his hands to his tied ankles.

Ounce of prevention, right? I didn't want to have to hit him on the head with that shovel again.

"Cleo, do you feel up to holding the gun on Kyle? I want to check his pulse again and call the police and an ambulance?"

"Sure," I lied. I took the rifle.

I held the gun on Kyle while Luc checked his pulse, relieved when he told me it was strong. Luc also checked the ropes to make sure they were tight before he pulled out his phone and dialed his first call. My hands shook. I was not skilled with guns. I never liked them. I faced away from the dirt road that led to Luc's house and I thought I heard a couple of cars coming down the road toward us. I had texted Special Agent Rivera, and maybe cops were on the way.

Luc finished calling 911 and telling them we needed an ambulance. He tested the ropes on Kyle again to be sure they were secure.

Kyle groaned and started flexing his fingers. His eyes opened.

Luc looked at me. "It's okay, Cleo. You can put the gun down."

He said it twice before the words sunk in.

Kyle was awake now.

I slowly lowered the gun to point it at the ground.

A car came around the final bend of the road. I

thought I had heard two cars, but I was stressed. It must be Rivera on his own.

But when the car door opened, it wasn't the FBI agent, and no backup second car. There were tire tracks in the snow where a second car had pulled into the driveway of a neighboring house, but the vehicle was hidden behind trees.

No, instead of law enforcement, here to rescue us was Mimi, bright and perky as ever.

"What's up guys?" she asked.

The buoyant smile on her face unnerved me after what we had just experienced, being run off the road, hunted cross country, and Luc held at gunpoint. It had become clear that Kyle had killed Ginger. The ugly cruelty of wanton death assaulted me, and Mimi's freakishly oblivious smile revolted me.

Luc frowned. "You don't want to know, Mimi." He stepped toward me and put a hand on my shoulder, the one not holding the gun. "Are you okay, Cleo?"

"Yes." I started to hand the gun to Luc. Holding this rifle probably creeped me out, not Mimi. A glance at Kyle stopped me. He appeared fully recovered and struggled to sit up, rolling onto his side. I lifted the gun again.

"Stay where you are, Kyle. I don't want to shoot you, but I will if I have to," I said.

Kyle stopped struggling and sneered at me. "You still haven't figured it out yet, have you? You stupid bitch. I'm not the one who's in trouble here." His smile broadened in triumph as his eyes turned to Mimi.

I glanced at her to see where his bravado came from, and terror snaked into my heart.

Mimi stood as before, the cheerful smile on her face.

But now she held a gun, casually pointed at me. "You need to put that gun down, Cleo. I've got this." Mimi's smile grew broader. "I'm an excellent shot, remember. I go to target practice. You're clearly an amateur. You'll hurt someone by accident if you aren't careful."

I almost lowered the gun, eager to turn shooting responsibilities over to someone else. But… something didn't feel right. Why was Kyle so confident? And why was Mimi's gun aimed at me?

"Don't do it," Luc said softly. He stepped in front of me, placing himself between me and Mimi. "Cleo's doing fine, Mimi. You can put your gun away now. We've got this."

His back was to me and blocked Mimi from my view. I kept my eyes on Kyle.

He tried to sit up again and managed it this time, laughing. "They still don't—"

Crack.

Kyle slumped down. A gurgle replaced his taunts as he coughed up blood. A confused look clouded his eyes before they closed and the gurgling stopped.

What happened? I stared at the gun in my hand. I didn't shoot him. I'd know if I had, right? I pulled the gun in to inspect it more closely, being sure not to point it at anybody. It didn't feel warm. Was it supposed to?

"Put the gun down, Cleo." Mimi's voice chilled me. *Oh.*

Luc had figured it out before me. Mimi was a killer. She shot Kyle. And now she was going to kill Luc. And me.

"Mimi, we can work this out. I'm sure you have a good reason for what you've done." Luc lifted his hands and took a slow step toward her.

"Stop right there, Luc. Don't try to play the hero. I am a very good shot. I could shoot you and Cleo with one bullet." Mimi's voice sliced through the frigid air.

The temperature had dropped and numbed my fingers. I held the gun, but it didn't do anyone any good with Luc standing in front of me. He wanted to shield me from Mimi. But she could be right. For all I know about ballistics, she might be able to shoot Luc and have the bullet go through and hit me too. I took a step to Luc's right side and held the gun with both hands to steady it, pointed at Mimi.

"Walk away, Mimi," I said. "No one else needs to die today."

"But you're wrong, Cleo. You and Luc know too much. How am I going to enjoy Aunt Ginger's money if you two are alive to tell the tale?" Mimi smiled with confidence. "And now I don't have to share it with dufus there." Mimi laughed. "Things are turning out better than I planned."

My heart stuttered at her words. We needed to keep Mimi talking while we figured out how to escape. The house was only twenty feet away. But Mimi was only forty feet away in the other direction. Perhaps we could make it. But I needed to distract her.

"I don't get how you pulled it off. You were on the East Coast and Kyle was here in Santa Fe…". *Oh, that's how they did it.*

The pieces clicked in place. Kyle wasn't in Santa Fe. He secretly flew to Phoenix and sabotaged Ginger's car. We only had Kyle's word that he had been working in his studio. But we needed to keep Mimi talking. "And that day on the ski mountain?"

Mimi smiled. "Yes, Kyle was eager to prove his love

for me. All I had to do was hint at a way to make a problem go away, and he would do it." She shrugged. "I usually had to break it down into step-by-step instructions, but he was competent enough." Mimi's smile disappeared and she cocked an eyebrow. "Except with you, Cleo. I needed you to quit digging into those files. He was supposed to knock you off the mountain. I thought that would at least break your leg. And he failed to crush you at that store. Even after I managed to get you there." She shook her head.

"And the coded files from the Center, you took one didn't you. Why?" My arms tired of holding the gun. After snow shoveling and running the hilly trails in snow, I was exhausted. Fatigue made my arms and the gun I held shake.

Mimi noticed it and her eyes became frostier. She relaxed her shoulders, but there was no tremble in her arm.

"I had my reasons. But that's enough of that. Poor little Cleo's getting tired." Mimi stepped forward and lifted her second arm up to steady the gun.

"No," Luc yelled. He wrapped his arms around me and with a step to our right pulled me into a dive to the ground behind one of the large boulders in his yard.

A shot rang out. I could feel Luc on top of me, still breathing. I felt his heart beating against my back. Did she miss him? I struggled to free my arms and the gun, so as soon as Mimi stepped around the boulder to finish us off, I would be ready.

"F.B.I. Drop your weapon. Now."

Special Agent Joe Rivera to the rescue.

Chapter 45

Before the Coffee Gets Cold!

I eased awake after the first good night's sleep I'd
had since the Kyle/Mimi stress-a-thon. Luc and I had
spent almost two days at the police station, telling and
retelling our story. Finally, after both of our stories had
been checked and rechecked, the police seemed to
believe us. Special Agent Joe gave us our last interview
and actually answered some of our questions.

Kyle had assaulted a native woman in Indian
Country. But the woman hadn't come to Ginger, and
Ginger didn't know anything about it. Some years after
the assault, Kyle had caught Ginger's eye at an art show
and they began dating. Soon after Ginger had invited
Kyle to move in. Everything was fine until Mimi came
for a visit.

Joe was still putting the pieces and the evidence
together, but his working hypothesis was that Mimi was
impatient to inherit from her aunt. Mimi also worried that
her aunt had become a little too infatuated with Kyle, and
Mimi might lose most, if not all, of that inheritance if
Ginger decided to marry him. Special Agent Joe Rivera
believed Mimi deliberately seduced Kyle. On one of her
visits, Mimi got him ridiculously drunk while Ginger
attended a board meeting. She lured him into bed. And
when Kyle got drunk he reminisced about his past, a

bonus for Mimi. In his drunken, guilt-induced stupor he blathered on about his regret for his assault on the native woman.

Mimi was delighted. Her original plan, to get photos of Kyle in bed with her and take incriminating photos of their sexual encounter in Ginger's bedroom, was risky. In reviewing the photos, she'd kept her face out of the pictures but worried her aunt might recognize some identifying feature on her body. And if Ginger realized the woman in the pictures was Mimi, then her aunt would disinherit her and Mimi would lose everything. Blackmailing Kyle over his past was much better.

Evidently the police had found the photos, and a copy of a file that Mimi had forged with the woman's name blacked out, and most of the details blacked out, but Kyle's name in it. Mimi admitted it was a fake she'd doctored after stealing a file when she pretended to help Samia and me. It backed up the story she had been telling him that she had evidence. And, Kyle had believed the file was real.

When Mimi suggested that Kyle kill Ginger, he hesitated. He only acquiesced when Mimi pointed out that Ginger would eventually get around to reading that file and not only would Kyle be out the door and lose his grand lifestyle, but he could be convicted of rape. Mimi promised Kyle that she would marry him and share her inheritance after Ginger was gone.

Joe shook his head. "Criminals can be really stupid sometimes."

"So was it Mimi or Kyle who killed Ginger?" Luc asked.

"Kyle, right?" I looked at Joe.

He smiled and signaled me to continue. "Go ahead,

tell me why you think that."

"One day he told me he had worked in a garage, but hated it. But he would've known how to sabotage a car to break down after working fine for miles."

Joe smiled in agreement.

"And…" I switched my gaze to Luc, who sat next to me. "Remember the email that gave Ginger the wrong directions, directing her to hot, arid land where she would be unlikely to find help?"

"Yes."

"Kyle was a tech expert. He could figure out how to make it appear to come from Jon's email, or I don't know, maybe hack into Jon's account and send it from Jon's email."

I looked back at Joe. "Am I right?"

"Yes. He hacked into your friend's account. Which is what made me suspect Jon Suvorov initially. But then he probably wasn't stupid enough to send something so incriminating from his own account and I broadened my investigation."

"What I still don't get is why Ginger changed her plans and drove south instead of north," I said.

"We checked Kyle Paige's phone. Ms. Hanlon texted him that the Rez Golf was closed when she got there. Her meeting in Holbrook wasn't for a couple of days, so she decided to detour to Tohono O'Odham lands to see a woman about some baskets. Kyle suggested he meet her in Phoenix for a romantic make-up night and caught a flight there. Mimi claims the next morning when Ginger and Kyle checked out, he told Ginger he wanted to make sure her car was safe. That's when he sabotaged it, just before picking a fight with her and taking an Uber to the airport. Leaving her to drive off into the Sonoran Desert with a damaged car."

We sat in silence, letting that sink in.

"And the Center's books? Was there any embezzling going on, or was that just Mimi, stirring up trouble and deflecting suspicion toward Samia?" I asked.

"Our forensic accountant said they were clean as a whistle."

I was relieved, but something else niggled at me. "By any chance did you find any burner phones at Kyle's place with calls to Samia Keller?"

Rivera frowned. "How would you know that?

"I know she was getting threatening calls, and they always seemed to happen around the time we planned to read through the Center's files."

Rivera smiled. "Well that clears that up. I am heading over to speak with Dr. Keller after I finish here. It's always nice to ask a question when you already know the answer." Joe winked at me.

Luc cleared his throat. "I understand Kyle and Mimi's motive to kill Ginger. And threaten Samia. But why did they try to kill Cleo?"

Joe's brow furrowed. "Ms. Cooper kept pushing to investigate the files. Arranging for her and Samia Keller to go through them. That frustrated Mimi and Kyle. Mimi, who didn't want her false claim that there was a file on Kyle exposed. And Kyle, who believed that there was a file that not only incriminated him in a rape, but also gave him a motive for murdering Ginger. Mimi egged him on. She told Kyle he wouldn't be safe unless he got rid of you. We found her texts and emails to him."

Joe's deep, mournful eyes focused on me. "You need to be more careful. Leave murder investigations to the professionals."

And with those final words yesterday, Special Agent Joe Rivera walked out of the interview room.

This morning, the sun streamed through the bedroom windows as I stretched luxuriously. One look at my phone told me I had slept scandalously late. I hopped out of bed and pulled on jeans and a sweater. Faint voices floated up from downstairs through the closed door. Luc was not alone. I ran a brush through my hair and went down to greet the world.

The puppy rushed over to greet me and lick my shoes. A heavenly scent of coffee delighted my nose and laughter tickled my ears. Luc, Samia, and Jon were seated around the table. Would wonders never cease? Samia and Jon laughed together. When Jon saw me, he jumped up.

"Let me make you a coffee. And I brought empanadas. They're on the table, if Samia hasn't made a pig of herself." Jon stepped briskly into the kitchen, all business.

"I *have* made a pig of myself as Jon so gentlemanly put it." A rueful smile on Samia's face. "But we made sure to save some for you."

I stood behind a seated Luc, laid a hand on his shoulder, and kissed the top of his head. "Was there a party I forgot about?" I pulled out a chair and sat between Samia and Luc.

Samia laughed, "No. The paper today came out with full coverage of the crimes of Mimi and Kyle. And how you," Samia looked at me with raised eyebrows, "were almost killed because you were trying to save Jon and Luc. You are Santa Fe-mous."

I smiled and reached a hand to Luc. "I didn't save Luc; we saved each other." Luc closed his hand over mine and squeezed it. My stomach flip-flopped at the smoldering, sad, scared look in his eyes.

Jon walked in carrying a steaming mug. "Ta daa, a world class coffee for a world class amateur detective."

"Now, Jon's butt I saved." I laughed and wrapped my hands around the mug before he could pull it back and make me beg for it. And I would have begged. Jon had remembered how I adulterated my coffee, and it was perfect.

A knock came from the door. Luc answered and Special Agent Joe Rivera followed him back into the room.

I stood up. "Good morning, please come in and pull up a chair. We have empanadas and Jon makes fabulous coffee."

"Not for him, I don't," Jon said.

"No, thank you. I didn't know you would have guests. I'm driving back to Gallup and wanted to stop in to say goodbye." He nodded in Jon's direction. "I'm sorry for the trouble I put you folks through, but in a murder investigation…" He shrugged, then tipped his hat to me before shaking Luc's hand.

"I'd keep an eye on that *wahine* of yours. She's a keeper," Joe Rivera said. He waved and walked out the door.

"That man speaks truth." Samia winked at Luc.

"What? No, I'm not really a *wahine*. I'm considered a *malahini,* a newcomer. *Wahine* refers more to Native Hawaiian or…" I stumbled to a stop as Samia laughed.

She stood up, patted my cheek, and looked at Luc. "Is she not cute?" Samia suddenly turned back to me. "Oh, I saw on the news last night that your volcano calmed down. Is that right?"

"Yep. Rikki texted me. The caldera is deflating and fissures have stopped flowing. Pele is going back to sleep."

"That is good," Samia said. "I am out of here, folks." She waved a hand to the room to include Jon. "I have a husband at home. I will have to pick up empanadas for him once he hears I had them here."

"Thanks for stopping by, Samia," I said.

"Ah, Cleo, you missed my announcement. I was notified early this morning that since Mimi is implicated in Ginger's death, most likely her bequest will go to our Foundation. So if none of the grants come through for Luc's program, I will be hiring." Samia winked at me again and waved to Luc before leaving.

"I've only been downstairs fifteen minutes and two guests have left. Is it me?" I said as I returned to my seat and Jon's divine coffee.

"Most likely," said Jon. "I make you one of the best coffees you will ever taste and after a few sips you let it cool to a not-optimum temperature."

I laughed. Jon's curmudgeon attitude was growing on me. I also reached to drink the rest of my coffee before it cooled any less optimally. I have respect for a master craftsman.

"Oh, and I've brought you a gift, Cleo. You made a moderately good effort of clearing my name. And I appreciate that." Jon handed me a package wrapped in purple wrapping paper and orange ribbon.

Jon benignly sipped his coffee as I unwrapped it.

And found a copy of *The Complete Idiot's Guide to Private Investigating*, by Steven Kerry Brown.

As I held it up to show Luc, Jon smiled brightly. "Can I not find the perfect gift for any person?"

A word about the author…

DK lived the dream as a cross-cultural psychology professor in Hawaii for many years before leaving that to write and forecast geopolitical events. She is a superforecaster with GJI https://goodjudgment.com/ and the Rand Forecasting Initiative (RFI) https://www.infer-pub.com/ Her first mystery, Evil Alice and the Borzoi, was released by The Wild Rose Press in 2023. She loves traveling, writing, her dog Beasley, and her husband (not necessarily in that order). For more information https://www.dkcoutant.com/

Thank you for purchasing
this publication of The Wild Rose Press, Inc.

For questions or more information
contact us at
info@thewildrosepress.com.

The Wild Rose Press, Inc.
www.thewildrosepress.com